P9-DHI-076

THE LONG FALL

ALSO BY WALTER MOSLEY

EASY RAWLINS MYSTERIES

Blonde Faith
Cinnamon Kiss
Little Scarlet
Six Easy Pieces
Bad Boy Brawly Brown
A Little Yellow Dog
Black Betty
Gone Fishin'
White Butterfly
A Red Death
Devil in a Blue Dress

OTHER FICTION

The Tempest Tales
Diablerie
Killing Johnny Fry
The Man in My Basement
Fear of the Dark
Fortunate Son
The Wave
Fear Itself
Futureland
Fearless Jones
Walkin' the Dog
Blue Light
Always Outnumbered, Always Outgunned
RL's Dream
47
The Right Mistake

NONFICTION

This Year You Write Your Novel
What Next: A Memoir Toward World Peace
Life Out of Context
Workin' on the Chain Gang

RIVERHEAD BOOKS a member of Penguin Group (USA) Inc. NEW YORK 2009

WALTER MOSLEY

THE LONG FALL

RIVERHEAD BOOKS
Published by the Penguin Group
Penguin Group (USA) Inc., 375 Hudson Street, New York, New York 10014, USA • Penguin Group (Canada), 90 Eglinton Avenue East, Suite 700, Toronto, Ontario M4P 2Y3, Canada (a division of Pearson Canada Inc.) • Penguin Books Ltd, 80 Strand, London WC2R 0RL, England • Penguin Ireland, 25 St Stephen's Green, Dublin 2, Ireland (a division of Penguin Books Ltd) • Penguin Group (Australia), 250 Camberwell Road, Camberwell, Victoria 3124, Australia (a division of Pearson Australia Group Pty Ltd) • Penguin Books India Pvt Ltd, 11 Community Centre, Panchsheel Park, New Delhi–110 017, India • Penguin Group (NZ), 67 Apollo Drive, Rosedale, North Shore 0632, New Zealand (a division of Pearson New Zealand Ltd) • Penguin Books (South Africa) (Pty) Ltd, 24 Sturdee Avenue, Rosebank, Johannesburg 2196, South Africa

Penguin Books Ltd, Registered Offices: 80 Strand, London WC2R 0RL, England

Published simultaneously in Canada

Library of Congress Cataloging-in-Publication Data

Mosley, Walter.
The long fall / Walter Mosley.
p. cm.
ISBN 978-1-59448-858-0
I. Title.
PS3563.O88456L66 2009 2008046238
813'.54—dc22

Printed in the United States of America
1 3 5 7 9 10 8 6 4 2

BOOK DESIGN BY NICOLE LAROCHE

In memory of
St. Clair Bourne
documentarian extraordinaire

THE LONG FALL

I'm sorry, Mr. um? . . ." the skinny receptionist said.

Her baby-blue-on-white nameplate merely read JULIET.

She had short blond hair that was longer in the front than in the back and wore a violet T-shirt that I was sure would expose a pierced navel if she were to stand up. Behind her was a mostly open-air-boutique-like office space with ten or twelve brightly colored plastic desks that were interspersed by big, leafy, green plants. The eastern wall, to my right, was a series of ceiling-to-floor segmented windowpanes that were not intended to open.

All the secretaries and gofers that worked for Berg, Lewis & Takayama were young and pretty, regardless of their gender. All except one.

There was a chubby woman who sat in a far corner to the left, under an exit sign. She had bad skin and a utilitarian fashion sense. She was looking down, working hard. I immediately identified with her.

I imagined sitting in that corner, hating everyone else in the room.

"Mr. Brown isn't in?" I asked, ignoring Juliet's request for a name.

"He can't be disturbed."

"Couldn't you just give him a note from me?"

Juliet, who hadn't smiled once, not even when I first walked in, actually sneered, looking at me as if I were a city trash collector walking right from my garbage truck into the White House and asking for an audience with the president.

I was wearing a suit and tie. Maybe my shoe leather was dull, but there weren't any scuffs. There were no spots on my navy lapels, but, like that woman in the corner, I was obviously out of my depth: a vacuum-cleaner salesman among high-paid lawyers, a hausfrau thrown in with a bevy of *Playboy* bunnies.

"What is your business with Mr. Brown?" the snotty child asked.

"He gives financial advice, right?"

She almost answered but then decided it was beneath her.

"I'm a friend of a friend of his," I said. "Jumper told me that Roger might show me what to do with my money."

Juliet was getting bored. She took in a deep breath, letting her head tilt to the side as she exhaled.

It wasn't my skin color that bothered her. People on Madison Avenue didn't mind dark skins in 2008. This woman might have considered voting for Obama, if she voted. She might have flirted with a rap star at some chic nightclub that only served imported champagne and caviar.

Roger Brown was black. So were two of the denizens of the airy workspace. No. Juliet didn't like me because of my big calloused hands and no-frills suit. She didn't like me because I was two inches shorter and forty pounds heavier than a man should be.

"If I leave you my card, will you make sure that he gets it?"

After another sigh she held out a hand, palm up.

My fat red-brown wallet was older than the child, no doubt. I opened it and rooted among the fake business cards that were the hallmark of my trade. I decided on one that I hadn't brought out since a woman I hardly knew had died at my feet.

ARNOLD DUBOIS

Van Der Zee Domestics

and In-home Service Aides

I went down on one knee, taking a pen from the red plastic desktop.

"Excuse me," Juliet said in protest.

I scrawled *for Roger (aka B-Brain) Brown* across the bottom. Beneath that I added a number from a lost, or maybe stolen, cell phone that I had purchased specifically for this job. I stood up easily, without grunting, because, unknown to Juliet, most of my extra weight was muscle. I handed her the card and she took it gingerly by a corner.

"Is that all?" she said.

The chubby woman in the corner looked up at just that moment. I grinned at her and waved. She returned the gesture with a slightly puzzled smile.

"Thank you for your time," I said, pretending I was talking to the woman under the exit sign. "This means a lot to me."

Juliet sucked a tooth and pulled in her chin.

I remember a time when only black women did that.

STOMPING DOWN THE two flights to the street, I was thinking about when I would have pushed harder to get past that girl. All I had to do was get a look at Roger Brown. I had never even seen a photograph of the man but I knew he was black and in his thirties with a small crescent scar under his right eye. All I needed was one look.

At an earlier point in my career I would have probably done something extreme to achieve that simple goal. I might have raised my voice and demanded to see her supervisor, or just walked past her, looking into offices until Roger Brown showed his face, or not. I could have pulled the fire alarm in the hallway or even put a smoke bomb in a trash can. But those days were pretty much over for me. I hadn't given up on being a private detective; that was all I knew. I still took incriminating photographs and located people who didn't necessarily want to be found. I exposed frauds and cheats without feeling much guilt.

In other words, I still plied my trade but now I worried about things.

In the years before, I had no problem bringing people down, even framing them with false evidence if that's what the client paid for. I didn't mind sending an innocent man, or woman, to prison because I didn't believe in innocence—and virtue didn't pay the bills. That was before my past caught up with me and died, spitting blood and curses on the rug.

I STILL HAD a family that looked to me for their sustenance. My wife didn't love me and two out of three grown and nearly grown children were not of my blood. But none of that mattered. I had a job to do, and more than one debt to pay.

So I had contracted to find four men. I'd already located three of them. One was dead, one in prison, and the third was awaiting trial. Of the four, only Roger Brown, if this was indeed the Roger Brown I was looking for, had made some kind of life for himself, the kind of life where a pretty young white girl protected his privacy and called him Mister in an office of first names.

Maybe I went easy on Juliet because I was worried about Roger. The job was presented as a straightforward case, with no criminal prosecution involved. But if you find three bad apples, you know there's got to be something rotten somewhere.

I walked down Madison in the bright summer sunshine, hoping that this Roger wasn't the Roger I was looking for; and even if he was, I would have been happy if he never called.

From the Sixties on the East Side of Manhattan I took a yellow cab down to Thirty-fourth Street, a little west of Penn Station. Gordo's Gym took up the entire fifth floor of a dirty brick building that was built sometime before Joe Louis knocked out the Cinderella Man. At noon on a Wednesday the ring was empty, as most of Gordo's hopefuls were out plying day jobs to pay for their protein and locker space.

I set myself up in the corner where a heavy bag hung. That particular piece of real estate was next to a big window that was painted shut and so murky that you couldn't see a thing through it. But I didn't go to Gordo's Gym three days a week for the view or the smell of men's sweat, or for the company, for that matter.

I stripped down right there, put on my thick leather gloves (which were also older than Juliet), and started in on a rhythm of violence that kept up my balance in the rotted infrastructure of my city and my life.

Throwing a punch is the yang of a boxer's life. The yin is being able to avoid getting hit. I'm pretty good at the yang part. Everybody knows but few can exploit the fact that a good punch comes first from the foot, moves in circular motion around the hips, and only then connects with the arm, fist, and if you're lucky, your opponent's jaw or rib cage. Fighting therefore is like the dance of a mighty Scot stamping and swinging in a dewy Highland morning.

For nearly twenty minutes I did my barbarian dance, punishing the big bag, allowing it to swing forward and hit me in the chest now and again. Since I'd given up smoking my wind was getting longer.

I needed anaerobic exercise to vent my anger.

I hated Roger Brown and Juliet along with so many things I had done over the years. At one time I had been able to live with myself because I could say that I only set up people who were already crooked, guilty of something—usually something bad—but not any longer.

I hit that bag with dozens of deadly combinations but in the end I was the one who was defeated, crouched over with my gloves on my knees.

"Not half bad," a man said, his voice raspy and familiar.

"Hey, Gordo." I didn't raise my head because I didn't have the strength.

"You still know how to give it yer all when you decide to give."

"And even with that I come up short nine times out of ten."

"You shoulda been a boxer," one of New York's unsung master trainers said to me.

"I liked late nights and cheap wine too much."

"Beard like you got belongs in the ring."

I'm a clean-shaven guy. Gordo was complimenting the iron in my jaw.

"Hit me enough," I said, "and I'd go down like all the rest."

"You coulda cleaned the clock of every light heavy in 1989."

"Somebody woulda beat me."

"That somebody was you," Gordo said with emphasis. "You hung back when you coulda stood tall."

"Lucky for the world that I'm a short man in inches and stature."

I straightened up and turned to face my best friend and toughest critic.

Gordo was a short guy too, somewhere between seventy-five and eighty-eight. He was black by American racial terminology but in actuality he was more the color of untanned leather informed by a lifetime's worth of calluses, hard knocks, and hollering. The blood had risen to his face so often that his mug had darkened into a kind of permanent rage-color.

I was still breathing hard. After all, I'm past fifty.

"Why you wanna put yourself down like that, LT?" the veteran trainer said. "You coulda been sumpin'."

He wouldn't have been talking to me if any of his young prospects were in the gym. Gordo hovered over his young boxers like a mama crocodile over her brood.

I slumped down on the floor, letting my wet T-shirt slap against the wall.

"That's just not me, G. I never could take any kinda order or regimen."

"You know how to hit that bag three times a week."

"Is that enough?"

The sour-faced little guy frowned and shook his head, as much in disgust as in answer to my question. He turned away and limped toward his office on the other side of the big, low-ceilinged room.

After five minutes or so I made it back to my feet. I pawed the bag three or four times before my knees and hips got into it. After a minute had passed I was in a kind of frenzy. Before, I had just been angry, now I was desperate.

I think I went to Gordo's just so that he could kick me in the ass. The foundation of our friendship was the simple fact that he never held back. I was a failure because I wasn't a boxer—at least in his eyes. He never cared if his boys lost, only if they didn't try.

I pounded that bag with everything I had. The sweat was streaming down my face and back and thighs. I felt lighter and lighter, stronger and stronger. For a moment there I was throwing punches like a real contender in a title match; the underdog who intended to prove the oddsmakers wrong. Everything fell into place and I wasn't anything but ready.

And then, in an instant, the feeling slipped away. My legs gave out and I crumpled to the floor. All that I had was spent.

Gordo leaned back in his office chair and glanced out the door in my direction. He saw me lying there and leaned forward again.

Ten minutes later I got to my feet.

Twenty minutes after that I'd showered and gotten dressed. A few guys were in the gym by then. Not boxers but office workers who wanted to feel what it was like to work out next to real athletes.

I was headed for the stairs when Gordo called out to me.

"LT."

The visitor's chair in his matchbox office was a boxing stool. I squatted down on that and took a deep breath.

"What's wrong with you, kid?"

"It's nuthin', G. Not a thing."

"Naw, uh-uh," the man who knew me as well as anyone said. "For over a year you been comin' in here hittin' that bag hard enough and long enough to give a young man cardiac arrest. You wasn't all that friendly before but now even the smart-asses around here leave you alone. Don't tell me it's nuthin'. Uh-uh. It's sumpin' and it's gettin' worse."

"I got it under control," I said.

"Talk to me, Leonid." Gordo never used my given name. He called me Kid or LT or McGill in everyday banter. But there was no humor in him right then.

"You once told me that you didn't want to know about what I did to make a living," I said in a last-ditch attempt to stave him off.

The old man grinned and tapped his forehead with the four fingers of his left hand.

"I got more dirty secrets up here than a slot machine got nickels," he said. "I didn't wanna know about your business 'cause I knew that you couldn't talk about it an' still come around."

In order to be a good trainer you had to be a teacher, a counselor, a psychologist, and a priest. In order to be a great trainer—add to that list, an irrefutable liar.

"You can do it, kid," the trainer says when his fighter is down on points with his good eye swollen shut.

"He's gettin' tired. It's time to pour it on," the trainer says when the opponent is grinning and bouncing on his toes in the opposite corner.

Gordo never wanted to hear about my shady doings before. But before ceased to exist and all we had was now.

But I couldn't tell him the truth. I mean, how could I confess that after twenty years a young woman had found out that I'd framed her father, sending him to prison and ultimately to his death? His daughter called herself Karma, and she framed me for her own murder using seduction and a hired assassin. I killed the killer but still the young woman, Karmen Brown, died in my arms cursing me with spittle and blood on her lips.

Karmen's last breath was a curse for me.

"Let's just say that I realized that I've done some things wrong," I said. "I'm tryin' to backtrack now. Tryin' to make right what I can."

Gordo was studying me, giving away nothing of his own thoughts.

"I got a kid tells me that he can be a middleweight," he said at last. "Problem is he thinks he's an artist instead of a worker. Comes in here and batters around some of the rejects and thinks that he's Marvin Hagler or somethin'."

"Yeah? What's his name?"

"Punterelle, Jimmy Punterelle. Italian kid. He'll be in here the next three days. If I put some fifty-year-old warhorse in front of him and point he'll put on a shit-eatin' grin and go to town."

I pretended to consider these words for a moment or two and then said, "Okay."

It was Gordo's brief smile that eased my sadness, somewhat. He was my de facto confessor, and Jimmy Punterelle was going to be my Hail Mary.

I checked my illegal cell phone for messages but Roger Brown hadn't called. So when I was out on the street again I felt lighter, easier. Maybe everything would be okay. It didn't matter if my client only found out about three lowlifes. It didn't matter at all.

I WALKED UP TO Thirty-ninth Street and over to the Tesla Building, between avenues Six and Seven.

"Hello, Mr. McGill," Warren Oh said in greeting. Warren was one of the daytime weekday guards who stood behind a green-and-white marble podium set under a huge dark-red-and-white plaster mural in the lobby of the most beautiful Art Deco building in the world.

The fresco was of big blocky men and women walking/marching under a Romanesque arch that stood against a tiled azure sky. Some of the people were clothed, others not. They were all white, but I accepted the racial wish-fulfillment of the thirties.

"Hey, Warren," I hailed. "I haven't seen you for a while. Where you been?"

"Down home. My mother was sick."

"How is she now?"

"Fine, fine. Thank you for asking, Mr. McGill."

"How's the kids?"

"Doin' okay, sir. My boy got into technical college, and Mary's expecting."

Warren was Jamaican by birth. His mother was a black woman and his father a Chinese descendant of a long line of indentured servants. Warren had a beautiful face and loyal eyes. Every time I saw him I thought that he would make a great con man. You almost had to trust him.

"Ms. Ullman is looking for you, sir," the copper-colored guard said.

"Oh?"

"Said to ask you to come by her office."

"She just said to ask me?"

Warren shrugged and I smiled.

MY OFFICE SUITE in the Tesla Building was the apex of my professional life.

The old real estate manager, Terry Swain, had been siphoning money out of the maintenance fund for years. He never took much at any one time but it added up to quite a sum over twenty-six years. When my lease in the Empire State Building was about to lapse, I asked around and found out that Swain was being investigated by the Tesla's new owners for having stolen one hundred seventy-one thousand dollars. So I did a little research and went to his office on the eighty-first floor.

Terry was tall and thin, sandy-haired even at the age of sixty-one. At fifty-three I'm already three-quarters bald and half the way gray.

"Hello, Mr. Swain, I hear you got some problems," were my first words to him.

"Not me," he said with an unconvincing smile.

"No? That's too bad, because I'm the guy to go to when the hammer is comin' down and you need to get out of the way."

My words brought moisture to the man's eyes, if not hope.

"Who are you?" he managed to ask.

"Peter Cooly used to work in here with you, right?" I replied, gesturing to an empty desk in the corner.

"Peter's dead."

"Yep. Died just this last March. His second heart attack in two months. Last day he worked was February nine."

"So?"

"Did he have access to the books, bank accounts?"

Terry Swain had gray eyes that were very expressive. They widened as if seeing the rope that could save him just inches out of reach.

"Pete was honest."

"He was that. But he was a loner, too. No parents or wife, not even a girlfriend."

"So?"

"You got any money, Terry?"

"What's your name?"

"Leonid McGill is my name. Jimmy Pine sent me."

Jimmy was a bookie. Terry was one of his best customers.

"Leonid? What kind of name is that for a black man?"

"My father was a Communist. He tried to cut me from the same red cloth. He believed in living with everybody but his family. McGill is my slave name. That's why I got to do business with fools like you."

"What kind of business?"

"You ever hear of Big Bank?"

"On Forty-ninth?"

"Peter Cooly had a savings account there. I got a guy, a business associate owes me a favor, who works with a guy who works there. The guy in the bank can make it look like Pete deposited an extra twenty-four thousand in his account over the last six years."

"He can?" Terry passed gas then. He was a very worried man. "How?"

"My friend and his friend need six thousand apiece and then there's the twenty-four."

"I don't have that kind of money." Terry was so upset that he rose to his feet. "They're gonna prosecute me, Mr. McGill. They're gonna send me to prison."

"Say the word and I'll throw just enough suspicion on Pete so that any half-decent lawyer could keep the new owners from dragging you into court. Hell, they won't even be able to take your pension."

"Where am I gonna get thirty-six thousand dollars?"

"Forty-six," I said, correcting his perfect math. "You need ten for the lawyer."

"And what about you? What do you get out of this?"

"You got a jeweler vacating a suite of offices down on the seventy-second floor. Six rooms with views south and west. I like having a big office with a good view. People look at you differently when they think you're livin' large."

"So?"

"You're still the building manager. Give me a twenty-year lease at eighteen hundred a month and I'll pull the trigger on Pete."

"The Melmans are paying eleven thousand," Terry said.

I shrugged.

"I don't have the money," the sandy-haired fraudster complained.

"Jimmy Pine said that he'd advance it to you. I mean, you'll have to get another job to pay him back, but I bet you'd rather run a hot dog stand than spend your sunset years in prison."

We haggled for over an hour but in the end I got everything I wanted. Hyman-Schultz, real estate developers, dropped the charges when Breland Lewis, attorney-at-law, brought evidence to their attention that Peter Cooly was just as likely a candidate for the crime, even more so because Terry was always broke.

Swain retired early and bought a hot dog cart. Whenever I see him he gives me a hot sausage on the house.

Some people, when they see my office, think that I'm putting on airs. They want to know what I pay for rent but I never say. Others are quietly impressed, believing that there's more to me than they at first thought. The reaction to my posh workspace could be anything but whatever it is I'm left with an edge.

WHEN I GOT OFF the elevator on the seventy-second floor I felt a rush of satisfaction. The light fixtures along the hall are polished brass, and even the floor is a complex design of purple, green, and white marble tiles. The Tesla has wide hallways and the doors are heavy, hewn from solid oak. I got to the end of the hall and turned left. It was no surprise to see Aura Antoinette Ullman at the far end, waiting at my front door. Warren Oh had probably called her.

Aura was a tall woman, the color of dark burnished gold. She was near forty with a womanly maturity about her that always made me feel a thrumming somewhere near my heart. Her wavy hair was blond, naturally, and her cool-colored eyes defied definition by the color wheel. Her mother was Danish and her father a black man from Togo, an ambassador to some east European nation. Her father's Christian name was Champion. Aura had told me that her mother, Helene, married him for his name, but was let down.

She, Aura, took her mother's maiden name and came with her to New York when she was fifteen. She majored in business at CCNY and took over Terry Swain's job when he went into the hot dog business.

"You're seventeen days late on the rent," she said when I reached her.

I pulled out a keychain that held the seven keys I needed to open the locks that secured the outer chamber of my inner sanctum.

Hyman and Schultz had figured out that I was the likely cause of their problems, but they didn't have proof. So when they hired Aura they told her that her top priority was breaking my lease.

"The landlords want their money," Aura said. Her voice was also golden—sexy with an added vibration that sent chills down into my shoulder blades.

I had opened three locks.

"I will start eviction proceedings tomorrow if I don't have the rent by tonight."

Five locks.

"You know that your lease is a crime, Mr. McGill."

So's that black dress you're wrapped in, I thought.

Seven locks and the door came open.

When we walked in, the lights came on automatically. A tripped switch turned on three silent cameras that took digital pictures every eight seconds. The cameras were installed on a rare site-call by Tiny "Bug" Bateman himself, and so they were foolproof. I would look at the pictures of Aura later, after she'd finished threatening me and went back to her own office.

I leaned against the receptionist's desk while Aura shone her stern visage down on me.

"I got a job I'm just finishing up right now," I said. "I can pay you by tomorrow night."

She appraised my words with her stormy, sky-colored eyes and smirked. Then she shook her head.

"My number-one job is to get you out of here."

"Isn't there anything I can do?" I asked, standing up straight.

Aura was three inches taller than I but it seemed like a foot. She pulled her head back and sneered, shaking her head ever so slightly.

"Come on," I said. "Just one day. You know that you can't evict me if I pay by tomorrow anyway. It'll just be a lot of paperwork."

"The owners would like to see it."

"One day."

"One day," she said, "for one kiss."

It was astonishing to me that something so sweet could hurt so bad. Holding that woman in my arms, I ached for a whole other life, a life that I would never have. When she pressed her shoulder against mine I moaned as much from the pleasure as from the ache.

I pulled away, trying to remember how to breathe.

Her gaze was triumphant.

"I could tell you liked that, Leonid Trotter McGill."

I hadn't caught my breath yet.

"You don't love her," Aura said. "She's done you dirt again and again. Why would you stay there when it's obvious where you want to be?"

"Georg and Simon would fire you if they thought we were together," I said lamely.

"I can always get another job."

"I'll have your money before six o'clock day after tomorrow."

"I only gave you one day."

I went to the door, opened it, and looked down at her feet.

After Aura had gone I sat down in the receptionist's chair and put my feet up on her ash desk. I didn't have a receptionist but it was important to keep up appearances. I might become successful one day and need someone to greet my long line of wealthy clients.

Sitting there, gazing out the window at New Jersey, I wanted nothing more than to have Aura in my life. I wanted her to be my woman in a world where I was an upstanding and respectable citizen with a receptionist who only allowed honest civilians like myself past the front office.

These bouts of fantasy were always bittersweet because thoughts of what I didn't have always brought me back to the chain around my neck—my wife, Katrina.

"I'M GOING TO leave you, Leonid," Katrina had said to me one evening eleven months before. We were sitting in the dining room of our West Side apartment, alone.

I looked at her, trying to decipher the meaning of her words.

"Did you hear me?" she said.

Some months earlier Katrina joined a gym, had a surgical procedure that transformed her face from middle-age sag into something quite lovely. I had hardly noticed but by an act of supreme will Katrina had regained much of her youthful beauty.

"I've met someone," she'd said, wanting to keep the conversation going. "His name is Andre Zool."

"Uh-huh," I managed to say.

"He's an investment banker and he loves me."

"I see," I said but Katrina heard something different, a complaint.

"You haven't slept in our bed more than two nights in a row in half a year," she condemned.

"I've been sleeping in the office. I've been . . . been thinking."

"I need a real man in my life. Not a zombie."

"When are you going?" I asked, wondering about the silence in our seven rooms.

"There's no use in arguing," she said.

"I'm not arguing. I'm asking you when you're leaving."

"Dimitri is going to stay with Andre and me until he finds a dormitory," Katrina said, having a conversation in another dimension, with a different Leonid. "Shelly and Twill both want to stay with you."

"But I had blood tests done," I said from my separate reality. "Dimitri is the only one that's mine."

Katrina, in all her Nordic beauty and savagery, stood up from the table, knocking her chair to the walnut floor.

"You bastard!" she said and then stormed out of our apartment.

That was on a Wednesday, too. For six months I had been brooding over the corruption of my life. Katrina leaving meant nothing to me. We hadn't loved each other for a very long time. We hadn't ever lived in the same world.

On Monday Terry Swain announced his early retirement.

On Friday Aura Ullman put me on notice for Hyman and Schultz.

By Sunday Aura and I were lovers and I had decided that the only thing I could do was try to make right what I had done wrong. At night Aura and I slept wrapped in each other's arms. I begged her to come live with me but she had an adolescent daughter and thought that we should give it some time.

EIGHT MONTHS LATER the real estate market crashed.

Andre Zool had been instrumental in getting his company to buy up fourteen percent of Arizona's recent mortgage debt—and there was some question of kickbacks. He lost over a billion dollars. Zool got on a plane bound for Argentina, where his family had migrated after World War II.

The next morning I came home from work to find Katrina in our living room with our dour son Dimitri at her side.

"Forgive me," were her only words.

If she had said anything else, anything, I would have been able to send her away: I would have been able to go off with Aura to start a new life.

MY PRIVATE CELL PHONE, the legal one, rang. Actually it made the sound of a growling bear, the special tone I had given to anyone whose phone number came through as private.

"Mr. McGill?" he said. "Ambrose Thurman here. I tried your office phone but got no answer."

"Mr. Thurman. I was just about to call you."

"With good news, I hope," the fop detective said.

"Yes, very good news. I have located three of the four men you're looking for."

"What are their real names and addresses?" he said, his voice brimming with formality.

"There's a question of remuneration."

"A question of what?"

"You know what I'm saying—I need my money first."

"Oh, yes, of course. Yes—remuneration," he said, repeating the word carefully. "I will have to have all four names before I can pay you."

"Well, then I'll call you later."

I pressed the hang-up button on my phone and sat back in the phantom's chair.

There was something odd about Ambrose. He was an Albany detective working for an upstate client. This client wanted definitive information on all four subjects before he would pay.

I decided that I'd need more information before handing over what I had to the persnickety, overly formal Albanyite.

But I appreciated his call. Moping over lost love, a loveless relationship, and other things was no good. It tended to give me bad dreams.

In order to keep the momentum toward a healthier state of mind, I entered the code on the electronic lock that allowed entrance to my interior offices. Once I was ensconced behind my ebony desk, looking down over lower Manhattan, I logged onto a specially constructed computer using the ID $$Twillhunter@twilliam.com. This allowed me secret entrée to my favorite son's personal domain.

Once a week or so, as a rule, I perused Twill's personal e-mails. I did this because Twill, for all his superior qualities, was a natural-born criminal. He didn't hurt people physically but he was a whiz at getting in and out of locked rooms, performing Internet scams on children of his age, and putting A in touch with B to garner C. He had at least seventeen separate e-mail addresses, all of which were forwarded to Twill@twilliam.com. He had to have a pretty good hacker who helped him with all this, but I had Tiny "Bug" Bateman, and Tiny, by his own estimation, was the best in the world. Tiny had set me up so that by using the double dollar sign and the word "hunter" I could shadow Twill's every communication.

Most of the handsome teenager's e-mails were innocuous enough: young men talking about sports and girls, girls offering to do things that most of the children of my generation never even imagined, and minor criminal activities that I ignored because I had my shadow on Twill to rein him in if things started going seriously wrong.

The bear growled in my jacket pocket but I ignored it. If it was Thurman again he could cool his heels wondering if I was going to let him walk all over me. If it was someone else they could leave a message, because for the past few days my son had been getting some worrisome communications on his private address.

Someone, a teenage girl calling herself "M," had been sending Twill distressed and depressed messages. She'd even mentioned suicide. Twill was very good with her. He told her that she was a good person in bad circumstances and that he would be there for her anytime she needed. They never discussed the exact nature of her troubles but it had something to do with her family.

The problem was that Twill was more like a man than a sixteen-year-old boy and was apt to take on more than he could accomplish. So I had been signing on as his shadow once a day for the past week.

There was a message from M and a reply that day.

> Hey T, Thanks for your note. I really appreciate it but things are getting worse around here. Much worse. I really do think it would be better if I stopped him myself. I know that you have connections with people and if you could just give me a name of somebody who could sell me a gun that's all I need. Please do this for me. I have to do something.
>
> M

If that wasn't bad enough, Twill had an answer that set my teeth on edge.

M. I hear you girl. But you can't do something like that. You'll probably just hurt yourself. The street fair is just two weeks from this Saturday. You hold on till then and I'll take care of it for you. No one will know.

T

One of the many good qualities Twill had was that he never made idle promises. If he said he'd do something, he always tried his best. And I was absolutely sure that his best in this case was the death of someone. I had more than two weeks to defuse the situation. Looking on the good side—at least it gave me something positive to do.

5

Gazing at the gap in the skyline left by the World Trade Center, I thought about Twill. Not of my blood, he was tall and lithe, handsome and quick to smile. The only thing we had somewhat in common was our dark coloring but even there our skins were different hues. I had more brown to my blackness.

But blood relations are overrated. Twill had a way of making you feel good. His greeting—morning or night, being picked up at the police station or after a school function—was always friendly and sincere. His head was cool and his heart warm. Twilliam was one of the finest people I had ever met. And so it was my self-appointed duty to make sure that he wasn't pulled down in the wake of his own superiority.

A solitary seagull cried. That was the sound I had Tiny program into the stolen cell phone he sold me.

"Hello?"

"Who the hell is this?" an angry voice demanded.

"You called me, young man," I said trying to sound pleasant.

"Are you Arnold DuBois?" he asked, pronouncing the last name in French fashion.

"Du Boys," I said, correcting him on the pronunciation of my alias.

"Why are you trying to get in touch with me, Mr. Du Boys?" Roger said, maybe hearing some of the iron in my jaw and moderating his tone appropriately.

"Are you the Roger Brown that they used to call B-Brain back in the day?"

"Who *are* you, man?"

"My real name is Ambrose Thurman," I said. "I'm a private detective. And I have been retained to get in touch with you."

Three tiny blips sounded and I knew that Roger had hung up on me. It didn't matter. I had a hook into him now.

WHEN AMBROSE THURMAN came to me all he had was a short list of street names—Jumper, B-Brain, Big Jim, and Toolie —along with a few descriptive details. The last time his client had seen them they were kids, not much older than Twill. He needed their real names and current whereabouts. They all had had records as juvenile offenders but the bureaucracy of New York's judicial system wouldn't allow him to invade the privacy of minors.

Ambrose asked me if I could do what he could not.

That's where Randolph Peel came in. Randy had been a detective in the NYPD until they found him trading favors for sex at a posh midtown hotel. At one time he was the partner of a cop named Carson Kitteridge. Kitteridge was an honest cop, and it had been speculated that he was the cause of Peel's downfall.

Randy was out of a job but he still had a few friends in the department. For three hundred dollars a head, the former policeman broke the seals of justice and delivered the identities to me; three of them, at least. Jumper, Big Jim, and Toolie had gone on to commit adult crimes, but B-Brain was clean. I had a name, Roger Brown, but there was no practical information, like a current address. There were no adult records on him and the details of his adolescence were all cold as far as an investigation was concerned. His father was nowhere to be found, and his mother, Myra Brown, as far as I could tell, had died in 1993.

THE SEAGULL CRIED three times before I answered the phone again.

"Hello?"

"Who hired you?"

"It's not polite to hang up on a brother, Roger."

"I'm not your brother."

"You still hung up on me."

"Excuse me," he said, maybe even meant it. "I'm not used to private detectives calling me on the phone."

"You called me," I reminded him.

"You came to my office."

"It's not so bad," I said, "being sought by a PI. Nobody said you did anything wrong."

"Who hired you?"

"Are you the Roger Brown who was once known as B-Brain?" I asked again.

The silence was long and painful. Roger didn't want to hang up a second time. He didn't want to answer my question either. There was music playing in the background of whatever room he was in; thuggish hip-hop with an insistent beat.

"How much they payin' you, man?" a slightly different Roger Brown asked. This young man didn't wear a suit and tie or collect a salary that had taxes taken out.

"My regular fee."

"I'll double it."

"You don't know what it is."

"I'll pay you a thousand to forget me."

"Are you in trouble, Roger?"

"Naw, man. I ain't in no kinda trouble." His descent from Madison Avenue to the Lower East Side continued.

"Because," I said, "I only ever charge my standard fee. I never take more. That way I keep my nose clean."

"Why you up in my grill, man?"

"All I need to know from you is if you are the Roger Brown known as B-Brain."

"Why?"

"I'll tell you what, Roger," I offered. "I'll come over right now and meet you at that little espresso place across the street from your office or anywhere else you say. We could talk."

"Uh-uh. No way, man. I ain't meetin' you nowhere, no kinda way."

I had already been to his office. He didn't know what I looked like. Even if Juliet had described me, he didn't have my picture in his head. But Roger wasn't being rational. He was afraid of something, and I wanted to know what that something was.

I made a few sounds that were meant to express hesitation.

"I'm not used to giving out information on my clients," I said. "That kind of breach in confidentiality is not looked upon kindly in my profession. But maybe if we got together you might convince me."

"I already told you, man. No."

Roger wasn't going to trust me even though I was telling him the truth. I wanted to meet him face-to-face so that I could judge for myself if he was in some kind of fix that Ambrose had not informed me about.

"Frankie Tork," I said and the line went so silent that for a moment I thought the connection had gone dead.

"S-say what?"

"Frank Tork. He's in the Tombs right now awaiting trial on B and E. They caught him trying to burglarize a pawnshop on Second Avenue."

"Frankie hired you?"

"I AIN'T SEEN B-Brain in years, brother," Frankie Tork had told me through a Plexiglas window in the visitor's area of the New York City jail. "His moms and them moved somewhere out in Brooklyn right before his last year in high school. She said that we was a bad influence."

Jumper was small and wiry, brown like a walnut is brown, with tar-stained teeth and bloodshot eyes. He had the kind of smile that frightened children—and their mothers.

"What was his mother's name?" I asked, trying to corroborate the sketchy information I'd gotten from ex-officer Peel. Roger, aka B-Brain, and the others had been arrested for trespassing in 1991.

"Mrs. Brown," Frankie said.

"You don't know her first name?"

"You still gonna gimme that twenty dollars, right?"

There was an account I could credit. I would have given him the money even if he wasn't any help.

"What was B-Brain's first name again?" I asked.

"Roger."

"Yeah, I'll give you twenty bucks."

"Maybe I could ask around, about his mom's name, I mean."

"No thanks, Jumper." I made to rise.

"Hey, hey, man."

"What?"

"They say around here that you the kinda dude get a brother out of a jam."

"I used to do that. Not anymore."

"How much?" Jumper asked, ignoring my claim of retirement.

"Twenty thousand was my lowest fee." That was a lie. No one

had ever paid me that much. But I didn't want to give Jumper false hope.

"Damn, man. All I got is the twenty dollars you payin' me."

"See you."

". . . WHY JUMPER WANT you to find me?" Roger asked, admitting that he was the man I was looking for.

"His lawyer, Matrice Johnson, is a friend of mine. Professional. She asked me to find somebody who could be a good character witness for Frankie, said that it might make a difference between three and seven years in the sentencing."

"I haven't seen Frankie in sixteen years, man. How'm I gonna be a character witness for somebody I don't even know no more?"

"Well," I said, "if you're not willing to help a brother out . . ."

"He's not my brother. And how the hell you even know how to find me?"

"Some girl," I said.

"What girl?"

"A friend of Jumper's—Georgiana Pineyman. She saw you come into Berg, Lewis & Takayama a few months ago but when she tried to get to you they turned her away at the front desk."

"Well, you found me but I can't give Jumper a reference. I can't. I don't even know him anymore." Roger was feeling some relief. His language drifted back toward the semi-sophistication of an investment advisor.

"Okay. My job was to find you and ask for your help. That's all."

"So we finished?"

"Goodbye, Roger."

Just a year and a half before I wouldn't have had the slightest compunction at turning Roger's name over to Ambrose Thurman. Even that day, if Roger was a hood like his old friends, I wouldn't have been bothered.

But as things stood I had misgivings.

On the one hand Roger sounded scared, on the other the rent was due and there were no new jobs on the horizon. Aura liked me, maybe she even loved me, but she was going to do her job. I'd be on the street by the end of the month if I didn't pay the landlord's fee.

"Money is a chain that the worker willingly wraps around his own neck," my father had said many a time. "It chokes him and weighs him down until finally, one day, he would kill his own brother for just a few minutes' relief."

Maybe if my father, Tolstoy McGill, hadn't gone off to South America to fight the fascists or the capitalists or whoever, maybe if he'd come back and been a parent to me, I would have tried to live by the vision of his perfect world. Maybe if my mother, once she knew the love of her life was never coming back, hadn't gone to her bed and lay there until the doctors came and took her off to the hospital to die, maybe then I would have taken a different path.

But as it was I had to make my own way in a world

of chains and choking, imperfect choices and the fools who made them.

"HELLO?" AMBROSE THURMAN said, answering his phone on the first ring.

"I got all four names."

"What are they?"

"You want 'em over the phone?"

"Yes, indeed. Time is of the essence."

"You see, you and me got something in common there, Mr. Thurman."

"What's that, Mr. McGill?"

"I want my money."

"I can't give you your, your remuneration on the phone." He used the word as if trying to learn it, to integrate it into his vocabulary.

"And so I can't give you what I got."

"I can send it to you via overnight mail."

"I have a better idea."

"What's that?"

"Why don't you come down here this evening and we'll trade information and money across a table, face-to-face."

I wasn't my father or my mother. I wouldn't run away or lie down and give up.

"Meet me at the Crenshaw tonight at nine forty-five," Thurman said in angrily clipped words.

"That's what I'm talkin' about."

THE AFTERNOON PASSED quietly enough. I logged onto the BBC website and perused the world, starting in Africa. I always start there, looking to see what the news providers of American TV didn't deem important.

I had worked my way through South America and Asia before Twill came back to mind. I couldn't let him know that I had bugged his IP. Not that I was worried about him getting upset but because this wouldn't be the last intervention I'd have to make in his formative years. It wasn't the first, either.

At the age of fourteen he had already spent six months in a juvenile facility for stealing middle school property.

"I got the idea from something you said, Dad," he'd told me when we got home from the police station after his initial arrest.

"From me?"

"You were always sayin' how people in Africa and other places didn't have the tools they needed to compete, so I found out about the School Supply Fund and set up a fake office to sell computers to them."

"How much property did you move?" I asked. The boy had been arrested for stealing five computers and three microscopes.

"A lot," young Twill answered.

He'd organized a group of adolescent thieves at eleven schools, kids that he'd met through his sister's Leadership Camp the previous summer. They had cleared over fifteen thousand dollars and still gave the NGO a great deal.

Luckily the authorities didn't have enough of an imagination to delve into the depths of Twilliam's crimes. But I was put on notice to keep him out of trouble.

When I looked up, the sun was setting. Twill always gave me both worry and wonderment. He was the only person I'd known who met me halfway in life.

AT ABOUT 8:30 I walked across from the Tesla to the East Side and took a subway up to Eighty-sixth Street. From Lexington I walked two blocks north, and east for three. There I came to the Crenshaw, an exclusive little hotel that catered to an upscale clientele.

The doorman, clad in a red coat and black trousers, gave me a look like Juliet had at Berg, Lewis & Takayama. I smiled as pleasantly as I could, walked past him, and made my way to the bar. It was a dark room of red lampshades and dark-stained wood. I was half an hour early but Ambrose was already there at a small round table near the high bar. He was seated in a spindly chair with his hands clasped on his lap. I remember thinking that he was just sitting there, not reading a newspaper or a book, not searching his BlackBerry for e-mails and text messages. He wore a dark-gray suit with a bright-red vest and a checkered blue-and-white ascot. His glass frames were small and rectangular, and his blue, blue eyes didn't miss a thing.

"Mr. McGill," he said through a meaningless smile. "Have a seat."

He gestured at a sturdier chair across from him.

I sat, putting an elbow on my left knee and a palm on my right. I took that position to let Thurman know that I meant to get down to business.

"Wonderful weather, isn't it?" he said. "They talk about global warming but every year seems more moderate than the last, cooler and more habitable."

"Why does your client want these names?" I said.

Ambrose swiveled his head slowly, making sure that no one was listening.

"Why does anybody want anything?" he asked, moving his shoulders in a kind of bound-up shrug.

"I do it for the money," I said. "But not if it causes trouble for somebody who doesn't deserve it."

Ambrose smiled.

"I'm not joking with you, man," I said. "I need to know what you're going to use this information for."

Thurman was in his forties but looked older. He was bulbous, with a receding hairline and pudgy, pale hands. He used his little mitts to pull down the Ben Franklin spectacles, peering over the frames at me through the gloom of the posh bar.

"I was told that you were the kind of man who did a job with no questions asked," he said.

"Who told you that?"

"It doesn't matter who it was. What matters is that I seem to have been misinformed."

"I used to be a heartless kind of guy, Mr. Thurman," I said. "If a job needed me to be cold-blooded, cruel, or blind I was willing to oblige. But today I need to know what you plan to do with what I give you."

"Are you trying to up your remuneration?" he asked, missing the honesty in my tone.

"Not really."

Thurman pushed his foppish glasses up and sat back in his chair. Considering me, he took in a deep breath through his nostrils.

"A person, the name doesn't matter, had a son who died tragically and comparatively young. It was one of those quick and terrible diseases that come out of nowhere and leaves a happy home bereft.

"This person, the parent, was once a rough-and-ready sort with no money and few prospects. They lived on the Bowery and raised their son there. These young men were his friends. Next month will mark the first anniversary of the boy's death, and my client, the boy's parent, wishes to include his old friends together in the memorial service."

"Why would your client need all four names or none?"

"It was a promise they made to themselves. I'm not sure but I believe there's more than a little superstition involved."

"Names?" I asked.

"No names, Mr. McGill."

It was a plausible story. Whoever was looking for the young men hadn't known them since they were teenagers. Roger was upset by someone knowing about his old life, not someone who might be after him today. And, anyway, I was broke and the rent was due.

"It cost me twelve hundred dollars to get this information," I said. "So before I hand it over to you I need to see eleven thousand, two hundred dollars, right here, right now." I tapped the table in a fast two-finger tattoo, like some bongo drummer from the fifties.

"Here?" Thurman said, gazing around.

There was no one else except the bartender in the room. She was a young thing with red hair and a sharp nose.

"Have you got a room upstairs or do you have people meet you here just to impress them?" I asked.

There were two dark-wood elevator doors next to the front desk. Ambrose pressed the button and we stood there in silence, waiting for a car to come. Two very young women wearing extremely short and sheer party dresses were talking to the dour, gray-headed man who stood behind the reception desk. The girls were shadowed by two older women, one wearing a fox stole, in June, the other attired in a coral Chanel dress, the cost of which would have paid my office rent through Christmas. The older women were visibly disturbed by the particular manifestation of youth before them.

The man behind the desk was acutely aware of the older ladies; he probably knew them by name.

"Are you sure?" the young brunette was saying to the skeptical night manager. "Did you look under Mr. Charles, um, Smith?"

The man shook his head, forcing a smile from somewhere deep down where there had never been levity or light.

"No, Frankie," the blonde of the two said. "Smythe. Chandler Smythe. He's in the Coolidge Suite."

The blonde didn't look at the man. Her relationship was bonded to the brunette with the bad memory.

"That's right, Tru."

"This is unbelievable," the woman with the dead canine wrapped around her throat said.

The night man was already on the phone, already talking to rich Mr. Smythe. With the receiver still to his ear he managed a constipated grimace, then said, "You can go right up," to the girls. "It's on the eleventh floor."

At that moment a muted chime sounded and the elevator doors opened. I moved inside the chamber, followed by a slightly distracted Ambrose Thurman. The door was already closing when one of the children—I think it was Tru—cried, "Hold that door!"

I heard the call but it didn't move me. I was conducting business. When I was on the job I resisted any diversions. But Ambrose's arm shot out and a new kind of smile, a grin actually, restructured his pear-shaped face.

"Ladies," he said as Tru and Frankie joined us.

"Eleventh floor, please," Tru replied in a surprisingly businesslike tone.

The elevator car was stylish with lobster-pink velvet walls and an actual crystal chandelier hanging above. The metal fittings were gold-plated and brilliant, but the mechanism was clearly from the same era. The car climbed slowly as the not-so-subtle scent of the girls' perfumes filled the space.

"You're a boxer, huh?" brown-haired Frankie said to me somewhere around floor three.

"Say what?"

"I can tell by your hands. It's those big knuckles and scars." There was a severe cast to her topaz-brown eyes.

"I coulda got that from bar fights," I speculated.

"Uh-uh," Frankie said, dismissing my words as only a woman thinking she's beautiful could. "You've got strong hands and a boxer's shoulders. I could tell just by the way you stand there, so easy."

With just those few words the child had gotten past half of my natural defenses. She had named me for what I was with a lazy kind of intensity.

"I had an old man was a boxer," she said. "He had a middleweight belt for four months—twelve, thirteen years ago."

"What's your name?" Ambrose asked Tru.

She didn't answer him. She was too busy watching her friend dissect me.

"He was the nicest boyfriend I ever had," Frankie was saying. "He was real strong, but gentle as a girl."

The machinery of the elevator hummed softly. I took the wallet out of my back pocket and handed the girl my card, my real card with a cell phone number that I actually answered sometimes.

"Here you go, Frankie," I said, saying her name just to show her that I paid attention too.

She took the stiff piece of paper and opened her tiny purse, which was made from an actual jumbo clamshell. She put my card in and took out a pink one.

"Oh my God," Tru whispered.

I took the card and read the name printed in red letters on the pink paper—Frankee Tayer. There was a handwritten number across the bottom. The personal touch.

The elevator doors opened on the eighth floor and we left Tru and Frankee on their trek to the Coolidge Suite. My heart rate had increased and I was a little confused moving into the hall behind Ambrose.

"Are you going to call her?" he asked me as we got to room 808.

"No need," I said, watching him fit the magnetic keycard into the slot of the lock.

"Why not?"

"The high point of our entire relationship was just now."

The Albany detective smiled and pushed the door open. He gestured for me to enter, and I passed from one reality to another.

IT WAS WHAT they call a junior suite—a largish room with a small couch and a cushioned chair across from a queen-sized bed. Ambrose took the sofa and I sat in the chair. He didn't offer me a drink or any more small talk. He was ready for business.

The scent of the girls' perfume was still in my nose. I snorted once in order to get my head back into business. Ambrose was looking at me like a counterpuncher in the early rounds of a hard fight—waiting for me to make the first move.

I didn't oblige him. Tru and Frankee had thrown me off balance. I needed more time for my head to clear.

"What about the twenty-five-hundred advance?" the prig feinted.

"What about it?" I jabbed.

"Shouldn't that cover your expenses?"

"I told you that you had to give me the advance just for me to look into the case, that it was in no way against my fee or to cover expenses."

After a moment or two of this face-off Thurman pulled a huge wallet from his breast pocket, producing a thick stack of hundred-dollar bills. One at a time he began putting bills on the low coffee table before us. As he stacked the notes, we both counted. I was experiencing the lust for women and the need for money (or maybe it was the other way round). When Thurman reached one hundred twelve he stopped, put the rest of the stack back in his wallet, and returned the wallet to its pocket.

The heap of bills lay there before me, a come-on that was hard to resist. Through a supreme act of will I managed not to reach out for the cash.

"Just to know," Ambrose said, "what were the expenses?"

"Those street names you gave me were for underage kids," I

said. "The law, as you know, tries to protect their identities. But I know a cop, got drummed out of the force for an injudicious liaison."

Thurman smiled at the last two words. He liked pretentious language.

"My friend," I continued, "has contacts that can get to information without bothering with judges and writs and all that nonsense."

While paying close attention to my every word, the detective still had the concentration to take a cigarette from a pack in his vest pocket. He picked up a lighter from the table.

"What was this detective's name?"

He set fire to the cigarette. My nostrils widened, pulling in the aroma. I hadn't had a cigarette in ten months and I missed them every single day.

"No names," I said, "remember?"

"Okay. What do you have?"

"Toolie's real name is Theodore Nilson. He's doing eighty-six years upstate for aggravated assault."

"Eighty-six years?"

"Ain't that a bitch? Poor kid gets his day in court with a defense attorney just outta college and the judge gives him triple-time just for being stupid.

"Jumper's name is Frank Tork. Frankie's in the Tombs right now awaiting trial on B and E."

Thurman was staring hard at me, submitting my words to memory. I wasn't worried about being cheated; the money was on the table. The only problem I had was finishing the list.

"Big Jim was born, and died, under the name James Wright. He succumbed to complications from a hot spike on the same day that we invaded Iraq for the second time. I don't know if the two had anything to do with each other—the heroin could have come from Afghanistan."

I stopped there, inhaling the secondhand smoke as best I could.

"And B-Brain?" the detective asked when he could see that I was stuck.

The question tightened my eyes.

"B-Brain was the hard part," I said, stalling now with superfluous information. "He had no record and so didn't have a floater file in the police records. The other three had other friends. There was a guy named Thom Paxton who they called Smiles, and a girl, there's always a girl, named Georgiana Pineyman. She called B-Brain Pops for some reason. Georgiana was Smiles' girlfriend from September to June, but she hung with Pops in the summer because Smiles went away with his family during school break.

"I got it all right here," I said, taking a thick envelope from my jacket pocket.

"B-Brain's real name is in there?" the upstate detective asked.

"Yeah."

Ambrose put out his cigarette and smiled. He lit up another and, taking a deep breath, I sucked up as much of the smoke as I could.

"You know this is just a normal job, don't you, Leonid?" he said. "It's not cloak-and-dagger. The client is known to me."

"Uh-huh."

At that moment Thurman proved that he was a shrewd judge of human nature. He offered me a cigarette. I really needed one right then. He lit me up and I was genuinely grateful.

Handing me the pack, he said, "Keep 'em. There's some matches in the cellophane."

I traded the history of four troubled young men's lives for nine filterless Camels and eight red-tipped matches.

I got back to my street, a block east of Riverside Drive, at a few minutes past eleven. Katrina was at the door before I could get my key out of the lock.

Her presence annoyed me. In all the years of our less than loving marriage Katrina never waited up. She didn't want kisses or make overtures for sex. She never asked how I was doing or when I was coming back home. She maintained the house and looked after her children and mine. We had a balance, a home life that I could follow like a German train schedule.

"Leonid," she said, putting her arms around me, kissing my cheek.

She was wearing a frilly pink nightgown and lime-green slippers. Katrina maintained most of the beauty that she'd generated for Zool. She'd put on a few pounds but didn't look anywhere near her fifty-one years. Her green eyes were actually luminescent.

"I was worried," she said. She had a slight Swedish accent, which was a little odd since she was born in Queens and, even though her parents were Scandinavian immigrants, they hailed from Minnesota.

"I come home late two nights out of three," I said, moving away from the embrace. "What are you worried about?"

"You didn't call."

"I never call."

"But you should. I was worried."

She followed me down the hall to the dining room. I sat at the table, not knowing what to do in a house where I felt both welcomed and alienated.

"You want me to heat you something?" my bride asked.

Katrina could make anything in the kitchen, and it always tasted great. Even those years when we lived separately together she made a good dinner seven nights a week.

"What you got?" I asked.

"French beef, with those wide noodles you like."

"Red wine sauce?"

"Of course."

I nodded because I hadn't eaten.

"I'll get the children," she said.

"It's late, Katrina," I complained.

"Children must respect their father," she said, bustling off down the corridor that led to the bedrooms.

We had a big prewar apartment, more than large enough for our family of five. I had my own den, the kids each had a bedroom, and the rent never went up. The landlord and Katrina had an arrangement. I never asked what that was. I never cared.

In the momentary solitude, Roger Brown came to mind. I hadn't even met him but still I sold his name for the money bulging in my breast pocket. I tried to convince myself that this wasn't like the people I'd bushwhacked in the old days. It was just a job. Roger would probably thank me, or maybe he'd get a call from his old friend's parents and politely decline the invitation.

"Hi, Dad," Shelly said. She entered the room from the hallway that led to the bedrooms.

Shelly had dark olive skin and almond eyes, in shape and color. She didn't look like me in the slightest but that didn't keep her from expressing a daughter's love. She hugged my head and kissed my cheek. Shelly had been a daddy's girl since she was a baby. I loved her, after a fashion, even though we didn't have much in common.

"How are you?" she asked. There was still sleep in her eyes. She wore a T-shirt and jeans thrown on quickly in her haste to welcome me home.

"Workin' hard," I said. "Just finished a case tonight."

"We should celebrate. You want me to make you a martini?"

It was the one thing she could do that I enjoyed.

"Sure, babe."

As Shelly ran off toward the kitchen, Dimitri rumbled in. He was a shade or two lighter than I, with my body type but taller. He was brooding and heavy-handed. Dimitri was my blood, you could see it in every aspect of his personality and demeanor.

"Hey, boy."

He grunted and sat in the chair furthest from me.

"How's college?" I asked, intent on engaging him.

"I need my sleep."

"I know. Your mother seems to think that we have to eat together no matter when I get home."

"I already ate," he complained. "I was in bed at nine."

"I'm sorry," I said. "Really."

The apology got me another grunt.

I wasn't angry at the sullen junior. He didn't like me, but he was my son and I would be a father to him no matter how he felt.

"Hey, Pop," the youngest of the brood said.

He was standing in the doorway smiling and easygoing. Twill was a handsome teenager. Dark-skinned, he was sixteen but could have passed for twenty-one easily.

"Twilliam," I said, saluting.

"You work too hard, Pops. If they paid you by the hour you'd make minimum wage look good."

He took the seat next to me and slugged my shoulder.

"How's school?"

"I got passing grades and my teachers are just about trained good."

"You makin' it to class?"

"Yes sir. Almost every day."

I should have gotten mad but instead I laughed.

"Dinner is served," Katrina announced. She entered the room carrying a large tray bearing two big bowls and a breadbasket. Behind her came Shelly with a chrome shaker and a martini glass. In the old days she would have had a glass for her mother too, but since Katrina had abandoned our family for Andre Zool, Shelly refused to serve her.

"Dimitri, get us some plates from the cabinet," Katrina said.

"I'm not eating," he replied.

Before I could say anything Twill popped up and went to get our plates. He was a peacemaker, a very important trait for a career criminal.

"Don't give me one," Dimitri said, holding his hands over his little parcel of the table.

"I'm on a diet," Shelly said.

"Isn't anyone going to eat with their father?" Katrina asked the universe.

"I will," Twill said.

My wife served me and her son.

He only took one bite but I still felt good that he joined me.

Shelly chattered on about her classes and classmates, her teachers, and a cute boy named Arnold. Dimitri was silent and Katrina kept asking if I wanted more.

When the food was gone and the shaker half empty, Dimitri stomped off to bed. Shelly followed after kissing me goodnight. She was a lovely Asian child. Her father, I was quite sure, was a jeweler from Burma who'd had a yearlong affair with my wife.

"I'll help with the dishes, Mom," Twill offered when Katrina began stacking plates.

"No, darling. You keep your father company."

She carried off the plates and we sat, side by side, at the table for eight.

Twill had a small scar under his chin, a blemish from a tumble he took as a toddler. I often thought that that little protuberant flaw made him even more perfect, telling the world that this handsome representation of a man was human too.

"How's it goin', Twill?" I asked.

"Can't complain."

"You see your probation officer this week?"

"This afternoon. He said I was doing fine."

Twill always looked you in the eye when speaking.

"Any girls on the scene?" I asked.

He hunched his shoulders, giving away nothing.

Twill didn't call girls hos and bitches, as many of his friends did; not that he was outraged by that kind of language.

That's just the way people talk, he once told me. *I don't do it 'cause it don't sound right comin' outta my mouth, that's all.*

"Is everything okay?" I asked.

"It is what it is, Pop."

The setting of the dream changes slightly over time but in essence it remains the same.

I'm in a burning building, running through a maze of blazing hallways. In this particular nightmare I come to a staircase and wonder if it's worth trying to get down that way. But when I arrive at the door, flames vomit out at me. I run through an office door into a burning room. I run from room to room, breathing hard, choking on the smoke and hot air.

I come to another stairwell but it is blocked by smoldering timbers. I try to move them but orange embers burn my hands, sending me reeling backwards. I stumble and right myself again and again, running in between the stagger. All of a sudden I see a window at the end of a long, flame-licked hallway. I take a step and the floor under my foot gives way. Shifting my weight to the other foot, I spring forward, vaulting over the gaping hole in the floor. The walls and floor and ceiling are all flame now. At every step the floor gives way behind me. I keep on moving toward that faraway window, certain that I won't make it. I'm running. Smoke is rising from my clothes. My senses become confused with each other. I see the concussive cracking of flame and hear the bright heat. My mind is burning and it is my soul more than any other part of me that is racing for the liberation of the window.

Suddenly I am standing on a solid floor before the huge plate-glass frame. The window is occluded by smoke residue. There is no mechanism to open it. I rush back into the conflagration to retrieve a burning timber. And though I am being burned I batter the glass, again and again. It cracks and buckles, weakens and finally gives way.

As the window falls I am faced with the most beautiful blue sky I have ever seen. Below, the broken pane and flaming timber are still falling through thousands of feet to earth. Fire and heat pulse behind me. The day beckons. The wind is bracing, and the choice . . . no choice at all.

I don't remember jumping, just the sensation of falling through the frigid atmosphere, the cold wind freezing my burnt skin, clean air excavating the tar from my lungs. I expected that falling through space would be quiet, like the last moments in a film when the sound cuts out while the hero is being shot down protecting the town from a gang of bandits.

This fall is loud, however; it roars in my ears, a jungle beast hungry for prey.

The ground is racing toward me with deadly indifference.

I STARTED AWAKE, gulping for air, with my hands thrust out in front of me to stop the deadly fall. The television was droning on about some kind of new abdominal exercise machine. Katrina, who cannot sleep without the company of her precious TV, was unconscious there next to me.

Like a sprinter at the end of a race, I needed many deep gulps of air before I could breathe normally. My chest was hurting and I wanted more than anything to scream. I was shivering and cold, sweating too.

I never dreamt about my victims, but their memory is the mortar and stone of that burning building.

The alarm clock on my side of the bed said 5:06.

I couldn't bear the thought of another meal with my half-family and pretend wife.

I knew full well that Katrina was being so nice to me only because she had faced the real possibility of being set adrift in life at middle age. If she met a new Andre Zool tomorrow she'd be gone by the end of the week.

I rolled out of bed and went to my den, where I always kept a change of clothes.

Down on the street I lit one of Ambrose Thurman's Camels and walked toward Broadway. At a kiosk on the corner I bought the *Daily News,* which I started reading right there on the street. I might have made some headway but raindrops hit my nose and left thumb.

That's Jesus kissing you with his tears, my mother whispered from the grave. She loved my father unconditionally but never accepted his atheistic ideology.

I COULDN'T READ in the subway because the closeness in there brought back the desperation of my dream. I imagined fire rolling through the subway car and people screaming, battering the windows with their hands and heads.

THERE'S A DINER DOWN the block from the Tesla Building. I read my paper there while eating a scrambled-egg sandwich with American cheese, bacon, yellow mustard, and raw onions. I scoured the metro section of the paper, looking for news about people I knew in my previous life. There were killings and robberies, a kidnapping, and three major arrests, but none of it had to do with me.

My heart was still thrumming from the nightmare and so I did the crossword puzzle. I had just penciled the five-letter name for "Black crime writer" when I noticed that it was three minutes after seven.

I made my way down to the Tesla and took an elevator to the eighty-first floor. That's where Aura Ullman's office was. She was always at work by seven.

The ornate halls that I had loved the day before now made me nervous, the corridors so reminiscent of the dream. But seeing her door and the light through the frosted glass pane eased my tension a bit.

"Who is it?" she called in answer to my knock.

"Leonid."

"Come in."

A click sounded from the electric release of the lock. I pushed the door and walked in.

It was one big room. There was probably a window somewhere but there was so much stuff stacked along the walls that it was anybody's guess where it might have been. There were cleaning supplies and filing cabinets, three safes and five pegboards, with dozens of keys hanging from each one. Fire extinguishers, cartons of toilet paper, a dozen new mops, and cans of paint were stacked in such a way as to form an aisle leading to Aura's big black-metal desk.

The ceiling was lined with half a dozen rows of fluorescent lights, all of them glaring brightly.

"How can you bear this kinda light?" I asked when I'd gotten to her desk.

"I take life as it comes," she answered and I thought about Twill and his similar philosophy.

I sat in a dark green metal folding chair in front of her. She looked up from the big ledger she'd been writing in.

"You had that dream again, didn't you?" she said.

She looked into my eyes and I felt sick. Gazing across the expanse of the cluttered desk at a woman so aware of my mood seemed to be the symbol of my impossible life.

"Yeah," I said.

"What's it about?"

Many a night while sleeping with Aura I had started awake from that same dream. Every time she'd ask me what it was about but I couldn't answer. It felt like naming the dream would somehow make it real.

"I don't know, Aura. I don't know."

She got up and went to her old, old Mr. Coffee machine and poured the strong brew into a Styrofoam cup. She brought this to me and sat on top of the desk, looking down on my head.

For three or four long minutes we sat there. I appreciated the respite, the moments when I could be myself in silence, but with company.

"Why do you stay with her?" Aura asked at last.

"I don't—" I said and stopped.

I looked up to see her stormy eyes. She was smiling because she knew that I had stopped myself from lying.

"It's my sentence," I said. "It's what I owe."

"You don't love her."

"That's what makes it a punishment."

"She doesn't care about you."

"But I'm the evil she's familiar with," I said. "I'm the guy on the ground floor, so she knows I can't let her down."

"That doesn't make any sense," Aura said. "You're a good man, and even if you weren't, everyone should have some happiness in their lives."

I stood up and handed her an envelope with thirty-seven hundred dollars in it: two months' rent plus a hundred-dollar late fee.

Taking the money from me, she said, "I want you back."

"Thanks for the coffee, Aura. It means a lot to me."

I was behind my desk when the buzzer to the front door sounded. The image on the monitor in my desk drawer was confirmation of the rightness of my decision to stay out of Aura's life.

Tony "The Suit" Towers was slouching there, loitering in the hall the same way he hung out on the stoops of Hell's Kitchen when that area of Manhattan lived up to its name.

I made my way to the front door and opened up for the middle-management hood.

He was a tall white man of indeterminate middle age. Slim and green-eyed, Tony professed to own two hundred and forty-eight suits, and a different pair of shoes for each one. These outfits weren't very fine or expensive, but few people ever saw him wear the same ensemble twice.

That morning he had on sky-blue rags with a black shirt and yellow tie. His shoes were bone-colored, his short-brimmed hat navy. When he saw me he dropped the cigarette he was smoking and crushed it underfoot.

His moderately straight teeth were tar stained and uninviting.

"Hello, LT," he said. There was a torn quality to the habitual criminal's voice, an unpleasant gruffness.

"Tone."

It bothered me most that Towers came alone to my door. He usually traveled with two leg breakers named Lucas and Pittman. If they had come along I would have known that it was business as usual: a collection or maybe a simple interrogation. When Tony moved alone he was a shark on the hunt and that meant there was already blood in the water.

We shook hands and smiled politely.

I considered asking him his business right there in the hall, telling him without uttering the words that he was no longer welcome in my world. But pushing Tony Towers away would be like sweeping a rattlesnake under the bed before retiring. He wasn't in the top echelon of the New York underworld, but since I had vacated my position as a PI for the various mobs and crews I had no natural defenses against men like him.

So I backed away, allowing him entrée. Once he was in I trundled back toward my office. Tony followed close behind. I barely cringed. After all, a bullet in the back of the head was probably the best way to leave this world.

Tony didn't shoot me, though. He followed me into my office and took a seat in the blue client's chair, without an invitation.

As I made it around to my desk chair Tony was already conducting business.

"I got a problem, LT. It's the kinda thing you're good at, too."

Sitting down was a good thing. It left me with nothing to do but pay close attention to the criminal sitting there before me.

Tony had a long face, and now that he'd doffed his hat you could see the double spikes of his receding hairline. He placed a cigarette between his lips, lit a match, and then asked, "Do you mind if I smoke?"

"Burn away," I replied.

My unwelcome guest didn't like the answer but he lit his menthol and inhaled deeply.

"So I got this problem—"

"I'm not in the life anymore, Tony," I said, cutting him off. "I don't walk that side of the street."

"That's what they say. Benny told me that you're a straight arrow now. You know what I told Benny?"

I sighed.

"I told Benny," The Suit continued, "that LT knows that he's a little fish in a big ocean. I told him that the only little fishes that survive are the ones eat the parasites off from where the big ones can't reach."

Tony smiled, showing off his soiled teeth.

"I'm out, man," I said.

The smile dried up, which was both a relief and a worry.

"Don't get all upset," he said. "All I want from you is some legitimate private-detective work, not no criminal activity."

Tony had lived so long because he was crafty if not smart. What he needed was more important than putting me in my place. I didn't have the juice to turn down a legitimate request. If I refused to hear him out he would have to send Lucas and Pittman to talk to me.

"Let's hear it," I said.

The smile returned and Tony leaned forward in the chrome-and-cobalt-vinyl chair.

"There's this guy I'm lookin' for."

"What guy?"

"A Mann."

"What man?"

"That's his name. A Mann."

"What's the A stand for?"

"No," Tony said, waving his cigarette around. "His father named him A because he always wanted him to be at the head of the line."

"But the line goes in alphabetical order by the last name," I said consciously keeping my hands from becoming fists.

"His old man was a go-getter but nobody ever said he was smart."

I wanted a cigarette but worried that lighting up would show Tony that I was nervous. So I sat back and stared.

"I need to find Mann," Tony said.

"What for?"

"To talk to him."

"About what?"

"That's my business," the mobster said, an edge in his raspy voice, smoke rising up above his head.

"If it's your business, then you go find him." It struck me then that smoking Tony and his ilk were the fires that drove my dreams.

"What's wrong with you, LT?" he asked. "I'm willing to pay you to find a missing person. That's all. No cop could brace you over that."

"I'm not lookin' for somebody unless I know why, Tony. I'm just not doin' it. You got some problem with this guy, then go out and settle it. I'm not on your payroll."

"I could send Lucas and Pitts over here to convince you," he said.

"Send 'em, then."

"Just 'cause you're friends with Hush don't mean you can disrespect me, LT."

That was Tony's gauntlet. Uttering Hush's name meant that he was serious. Everybody who was anybody in our world knew that the ex-assassin and I were acquainted. Just mentioning Hush sent serious men on long-term sabbaticals.

"Tell me why you want to see this guy or get outta here," I said.

The gangster made a motion like he was going to crush his

cigarette out on my desk. If he followed through I would have had to do something; neither of us wanted that.

Tony dropped the butt on the floor and stepped on it.

"Eight, nine years ago I had a small job with the button and cloth union," he said, "handling disputes. The IRS is lookin' into my finances from that time and they need records from back then. Mann was my personal accountant, provided by the union, and he's the only one who's got those records."

"So you want the files?"

"I need to talk to the man himself," Tony said. "The feds will want to interrogate me and I need to get up to speed. It's been a long time."

I didn't believe a word of it but I couldn't call him a liar straight out.

"So?" Tony asked.

"I got a full plate right now, Tone. There's lotsa other PIs you could call."

"I know you."

"I'm busy."

"Don't make this a problem, LT. Find the guy for me. I swear to you it's legit."

Not for the first time did I think of my going straight like getting caught in an ant lion's sand trap. I could get past Tony, maybe, but the more people I got mad the more likely I was to be taken down somewhere along the line. Every step I took upward, it seemed, brought me two rungs down.

"I'll think about it," I said.

"I could send Lucas and Pitts," The Suit suggested again.

"I'll think about that, too."

"You want me to give you what I know?"

"I said I'll think about it, Tony. Don't press me."

We were at an impasse. I wasn't saying no but I wouldn't say yes until I had a little time to consider my options. Tony saw all this.

"I'll be calling," he said.

Without another word he stood up and walked out of my office. I let a few minutes pass and then checked to make sure that he was gone. After that I got the .38 out of the old jeweler's safe and made sure that it was clean and loaded.

One thing I've learned in fifty-three hard years of living is that there's a different kind of death waiting for each and every one of us—each and every day of our lives. There's drunk drivers behind the wheels of cars, subways, trains, planes, and boats; there's banana peels, diseases and the cockeyed medicines that supposedly cure them; you got airborne viruses, indestructible microbes in the food you eat, jealous husbands and wives, and just plain bad luck.

I once knew a woman named Gert Longman. She had a place down in SoHo. I used to stay there sometimes. One morning, when she had already left for work, I was drinking coffee on her fire escape when a car came careening down the street. A mother and her young son were crossing and the car slammed into them. For a moment it seemed that the car was going to stop to help but then he, or she, stepped on the gas, ran over the bodies, and was gone. I climbed down the fire-escape ladder, but when I got to them I could see that they were dead, very much so. I called 911 and the ambulance came crying. The police arrived a few minutes later and I told them everything I could.

That was a tough day for me. I was so upset that I went home. Katrina had taken the kids to visit her parents in their Miami retirement condo, so I brooded alone in the apartment, worried about Death behind the wheel of a red car, rushing up on you out of nowhere and then hurrying away like a coward. I got in the bathtub with a book but forgot my drink on the sink. I got one foot on the floor and slipped, did a James Brown split, flew up in the air, and landed hard. My skull grazed the edge of the iron tub. And even though the pain in my head and hip was excruciating, I lay there laughing at myself. I had forgotten that Death was watching from all sides; that it comes at you from the place you least expect.

And so even though a gangster had me in his crosshairs, I still had a life to live just like every other doomed soul walking this earth, wondering if he could make it across the street.

I TOOK A bus downtown and got off three blocks from Tiny Bateman's Charles Street address.

Charles was a narrow street of mostly four- to six-story apartment buildings built of brick and thickly coated with decades of city grime. Most had concrete stoops and little barred gates that led down to the basements. Tiny worked in an underground apartment half a block from Hudson Street. I descended the seven granite stairs and gave that week's secret code. I felt like a fool with a magic decoder ring but Tiny would never answer unless I tattooed the right sequence on his buzzer.

After three minutes there was a loud click and I pushed open the reinforced steel door that was painted a fanciful shamrock green.

It was more of a compartment than an apartment. Each room, even the toilet, had worktables along the walls. These tables were crowded with wires and chip boards, computers without casings and cameras that looked like ceramic dolls, single-cigar humidors, a copy of *The Old Man and the Sea*, and other, less recognizable items. There were clusters of cell phones on the tables; some were wired to computers, others wired together. Tiny could do things with modern technology that even the inventors had not yet imagined. He supplied people like me with surveillance tools, hacked information, and general advice. Most of his work was done over the Internet but he allowed a select few into his dark and dusty domain.

I passed through three packed rooms before coming to Tiny's office. This had once been the master bedroom of the subterranean abode. Huge light-gray, plastic-encased computers lined the southern wall. They were humming and throwing off a lot of heat, I was sure, but Tiny had enough air-conditioning running to freeze a penguin.

The fat young caramel-colored man was seated in a swivel chair perched in a cockpit cut into a round Formica table that was, by my estimation, eleven feet in diameter. Surrounded by keyboards, he wore overalls but no shirt and glasses with one blue and one green lens, both of them iridescent. There were twelve screens hanging from the ceiling, tilting so he could see them by turning his head or, at the outside, swiveling his butt. There was a huge screen behind him broken into various-sized boxes that displayed shifting TV images—numbers, foreign characters, and sometimes nothing but continually shifting and amorphous forms.

"Hey, Tiny," I said.

I didn't sit because there was no visitor's chair in Tiny's laboratory. He once told me that he only ever had four visitors. I didn't know the others' names but it was a good bet that one of them was his father.

Simon Bateman had introduced me to his nerd-to-the-max son. I helped the elder Bateman once when he was in serious trouble, and he paid me by getting Bug to agree to work for me now and again.

"How'd that phone work out?" the thirty-something misanthrope asked in a high voice that seemed to want to get higher.

"Fine. Fine. I think I might need another couple soon."

"The blue and pink ones near the front door," he said.

Bug owned, and slept in, the apartment above his workplace. The people he did business with dropped their deliveries and picked up their orders in a sealed antechamber that he constructed up there. That way he didn't have to see anyone for weeks at a time.

"I wanted to talk to you," I said.

"'Bout what?"

I explained about the e-mails that Twill had sent and received.

"I'm worried about my son," I said.

"Maybe he's got a good reason," Tiny said, removing the glasses that had earned him the insect nickname.

His eyes were small and his fleshy limbs chubby. He was both the technically smartest and physically unhealthiest person I'd ever known.

Tiny called himself a techno-anarchist. He believed that humanity would slowly separate into what he called *monadic particulates*: self-sufficient individuals who depended only upon technology and their relationship with it.

"I'm not gonna have my son out there murdering people, Tiny. No way."

"Twill's a smart kid," the self-made scientist said. "Maybe he could get away with it."

"I need to know everything about the person he's communicating with," I said, cutting off any further discussion.

Tiny drew up his shoulders and nodded, submitting to my demand. Despite his particulate aspirations, Tiny's father was his lifeline, and Simon owed me big.

I WALKED FROM Tiny's to a small bar on East Houston named the Naked Ear. It was a place where I used to drink with Gert before she was murdered. Back then it had been a neighborhood bar that sponsored poetry readings after ten but now it catered to twenty-something stockbrokers who made more in a week than I did in three months.

If I got there early enough I could get a corner table, away from the crowd of flirty children. There I would down my cognac, toasting a memory.

I DRANK UNTIL standing up was a serious challenge but still I managed to stumble out into the street and hail a cab.

That night I remembered to call Katrina, so she was in bed when I got home. I dropped my jacket in the hallway and kicked off my shoes in the dining room. On the way to our bedroom I looked in on Twill. I didn't do that because he was my favorite (even though he is) but because Twill often went out at night when the rest of us were asleep. And when Twill was on the prowl there was no telling what mischief he'd get into.

But that evening he was sound asleep under a thin blanket. I smiled at him and staggered off to bed.

KATRINA WAS SNORING and the TV was on. My wife could not sleep without the drone of the television, so I dropped the rest of my clothes on the floor and rolled into my side of the bed.

I lay there in an alcoholic stupor, not really worried about anything. I had to do something about The Suit's problem, and there was Twill to worry about. But there was nothing I could do right then and so I stared into the bright glare of the TV screen, hoping that sleep would ambush me.

". . . murder in lower Manhattan this evening," a woman reporter was saying. The image of a clean-cut and youngish black face appeared on the screen behind her. The face looked vaguely familiar. "Frank Tork, only hours out on bail from police custody, was found beaten and strangled to death in a small alley off of Maiden Lane this evening. Mr. Tork was awaiting sentencing on a burglary conviction. Police say that an investigation is under way . . ."

I lifted my head to get a better look but then the dizziness from seven or maybe eleven shots of brandy pushed me down into unconsciousness.

12

I didn't sleep long. Frank Tork kept entering my dreams, asking me for twenty dollars or maybe a lifeline.

"I ain't got no idea where B-Brain is, man," he'd said in the visitor's cubicle, and also in the dream. "Georgie Girl said that she seen 'im that one time but he could be dead for all I know."

That phrase roused me at 5:34. My body wanted either to be sick or allowed to return to sleep—I didn't give in to either urge.

AN ICE-COLD SHOWER numbers among the most painful experiences I've ever willingly experienced, but it does wonders for hangovers and fear. I came out of the stall shivering like a wet dog and ready for the hunt.

ON BROADWAY AT Ninety-first at a few minutes shy of seven I was smoking Ambrose Thurman's last cigarette and reading about Frank Tork's demise. He didn't make the *New York Times*, or even the *Daily News*, but they had Frankie on page eight of the *Post*.

Bail was filed in the early afternoon through an online system from a bail bondsman in the Bronx. Along with the article there was a shadowy digital picture of a man with a wide-brimmed hat taken from above. This allegedly bearded man paid ten percent of Frank's bail in cash: thirty-seven hundred, fifty-nine dollars, and thirty-two cents, including fees.

The body was found at ten in the evening (three hours and twenty-two minutes after his release) by a homeless woman rummaging through trash cans in an alleyway off of Maiden Lane. The young man was badly beaten before being strangled. The man in the hat had given the name Alan Rogers. He was required to show a valid ID with a picture, but the system, the bondsman said, had somehow broken down; either that or the benefactor had used a fake ID.

I stopped by the Coffee Nook on Eighty-first to get some caffeine. I bought a new pack of Camels on the way there. After my fifth cup I pulled out my wallet and rooted around, coming up with the card that Ambrose Thurman had given me the first time we met.

It was a yellow card with a high gloss, a little smaller than regulation size. There, smiling brightly, was Thurman's pear-shaped mug. It was a younger Ambrose, an Ambrose with a little more hair and a little less sag. Vain men irritate me.

I noticed for the first time that the address given was a post office box. It was printed in blocky address fashion in exceptionally small characters.

Using the pink phone I'd gotten from Bug I called Thurman's number—it was no longer valid. Next I tried Albany information. There was no Ambrose Thurman listed in the city, either as a residence or a business. The same was true for the outlying areas.

No Ambrose Thurman had ever been registered at the Crenshaw Hotel. I tried to sweet-talk the operator into remembering the chubby guy in the three-piece suit but she told me that they didn't give out information on their guests.

I called Roger Brown's office and got the automatic system. It guided me to the young man's answering machine, but I didn't leave a message.

Thurman had played me like a drum. It was my fault. I could feel that there was something wrong in looking for those four men. Who paid that kind of money to find drug addicts and low-class career criminals? Who would take on a job like that? Me. And I did it just to pay last month's bills.

I WALKED DOWN Broadway until getting to Forty-second Street and then cut over to Sixth. The police could find out about my visit to Tork in the Tombs. They could wonder, but there was nothing they could prove. The guy who bailed Frank out was white. I might get questioned but they couldn't pin anything on me.

I was clean in the eyes of the law, but the problem was that I had promised myself not to do this kind of work anymore. I had been made to betray my pledge by a man who had disappeared completely.

It was a nice touch showing me a business card with a picture on it. That way I felt that he'd given me a way to contact him if I ever needed it. It was a trick that I might have used myself if I were doing work in another city.

I called Roger's office again.

"Berg, Lewis & Takayama," a young woman's bright voice sang.

"Roger Brown, please."

The phone went silent as if a mute button had been pressed and then, out of electronic nowhere, a young man's voice said, "Mr. Brown's line."

"Arnold DuBois for him," I said.

"Mr. Brown isn't in at the moment, Mr. DuBois. Would you like his answering machine?"

"Um . . . wow. He's not in?"

"No, sir."

"Roger told me that he always got in to work early." He hadn't told me any such thing but it was possible that a kid from the hood worked harder to make sure that he kept up with the rest.

"That's right. He's usually here by seven-thirty, but not today. I guess he had a meeting or something."

"Really?" I said putting feeling into my voice. "Did he have a meeting scheduled? I mean, I'm not trying to get into his business but I had a morning phone conference set up with him from last night."

"I don't have anything written down," the helpful boy said. "Maybe he forgot."

"Yeah. Maybe. Have him call me, will you?"

"What's the number?"

"He has it."

WALKING USUALLY HELPS me work out difficult problems, but that day nothing came. I was in my office by 8:45, but Frankie Tork was still dead and Roger Brown unaccounted for. Ambrose Thurman had vanished, as had my new leaf.

I gave it another hour, searching the Internet for Ambrose Thurman, Albany detective, while calling Roger's office twice more. Once I tried to disguise my voice but I think Bobby, his assistant, knew it was me.

Finally I called Zephyra Ximenez on my dedicated "800" line. Zephyra was an exotic young woman—Dominican mother, Moroccan father—who lived somewhere in Queens. I met her one night at the Naked Ear. She was at the bar, waiting for her girlfriends. Zephyra was tall and coal-colored. Her face wasn't exactly beautiful but it certainly put pretty to shame. I'd had a few drinks and tried to convince her to ditch her friends and have dinner with me. She said no but kept talking.

Zephyra told me that she was a TCPA, a telephonic and computer personal assistant.

"What's that?"

"I try to maintain ten to twelve clients," she said, "who need services I can provide pretty much exclusively over the phone and Internet. I make reservations, answer calls, order anything from takeout to a new washer-dryer, or take care of bookkeeping and data-file maintenance. I charge fifteen hundred a month, plus expenses, and I'm available on a twenty-four hour basis in case of emergencies."

"What if somebody were to call you right now?" I asked.

"I have a cell phone and an OQO minicomputer in my purse," she said. "It's my office away from the office."

"Wow."

"What do you do?"

I told the young woman a little about my services.

"I never had a private dick before," she said. I think I might have blushed a little. "Do you need someone like me?"

"ZEPHYRA," SHE ANSWERED on the third ring. "Leonid Mr. McGill's office."

"Hey, Z."

"Oh, hi, Mr. McGill. What can I do for you?"

"I need a flight to Albany by mid-afternoon. Sooner if you can do it."

"Only puddle jumpers this time of day," she said in a friendly tone. "You told me you had claustrophobia issues."

"You haven't heard from issues."

"I see." There was a pause, and then she said. "I can get you on a flight from LaGuardia at three sixteen."

"Book it," I said.

"You have some voice mail on the machine here," she said before I could hang up.

For her other clients Zephyra listened to the messages, typed them up, and delivered them as a kind of running narrative of their phone life. We decided rather early on that she should probably leave my messages alone, that she shouldn't even listen unless I asked her to.

"I'll get to 'em later."

"Do you need a limo to the airport?" she asked.

"Yeah. Sure."

"Your usual?"

"No. I don't need Hush for something so simple. Anybody cheap'll do."

"Answer your phone while you're gone?"

"Might as well." When people spoke to an actual person they were less likely to say something incriminating. "I'll forward the calls from the office and the cell."

Getting off the phone, I felt like I needed another cold shower. Hell, I needed a dip in the Arctic Ocean.

A dinged-up dark-green Lincoln limo met me in front of the Tesla Building at 1:47. As the young Russian driver wound his way slowly toward the Midtown Tunnel, I stared through my reflection, wondering why I couldn't do right. This was not wallowing in self-pity. I didn't feel guilty—not exactly. I felt bad that Tork had died, and to some degree I felt responsible, but mostly I had the sensation of slipping further down into the sandpit of my own sins.

While I sat there in the long queue, waiting to get into the tunnel, Katrina and the kids entered my reverie. Not for the first time I thought that if it wasn't for them I could cut all ties and move to Hawaii with Aura. There she would get into real estate, and I might find a job selling surfboards, or training young amateur boxers.

The reason I kept veering off course was New York and the people who knew me there. Tony the Suit and dozens of others like him had my name and number. For a hundred-dollar bill or a chit or to pay off some minor favor they'd pass that number to a man like Thurman. And then that man would come to me, and what could I do? I had to make a living. I couldn't blame the kids for their parentage. I couldn't even blame Katrina for her desire to be loved in a way I didn't, I couldn't, understand.

And, anyway, there was the question of Roger

Brown. Roger had climbed out of the sandpit. His mother had stuck with him and given him a chance. In her last dying months she propelled him to safety. The fear in his voice should have made me keep his whereabouts a secret. There was a chance that he was still alive, and even though I would have been better served to keep my head down I had to go to Albany because Albany and a matchbook were the only clues I had.

I WAS SELECTED for extra security measures at the airport checkpoint and studied by a series of dogs, machines, and Homeland Security experts with six weeks' training. They sniffed me for bombs and scanned for metals, they even frisked me; probably because of something in my attitude. Maybe they could sense the rage in me. I don't know.

DISTRACTED AS I WAS by the security search I didn't worry about the plane until they walked us out on the tarmac and I had to duck my head to enter the cabin. My seat was a single on the left side of the aisle and my butt was wider than the armrests designed to contain it. The arcing wall felt like it was closing in and there seemed to be too many people in the small compartment. I counted seventeen.

There were propellers on the wings.

The pilot slid the plastic partition open and turned his handsome gray head to address us.

"It's a short flight today, folks," he said. "I'm going to have Marie, your flight attendant, strap herself in because it's gonna be choppy for a hundred and seven out of the eighty-two minutes we'll be in the air."

The stew, a forty-something bottle blonde with a penchant for exercise but not for dinner, smiled at us in a nauseated sort of way. I reached to undo the buckle of my seat belt but Marie closed the hatchlike door and folded her seat down. As she attached her safety belt, crossing her heart with thick nylon straps, I took in a deep breath and forgot how to let it out. I was no longer concerned with Frank Tork or Roger Brown, Ambrose Thurman or Tony the Suit. While the plane was taxiing out toward the runway I forgot about my conviction that Death would not come at me from someplace I expected.

I closed my eyes and sought a place of calm in my soul. I found it for a moment telling myself that it couldn't be so bad, that this flight was a commonplace event that passed without incident thousands of times around the world every day.

I was wrong.

There was nothing ordinary about that flight. From the moment we took off the airship was buffeted like a dead leaf in white water. My head struck the window and only the seat belt prevented me from bouncing across the cabin. I kept my eyes closed but that wasn't much help. The plane veered left and then suddenly went right. I knew that couldn't have been the pilot's intention. We bounced and shook for what seemed like a very long time, but when I peeked at my watch I saw that we were only nine minutes into the flight.

I looked around the cabin, expecting to see terror in the eyes of the other passengers. I was wrong there, too. Two ladies were having what seemed like a pleasant conversation. One guy was reading his newspaper, and the man next to him was sleeping.

The world outside my window was the same blue of the sky in my dream. For some reason the memory of the nightmare partially negated the terror of the flight.

At some point I was further distracted from my fear when an errant thought entered my mind. I remembered that I didn't even know what Roger Brown looked like. I had maybe doomed a man without ever seeing his face.

The flight banged on like an old truck without shock absorbers making its way down a rutted country road. But the tumult and roar receded in my mind. I'd never been in the armed forces, but I had been through a war or two. This ride, I came to feel, was little more than one of my cold showers, a prelude to a weeklong day of adversities. I grinned at the fear roiling inside me. I didn't owe it anything but my company.

As soon as I got off the plane my hands began to tremble. The fear that I'd held down blossomed, forcing me to walk slowly so as not to stumble. It was a small airport with a magazine rack and a hot dog stand but it felt like nirvana to me.

Zephyra had reserved a car at the best rental service. Somehow she had pooled the various credit-card air miles and rent-a-car points of all her clients so that we usually got good deals on flights, rentals, and even some hotels.

A pleasant young man with pimples and big teeth gave me a map and the keys to a downsized red SUV. I sat in the driver's seat for a long time, studying the city streets. I'd been to Albany many times before because that's the state capital and a large percentage of your politicians are crooks. I'd done cover-ups and smears across the board up there but I didn't know the city the way I knew New York, so I took the time to refamiliarize myself with the general lay of the town.

The car radio was playing "Smooth Operator" by Sade when I turned my attention from map to matchbook. It was a wonder to me that with all the searching by security experts they couldn't come up with a book of matches. Luck, more than anything else, is what saved you up in the air.

Oddfellows Pub, the matchbook's advertiser, was on the north side of town. It seemed like a straightforward deal: I'd go to the bar, flash Ambrose's card along with a story, and they would have some memory, allowing me to get that much closer to this pretender's throat. But there again I was mistaken.

That stretch of North Pearl Street was lined with businesses that were slowly being crushed by mall culture. There was OK Hardware with its cracked glass door held in place by reinforcing wire, a dowdy chain convenience store, two dress shops, some squat brick office buildings, and Oddfellows Pub. The bar had a plaster façade pretending to be bricks that were too red and mortar that was toothpaste white. There was a small window with a blue-and-red neon beer stein that shivered as if it wanted to complete the circuit of some long forgotten animation. The front door had a regular knob on it, making it seem as if you were entering a private residence rather than a place of business; that was my first misgiving.

Opening the door, I heard Patsy Cline singing pure notes through a scratchy jukebox needle.

There was no Confederate flag hanging over the bar, but then again, neither was there any love lost in the eyes of the patrons. They became aware of me entering their dingy domain the way an owl suddenly notices a snake moving in the grass below. The men, all of them white, had stopped their drinking and conversation to fix me on the pinboards of their minds. I counted eleven, including the bartender, and if it hadn't been a matter of life and death I would have turned around and walked out immediately.

It wasn't 2008 everywhere in America. Some people still lived in the sixties, and others might as well have been veterans of the Civil War. In many establishments I was considered a Black Man; other folks, in more genteel joints, used the term "African-American," but at Oddfellows I was a nigger where there were no niggers allowed.

As I said, I knew the right move was behind me but instead I walked into the dark room and up to the Formica bar, just a tourist stopping for a quick beer. The pale bartender was bald like I am, but taller. He wore a shirt with thick red stripes on white, strapped over by dark-green suspenders. There was an old Pabst Blue Ribbon name tag pinned to one strap. The tattered badge read, "Hi, I'm Jake."

Jake didn't like me.

"Whatever you got on tap," I said.

The bartender, who was about my age too, smirked and turned his back. As he moved away down the soggy corridor behind the bar I decided that, even if he did serve me, I would not drink.

But I didn't have to worry. I wasn't going to receive service in 1953 Albany. Jake moved down the bar, stopping at a customer who was sitting at the far end. They shared a few words, glanced in my direction, and then laughed.

In some ways the objective of the private detective is similar to that of the beat cop. You have an aim—the end of your shift—but there are many distractions along the way. You have to live completely in every moment, because if you get beyond yourself something will certainly blindside you and leave you face down in the street.

I wanted to save Roger Brown, which meant locating, and maybe dislocating something on, Ambrose Thurman. But before I could do any of that I had to get through Oddfellows. I considered walking around the room, asking if anyone had seen the face on the fake business card. But I rejected that approach. A room full of half-drunk men who wouldn't like you in the best of circumstances could easily ramp themselves up into a frenzy.

I decided that this was a dead end and that I should move on.

I had been in the pub for no more than three minutes.

Just as I was about to turn a tall and hale redhead stood up from a table in the corner. He was young, maybe twenty-five, and had the look of a kid who had just taken a dare. He smiled broadly and walked in my direction, so I put off my exit for one minute more.

"Hey," the young man said, grinning and friendly. He was

handsome like a fifties TV child star who had grown up losing nothing of the boyish charm that got him through.

"S'happenin'?" I replied, deciding to be who he thought I was.

"What you doin' here?" he said, still showing teeth. It was almost as if there was no threat in the room at all. Almost.

"S'posed to meet a guy."

"What guy?"

I took Ambrose Thurman's card from my jacket pocket and handed it to him. His fingers were pale and thick. The nails had some dirt under them, which made me like the person he might have been.

He studied the photo and name.

"Know him?" I asked.

He handed the card back to me.

"What's yer name?" was his reply.

"Bill. What's yours?"

"Jonah."

"Like with the whale?"

The kid smiled. We might have gotten along in other circumstances . . . on some far-flung planet. He glanced around, as if the eyes on us were about him.

"Maybe we should talk outside," he suggested.

I nodded and turned toward the door.

"Out back," he said. "Come on, this way."

Jonah moved toward a short hallway at the far end of the bar. After a moment's hesitation I followed.

Being a boxer, even just an amateur like me, can make a man reckless. I've stood in the ring, sparring with heavyweights, and held my own. But that was many years before, and there was more rust than iron in my joints of late. Still, I had the confidence of a man Jonah's age.

When I caught up to him he was opening the back door. He went through first and I paused to make sure there was no one coming up behind us. As I passed the threshold Jonah sucker-punched me with a right hook that had some smarts to it. The blow sent me crashing into a herd of aluminum trash cans. I was down, but the only thing that hurt was my sense of smell. Garbage had been festering on that dark alley floor for decades.

Jonah was wearing serious motorcycle boots. I could see the steel-shod heel of one as he tried to stomp my face with it.

A good thing about being a boxer is that you have reason to be confident. My reflexes were twice what they should have been. I grabbed Jonah's foot and rolled with it until he was down on the ground with me. Then I scrambled to my feet, slammed the back door shut, and wedged the edge of a metal trash can under the doorknob so that we wouldn't be disturbed.

Jonah rose to his feet effortlessly and grinned. I could see then that he was one of those adorable sociopaths that can love you or kill you with the same friendly smile on his lips.

My mind was a calculating machine right then. There were ten men behind a flimsy wooden door who would most likely be on the kid's side, and there was Jonah, who felt that he could make short shrift of me with three well-placed blows.

I wasn't worried about Jonah. What had me sweating was the clock back in the bar. In three minutes guys would be banging on the door, in five they'd either break through or come around the outside.

The first rule in the streetfighter's handbook is—when in doubt, attack.

I crouched down and moved forward, delivering a one-two combination to the kid's middle. He threw a punch that landed on the side of my head but I was ready this time and paid him back in duplicate. I hit him in the gut again and he felt it. His hands came down and I was able to get in two uppercuts before he moved backwards. My short legs have always been strong, and even at my advanced age I had a spring in my left. I leaped and connected with a straight right, got my balance, and delivered two left jabs and then another right.

Jonah was bleeding pretty good from a rupture on his left cheekbone. He was breathing hard, and I was, too. I stood back to catch my breath, counting off the seconds in the back of my mind. Jonah took a staggery step forward and then fell face down into a puddle of glistening gray glop.

My legs were ready to run but I stopped long enough to turn the kid over. It would have probably been saving some innocent's life to let Jonah die in that alley, but I had my new leaf to consider, and I was feeling some largesse after having won the test of arms.

I got way too much pleasure out of beating on Jonah. Running down the alleyway behind the bar, I felt giddy over my performance. I still had it. I was still in the game.

Still a fool, was more like it.

I was in my red SUV speeding away in less than the five minutes it would have taken for the Oddfellows to be after me. My knuckles hurt and I was breathing hard to work off the adrenaline that the fight set loose. When the blood pressure began to fall I became aware of the fact that I'd messed up the one clear chance I had of getting to Thurman. My contacts in the city and state police departments of Albany were pretty much useless at that juncture. One man had been murdered and another was missing. I couldn't make my connection to them public record. The police had to be kept out until I knew more.

The summer sun was still in the sky at six. I made my way to the South End. That part of town looked a bit seedier but was more to my sensibilities. There were black and brown peoples in among the whites, and so nobody would single me out for special treatment.

On Standard I passed a glass-and-plaster hotel named Gray Wolf Inn. It was a modern structure hemmed in by older, nondescript buildings that were neither offices nor warehouses, commercial spaces nor living lofts. These buildings had once been factories where Americans worked to feed their families and pay their bills. My father had spent his life organizing unions in places like this. They broke his bones and sent him to jail more than once, but he kept on organizing. Now the factories were all shut down and the unions reduced to rusty old buttons and yellowing membership cards in forgotten trunks. My father was long gone, as were the vestiges of his blood and hard work.

Gray Wolf had a glass door that opened onto a short hallway ending at a gunmetal elevator. On the right was a clear plastic cage where there sat an emaciated and sallow-skinned white lad whose eyes had seen more years than he had actually lived.

The young man didn't have a proper desk. He was seated on a swivel stool at a turquoise ledge that jutted from the ochre wall. When I cleared my throat he stood up and approached the plastic barricade that sealed him away from danger. I was thankful for the barrier, certain that if he got a whiff of the sour odor of garbage on my clothes he wouldn't have given me a room.

"How many nights?" the old-young man asked. He was wearing a blue shirt and blue pants but still the colors managed to clash—with each other and with the dirty yellow walls.

"Let's start with one," I said.

"Thirty-six ninety-six a night, including tax," the impossibly skinny and long-faced kid announced. "Two-night minimum. The second night is a deposit against damages. That's seventy-three ninety-two. Cash, no check."

"What if I gave you a credit card?"

"Huh?"

"Never mind."

"There's an extra fee of ten dollars," the kid droned on, getting back into the groove of his spiel, "if you have guests."

"No guests for me," I said.

Some feeling must have escaped with those words because the kid gave me a closer look then. He seemed to be gauging me, but I wasn't concerned.

He opened a sliding panel in front of him and placed a pen and registration form down on the plastic top, closed the panel, pressed a button, and then gestured for me to lift the panel on my side. I filled out the sheet, using the name Carter, with an address in Newark, New Jersey. I placed four twenty-dollar bills on the sheet and slid the panel closed (it locked shut immediately).

"Keep the change," I told the kid.

He didn't crack a smile or even nod in thanks, but I didn't mind.

He passed the keycard over for room 4B and flipped a switch that opened the elevator door. I didn't even have to push a button to go to the fourth floor. The kid did that, too, from his remote control.

I'VE BEEN IN third-class cruise-ship cabins that were larger than that room. Just one big bed that ended a few inches from a sliding, hollow pine door that opened onto the toilet. Standing at the sink, my butt was in the shower stall. To look out the window I had to get on my knees on the bed.

On the bright side, Jonah's two blows hadn't even caused my jaw to swell. It really didn't even hurt all that badly. I took two aspirin and a shower, lay down on the mattress, which felt hard like rolled canvas, and fell into a light doze.

The dream was oddly altered in that cubicle room. Fire blazed all around me but I wasn't frantic. My flesh was burning but that was of no consequence. When I got to the smoky glass I just pushed it out, effortlessly. On the other side, standing in blue sky, was the kid from downstairs. He gave me a calculating look and I waited for his request. He opened his mouth but the sound that came out was not in words; it wasn't even human. It was a kind of electronic static. This sound slowly transformed into an insect-like buzzing. I wondered if the alarm clock was going off, if it was morning and I had slept through the night. But I hadn't set the alarm. When I sat up I realized that the noise was coming from a telephone that had been left on the window ledge next to my head.

The buzzing stopped and I wondered who could be calling. It started again and I answered, "Hello?"

"Mr. Carter?"

"Who is this?"

"Jimmy from downstairs, sir."

Sir?

"What do you want, Jimmy?"

"I was just wondering if you needed some company."

"What kind of company?"

"You know," he continued, "a girl."

A girl. Jimmy had called to offer me a girl. I realized that I had moved from a light nap into deep sleep. I was confused about the material world but quite lucid in my mind.

"How much?" I asked.

"Hundred bucks a half hour," he said. "Five hundred for the night."

"Who pays the ten bucks for the visitor?"

"The girl covers that fee."

I was quiet for a moment or two, wondering about Jimmy being in the dream and at the same time on the phone interrupting the dream.

"I don't know," I said.

"They're all clean," he protested. "I don't let no junkies up in here."

I could have asked how he knew if a girl didn't have tracks between her toes but I didn't. I didn't care.

"Okay. All right. But I want someone young and black," I said.

"Pretty if it's possible, but with a sharp tongue. And she has to be black."

"I can do that, Mr. Carter," Jimmy said eagerly. "Gimme twenty, twenty-five minutes."

"Take your time, son."

"You need anything else?"

"Yeah. You got an Albany phone book down there?"

"I think so. It might be from a couple'a years ago."

"Send it up with the girl."

"Yes, sir."

The thought of Jimmy made me smile. He was an old, corrupt soul bunged into a young, inept body. The only thing that got his motor running was commerce. He didn't even care about the money, only the method by which he got it. The tip was an insult, but providing me with female companionship made him feel like he was getting something accomplished. I liked that. It had the stink of humanity about it, something akin to the bouquet of Gorgonzola cheese.

I opened my duffel and took out a rolled-up navy-blue suit that was an exact replica of the one that got soiled in the alley. I liked Jimmy's predictability, and anything else I could count on.

The room was barely large enough to accommodate the queen-size bed. I was sitting at the edge, still a little groggy, when a tapping came on the door. I didn't have to stand up to open it but I did.

The child was young, and even darker-skinned than I. She wore a yellow party dress but no smile. Slender, she was wider below the waistline than above it. She was hugging a well-worn phone book against her chest.

"Come on in," I said, moving to the side because the bed blocked a courteous retreat.

She walked in, leaving the door open.

"One hundred dollars up front," were her first words.

I took a fold of four fifties from my shirt pocket and handed them to her. She traded the tattered phone book for the money.

"Two hundred for one hour," I said.

She counted the bills twice, closed the door, then turned to look at me. Her gaze was clear but not innocent. Those big eyes weren't worldly but neither were they inexperienced.

"What's your name?" I asked.

"Seraphina," she said.

"S-a-r-a-f . . . ?" I asked.

"S-*e*-r-a-*p*-*h*-*i*-n-a," she said like a third-grade

teacher who had lost patience before her current crop of students were ever born.

"Beautiful name," I said. "Beautiful dress, beautiful skin, beautiful girl. Have a seat."

I sat on the south side of the bed while Seraphina took the east. If anything she was wary now. Compliments are often camouflage for hidden resentment, and I had just given out four tributes in quick order.

"What you want?" she asked.

"Talk."

"You could go to a bar an' buy a girl a drink if you just wanted to talk to somebody."

"Not with my luck."

"You unlucky?" she asked, allowing a little gruff friendliness to show.

I grunted a laugh and nodded.

"I'm from Newark," I said. "And I came here looking for a guy."

I handed her the business card and she studied it.

"That's a white man," she said, handing it back to me. "I cain't tell 'em apart. Sometimes, if they ask for me more than once, I could tell you about how they smell. But that's about it."

She was looking around the room, sneering at what she saw.

Jimmy had certainly delivered the girl I'd asked for.

"What you want him for?" Seraphina asked.

"He hired me to do a job and then didn't pay me."

"Oh. I see."

"I went to a bar looking for this Ambrose guy and a big white dude started a fight with me. I gave him better'n he gave me, but I still need to find this man."

"Where he hit you?" she asked.

I gestured at the left side of my jaw.

The child leaned over and touched my cheek with four fingers. My heart started thumping. I could feel my nostrils widen.

"Skin is hot but it ain't swole," she said.

The last time I'd had sex was about three months before, the night Katrina came back. There was nothing enjoyable about that evening. I had to take a pill to make it. It was the kind of pill that made you hard but not happy. I would have liked to get naked with Seraphina. She was young and I'd already paid for it. I wanted her and there would have been nothing wrong with it, at least not that time. But sex with that child would have been the first step away from the man I intended to be.

"You have a boyfriend, Seraphina?"

"Of course I do."

"You and him know a lotta people in the clubs and stuff?"

"Yeah?"

"You see," I said, "I think that this guy I'm lookin' for might know people. You know, dealers and gamblers, like that."

"Uh-huh."

"So I was wonderin' if maybe there was somebody somewhere who might know a lot of what's goin' on with the gamblers and hustlers around here."

I was being very careful. Seraphina was a young prostitute. She might not have even been legal. She was still sensitive and therefore, very possibly, on the alert for insults. I couldn't mention pimps or whores, but I needed a whore's connections.

"There's Big Mouth Jones down at Tinker's Bar and Grill," she said. "He know ev'rybody, an' he got big mouth, too."

"Black guy?"

"Uh-huh. But you better not get in any fight wit' him. He got a crew down there kill a man just like that."

I smiled as I almost always do when people suggest that they or someone else might kill me.

"You ain't scared?" she asked.

"Not really."

"You want me to take off my clothes?"

"Truth is, Seraphina, when a man is making love to a woman, he's also makin' love to himself."

"What do that mean?" she asked with barely a sneer.

"That he imagines himself powerful and manly next to her beauty."

"So?"

"You are beautiful. I can see that. But I'm old and chubby, not like some young man that a woman like you would want to see naked and straining."

"How you know what I wanna see?"

"Is your boyfriend strong and well built?"

"Yeah."

"And do you like that?"

"Yeah," she said with a slight smile. "But that don't mean nuthin'. I might like you anyway."

"It's kind of you to say, child. But I know better than to embarrass myself like that."

"I could make you feel good." She took my hand.

The words made me dizzy. My tongue went dry.

"You breathin' hard, Mr. Carter," she said.

"I can't."

"Can't what?"

"Can't be with you, girl." I pulled away, gently.

"If you afraida disease I could just use my hands."

"I'm more afraida you than I am of any bug."

"Me? I'm just a girl."

I stood up.

"Thank you, Seraphina. You've been a lot of help."

I handed her a fifty-dollar tip, then took her by the wrist to bring her to her feet. She put her hands flat against my chest and I flinched.

"You haven't been with a woman in a long time, huh?" she said.

"It's okay, you know. Like ridin' a bicycle. You don't have to win no race to have a good time."

She paused a moment to see if I had changed my mind. Seeing that I hadn't she kissed me on the cheek, opened the door, and walked away.

If I was another kind of man I might have cried.

AFTER MY SECOND SHOWER I sat down to the phone book, which was both residential and yellow pages combined into one. It was nine years old but that didn't matter.

I looked up Ambrose Thurman. He wasn't listed. I turned to the yellow pages and searched for Tinker's Bar and Grill under restaurants. It was right there on South Street, not six blocks away. My watch said 10:37. Big Mouth would probably be holding court. Maybe, if I was lucky, Seraphina would show up after a while. She was right—I hadn't been with a woman in a long time. I needed some kind of release.

The idea of going to the bar oppressed me. Finding Thurman might cause more trouble than it settled; not finding him would leave me without a paddle.

My resistance to the only avenue open to me, combined with the hope of seeing the young Seraphina again, caused a line of thought that brought me back to the baseless vanity of Ambrose Thurman. I turned to the yellow pages' section of private investigators. Many of them had ads. Some of these sported illustrations; a few had photographs. Norman Fell's pear-shaped face was smiling from the page just as it beamed off the yellow card I had in my pocket.

You got a screwdriver?" I called into Jimmy's clear cage.

"Supposed to stay here in case the porter has to use it," he replied, not bothering to rise from the swivel stool.

"You have a porter?"

"I'm the porter," he said.

"I just wanna borrow it. Twenty bucks?"

He turned his profile to me, opened a short door in the wall, and rummaged around until he came out with a screwdriver that had a translucent yellow plastic handle. It was eighteen inches long with a blue metal shaft that was a good eighth of an inch thick.

We traded cash for tool and I went out into the Albany night.

That was a standard round after eleven.

DECKER AVENUE WAS a drab block of old-fashioned brick office buildings. There were six streetlamps but only two of them worked. The traffic was sporadic and not one pedestrian passed by in the seventeen minutes I sat there.

The label with Norman Fell's buzzer next to it said that he was on the third floor: 3E.

I went around back, down a slender concrete pathway between Fell's building and the one next to it. The lock on the back door was reinforced with a thick metal guard but the entrance to the basement, five steps down, might have been blown open by a strong wind. I jimmied the lock and made my way up the back utility stairs.

Norman Fell's door was next to the exit. There was no light shining under the crack. I checked the rest of the offices down the hall. They were all lifeless and dark.

A knock on Fell's door brought no answer.

His lock gave me more trouble than the one downstairs, but nothing challenging.

His rooms were at the back of the building, so I chanced turning on the light.

It was a big room with a pine desk set in the exact center. There were bookcases behind and to the right of the blond desk, and a solitary green metal file cabinet to the left, next to a broad oak door. The door opened onto a huge white tile bathroom that had a big, footed iron bathtub standing upon what could only be called a dais, ten inches or so above the floor. It was an odd design. The building had always been for offices but maybe, I thought, the man who drew up the plans for this suite also had lived here.

I gave up my architectural conjectures and got down to the business at hand.

I was already wearing cotton gloves, had been since before I got out of my car.

There were two deep file drawers. But they were useless. Not in any kind of order, there were mostly printed forms, manuals, and things like tools and wires in the hanging folders. I went through everything, looking for some reference to the names I knew. No Frank Tork or Roger Brown, no Leonid Trotter McGill for that matter; nothing about the case, or any other job, that I could see.

The desk revealed little more than a pair of small shoes that sat under it. Norman Fell (aka Ambrose Thurman) didn't keep information written down. There was no computer, or even a typewriter, in evidence. The only thing he had was a recent phone bill on the desk and a handwritten bookkeeping ledger in a locked bottom drawer. I tore out ledger sheets as far back as a month before Fell had gotten in touch with me, then pocketed them along with the phone bill.

"A MAN'S BOOKCASE will tell you everything you'll ever need to know about him," my father had told me more than once. "A businessman has business books and a dreamer has novels and books of poetry. Most women like reading about love, and a true revolutionary will have books about the minutiae of overthrowing the oppressor. A person with no books is inconsequential in a modern setting, but a peasant that reads is a prince in waiting."

I don't know where my father got all that stuff. He was raised just outside of Birmingham, Alabama, born to parents who could neither read nor write. He said that he became a revolutionary at the age of thirteen when his parents were being evicted from their sharecropper's hovel and one of the white marshals spit on his mother. Soon after that he changed his name from Clarence to Tolstoy.

For all his humble beginnings my father was smart. But I think that even he would have been amazed at what Fell's library had to say.

There were volumes in Greek and Spanish, English and French; old books of poetry shoved up right next to modern popular novels. Many had been shelved upside down and they covered every obscure subject under the sun. There was a Chinese tome that, from the illustrations, I assumed was about sewing machine repair. There were other manuals and textbooks along with sultry potboilers and children's fairy tales.

In the end I decided that Fell must be functionally illiterate, though he loved the idea of reading and wanted to be seen as smart. That's why there was no casework in his files, no computer, not one sentence anywhere written by his hand. I guess he knew his numbers well enough to write them down along with codes and simple names that he probably transcribed or worked out phonetically.

I'd have to come after Fell in a more straightforward fashion.

I would either wait in my car outside or stay where I was, seated behind his desk, to greet him when he showed up in the morning.

He wouldn't want to call the police any more than I did. The problem was that he might be armed and shoot me where I sat. It was always better to come up behind your enemy. My father never told me that, but I learned it early.

Deciding on discretion over comfort, I went to the toilet to relieve myself before going back to the red SUV. I could sleep in the backseat and wake up with the sun. It had been a while since I had done anything like that.

Standing at the high commode, I sniffed at a sour tickle way back in my nasal passage.

I knew that tickle.

The man who had introduced himself to me as Ambrose Thurman was crushed into the bottom of the deep iron tub, eyes wide and lips drawn back over the small rounded teeth. The fingers of his left hand had all been broken—probably by a single blow. I couldn't tell if he died from strangulation or the broken neck, but there was no question that he had died violently. He was wearing a dark-green suit with a checkered black-and-red vest. His socks bore holes at the big toe of either foot. I considered searching him but thought better of it.

I gazed into his face for a good long time before deciding he had nothing to say.

JIMMY WAS STILL on his stool when I got back to the Gray Wolf a few minutes before two. I returned the screwdriver and he set the elevator to take me to the fourth floor of the landlocked cruise ship.

I didn't sleep that night, knowing for certain there'd be plenty time enough for rest when I was dead.

I got off on the seventy-second floor of the Tesla Building four minutes past eight o'clock the next morning. The leftover nervousness from the flight was nothing compared to the growing possibility of spending a couple of decades behind bars. Men were dying and all I had gotten out of it was a paltry wad of cash.

I found the seven locks that secured the outer office undone and the door ajar. I hovered in the hall a full thirty seconds, wondering if I should turn around and run to Brazil. I had one offshore account that was inviolable, and Twill could secret himself, and his mother if she wanted to come, down to Mexico for a rendezvous . . .

It was the thought of Twill that anchored me that morning. I had to stay around long enough to save him from his own nature.

The locks weren't broken so I pushed the door and walked in quickly.

Carson Kitteridge stood up from one of the golden chairs usually inhabited by phantoms visiting my non-existent secretary.

"Lieutenant," I said.

The cop smiled but there was no mirth in his eye.

In his late forties, Kitteridge was short and balding, slim and very white—pale. His eyes were gray, as was his suit and machine-washable tie.

"LT," he replied.

We'd known each other nearly twenty years and not once had we shaken hands.

"How can I help you?" I said, refusing to ask how he got in.

"Just stopping by."

"What? You were investigating some kinda buggery on the fifty-fifth floor and said, 'Hey, why don't I drop in on old Leonid?'" By this time I was entering the combination to my inner door.

"Something like that," he said.

We walked down the aisle of empty cubicles that led to my office.

"Why you got such a big place?" Carson asked as we went. "You never had anybody work for you in all these years."

"It's my imagination," I said, moving behind the desk.

"What is?"

"My imagination," I said again. "It fills up all these rooms. It's the only way I can think."

"Fatheaded, huh?"

Sometimes the policeman and I could go on like that for half an hour or more. We kidded each other to hide our hands. In reality I didn't like him and he cared even less for me. But we were stuck with each other like coworkers on an assembly line. I'd punch out a hole in an iron plate and he'd sand down the edges, complaining that he had to work at all.

I don't know how the NYPD works exactly, maybe nobody really does, but Kitteridge was on a list that got lit up every time the cops got a whiff of me. Usually when he appeared my name had been whispered and a few dollars had changed hands, or maybe a surveillance tape had caught my profile coming out of some bad guy's lair. We hadn't seen each other much since I'd been trying to straighten out, but once every few months or so he'd drop by just to let me know that I was still on their radar.

For him to show up so soon after Frank Tork and Norman Fell had been murdered could not be a coincidence.

"I got work to do, Detective," I said, unable to continue our banter. "What is it you want?"

"Can you fix the Lotto?"

With all the bile between us, Carson Kitteridge could still make me laugh.

"Naw, man. But I could score you enough crank to make you feel like you won it."

His grin downgraded into a smile, and then that was gone.

"I don't believe in coincidence, LT," he said, echoing my own thoughts.

"Neither me." I was hoping that he had gotten word on me going to visit Tork in jail. I was willing to give up Fell's pseudonym. But if they had something on me up in Albany, things might get close.

The policeman sat back in the blue and chrome visitor's chair. He put his elbows on the arms and laced his fingers. His gray eyes were like a hazy afternoon sky, they were so light and distant.

"You remember me once asking you if you knew a fella named Arnold DuBois?" he asked.

Fear blossomed in my lungs.

"No."

"You remember. There was that guy, Timmons I think his name was. Second-story man, lived across the street from a jewelry store got burglarized. We found some of the ice in his freezer. But the robbery division was sure it was some other guy. Pete the Finn. You remember. This DuBois guy was in Timmons's building just the day before the tip came down. Said he was looking for clients."

"I don't remember," I said calmly, hollering inside.

"I understand. That was seven years ago. We'd just started the criminal keyword database at that time. Thank God for Homeland Security.

"The doorman gave us a description that fit you to a T, LT. But we couldn't tie you to the Finn, and Pete's lawyer kept him out of court, so we had no excuse to bring you in. Even if it was you, that didn't make any direct connection to the robbery."

I should have had a pithy comeback. That was our shtick. But I was no longer the man he'd hounded. And all I could think about was what his visit meant.

"Why are you here, Lieutenant?"

Kitteridge's eyes tightened. I'd never been curt with him on an exploratory visit. We had our roles to play and for the first time in nineteen years I was stepping out of character.

"Camilla Jones," he said. It was almost a question.

"Who?"

"Roger Brown's fiancée. He was supposed to meet her night before last at a club on Fifty-seventh. When he didn't show she called him and he said that he was sick. She thought he sounded nervous but he said no. He didn't call her all the next day and so last night she went to his apartment and rang his buzzer. Nobody answered. She had the key, decided to use it, and found him dead on the floor. Strangled and beaten like a dog."

"So?" I whispered.

"So a few days ago the elusive Arnold DuBois left his card at Brown's office."

"So?"

"The next day some big white guy came there, looking for Roger. The receptionist, a Juliet Stilman, said that he threatened her. When Roger heard about the guy he begged her not to call the police and snuck out through a side door. He didn't come to work the next day, and now he's dead."

I waited a few moments before asking, "Is that all, Officer?"

"Are you going to tell me what you were doing there?"

I shrugged and made a meaningless gesture with my hands. "Freedom of speech also lets me keep my mouth shut."

Kitteridge's furrowed brow darkened his light-gray eyes. He sat forward in the chair.

"It's said around certain circles that you've changed jobs," he said, suggesting something.

"Soda jerk?"

"Point man for the killer—Hush."

Of all the things I could be blamed for, murder for hire was one of the few not on the list. I knew Hush. We were friends as far as friendship was possible for either of us, but he'd given up the assassination trade, and I had never been involved in his business.

The idea that I could be a button man brought laughter from deep down somewhere. If I wasn't sitting at a desk I would have doubled over in dark mirth.

This reaction enraged Kitteridge. He leaped up from the chair and for a moment I thought he might attack me. But the detective took on the role of policeman in a complete and ideal way. He didn't batter prisoners or produce false evidence. He hated me and mine for not being like him but would never cross his own line.

He turned away and stalked out of my office. I didn't need to check on his exit like I had with The Suit. I doubt if I could have risen from my chair anyway.

Roger Brown's death weighed on me.

I wanted to do something but there was nothing left. Fell was dead, and Frank and Roger, too. Each one of them was like a nail through my flesh, pinning me down in that chair.

"It's the housewives and plumbers," my father had told me and my brother, Nikita, "the law-abiding and pious, that allow the most heinous crimes to continue. They raise their children and pray to

God, while soldiers slaughter dark-skinned families in their country's name."

I wished my father were standing there before me right then. If he was, I could rise to my feet and slap his face. I'd tell him that his lessons put Nikita in prison and nailed me to that chair, wishing that I had become a plumber voting the Republican ticket and saluting the Stars and Stripes.

The online version of the *New York Times* had a picture of Roger Brown on the first page of the metro section: a dark and handsome face with doubting eyes. The scar on his right cheekbone reminded me of my handsome son. Roger's smile was of the unconscious variety, the kind of grin that makes a woman think he'd be attentive, if a little mischievous.

Roger had lived in a good building in the West Village, where murders rarely happened, so there was a splash of sorts. The journalist questioned neighbors and they all testified to how shocked they were.

"He was a nice man," Doris Diederrot, who lived on the fifth floor, said, "always helpful and friendly."

"I saw him coming home from the Gristedes just yesterday," Bob Hahn, the super, said. "He was a very nice, very courteous young man."

Fear filled the streets of the Village, if you were to believe the copy.

Somewhere around eleven o'clock, two nights before, someone had broken the lock on the front door of the building. There was no nighttime doorman. The assailant or assailants went to the sixth-floor apartment, probably knocked, gained entry, and then beat and strangled the thirty-four-year-old investment advisor to death. No one heard anything. No one saw the attackers leave the building.

I had broken into a nighttime building. I had climbed up and down the back stairs, to and from a murder scene.

Exhaustion from the sleepless night before hit me like a revelation. I got to my feet, staggered across the room, and fell on my hard-cushioned Swedish sofa. I was asleep before my body came to rest.

NO FIRE OR FALLING in that dream. I was in a vast flower garden at the height of the blooming season. Every kind of rose and peony, orchid and dahlia filled the field with their brilliance and scents. Huge and deadly Japanese hornets buzzed among the blossoms. Broad-headed scaly-skinned serpents coiled through the soil at my feet. There were vultures overhead and thorns aplenty but I passed through without a bite, stab, or sting.

Around the perimeter of this twisted Eden was a barbed-wire fence. Every ten feet or so, on the other side of the fence, an armed uniformed guard stood at attention. I wondered if they were set there to keep the unsuspecting public out or to protect the obvious riches from plunderers.

The giant hornets' humming was deep and sonorous. They hovered, oblivious to my presence. There seemed to be a message for me in all this profusion and threat. I couldn't discern the meaning, but I knew that if I suddenly understood, the creatures would become aware of me and the soldiers would get me in their sights.

So I took long steady breaths and waited for some sign. I appreciated the beauty not only of the flora but also the loveliness of the deadly bees and fanged snakes, the cut of the soldiers' uniforms and the effortless glide of vultures riding on thermals overhead.

WHEN I OPENED my eyes Aura was sitting in the blue chair six inches from me. Her smile said that she was happy to see me coming awake.

"I'm sorry I let that cop in but—"

"Don't worry about it," I said.

As I sat up a groan escaped my throat that spoke of all my fifty-three years.

"He could have gotten every building inspector in the city down here if I didn't let him in," Aura said, unable to stem the excuse.

"You'd think so, but Kitteridge doesn't work like that. He might be the only truly honest cop in the whole city. Imagine that? One clean cop and his major goal in life is putting my ass behind bars."

"He wanted the combination to the inner door but I told him I didn't have it," she said.

Aura and Twill were the only ones who knew the access code to my inner doors.

"Don't worry, babe. Tryin' to stop the law is like holding back the rain. It's what they call an exercise in futility. If you'd made him wait in the hall he would have probably taken it out on me."

"What does he want?" she asked, her bronze visage somber yet calm. It wasn't what an aficionado would call beautiful, but still it was the kind of face that gave you hope.

I told her everything, about my search for the four young men and the three ensuing deaths. Talking to Aura was like opening a vein.

The first thing you learned in my line of business was that you never give up any information that you don't absolutely have to. Katrina knew nothing about my business. But Aura represented a whole new movement in my life. The time I spent with her was painfully honest. I never lied, except about my recurring dream. Sometimes, when something was just too secret to share, I'd say, "I can't talk about that, babe. So please don't ask me."

"WHAT ABOUT THE dream?" she asked after I'd told her about coming upon the corpse of Norman Fell.

Her question had a two-tiered design. First, she was telling me that she accepted my story and was on my side. Secondly, since I seemed to have let her deeper into my life, she wanted to know more.

"I'm in a building," I said, relieved to finally put the nightmare into words. "It's burning, burning, and I'm running from room to room. I think that maybe I'm the last man left alive but that doesn't matter because soon I'll be dead, too . . ." I told her about the window and the long fall. "It's like my life is one long tumble off the side of a mountain. I'm falling through the air and certain to die. There's no way that I can be saved. No cushion or twist or turn."

Aura took one of my hands in hers and squeezed.

"I love you, Leonid McGill."

"I don't understand that."

"You don't know what love is?"

"Maybe I do, maybe not. But what I don't understand is how you can listen to all this and still have any feelings for me whatsoever. I left you for another woman. I caused the deaths of at least two men. And you know I've done much worse in years gone by."

Aura's smile was in another place than the one I was addressing. She nodded at something, not what I'd said, and then waited as this unspoken knowledge settled around us.

She took my other hand, leaned forward, and kissed my lips lightly.

"You are a man on the road," she told me.

"What does that mean?"

"My father murdered many men back in his country. But I would have still loved him if only he could face what he had done. Instead he lied and blamed others for his crimes. He ran off the road, out of the sun. But you are right out there in the light of day. That's all I want from my man."

Her man.

I took in a breath but it didn't work. I took in another.

"What time is it?" I asked.

"Twenty after one."

"In the afternoon?"

Aura nodded and gave me that enigmatic smile.

"I've been sleepin' since nine?"

She nodded.

"How long have you been here?"

"I came up a little while after the policeman left," she said. "At first I just wanted to make sure that you were okay. Then I stayed to watch over you while you got some rest."

Aura kissed me again. It would have been the perfect moment for us to come together once more if it wasn't for the madwoman running around the couch, shrieking at the top of her voice. That madwoman was my life.

Aura stood up, pulling my hands and bringing me to my feet.

"I'll be in my office if you need me," she said.

Watching Aura leave was never an easy thing. But I didn't have the time to brood.

THE ILLITERATE NORMAN FELL kept pretty good bookkeeping records. Most of the entries were expenses. He knew a few awkwardly spelled words, like "offiss supplys" and "offiss expens." Now and then he took in some cash. There was a four-hundred-dollar payment from someone designated as *TR*. Another, two hundred dollars, was attributed to *Jo M*. The fees were all paltry except for those received from one set of initials.

Norman had received four payments of twenty-five thousand dollars, the last of which was paid on the day, or maybe the day before, he died. The initials next to these entries were simply *VM*—except for the first entry, where, next to the *VM,* there was a *BH* in parentheses.

I imagined the joy the untutored Fell must have felt when he could use a symbol like the parentheses. I would have felt sorry for him if it hadn't been for Gordo's hammer.

It was a story the boxing trainer had told thirty-some years before.

I'd just had a club fight with a sturdy journeyman light heavy from Philadelphia named Mike "Big" Pink. It was just an unsanctioned exhibition bout, neither amateur nor professional. Pink was almost twice my age and had slowed down quite a bit. But in the fourth round he hit me so hard that I was lifted up off my feet. I fell on the ropes and then bent down as if I were inspecting my feet for stink. He chased me for that round and the next two, looking for the knockout. That was the day I decided not to be a professional boxer. I managed to stay on my feet. And even though Big Pink beat me, it was a split decision on the cards. But I felt that blow for weeks afterwards. It was in my fingers and knees, my chest and back. I never wanted to get hit like that again.

When I informed Gordo of my decision was when he told me about the hammer, in an attempt to talk me out of quitting.

"There's a big fat hammer up above, beyond the blue in the sky," he told me. "It's just up there waitin'. One day, when you least expect it, that hammer comes streakin' down on you like Big Pink's fist. That's the ultimate test for a boxer, for any man. It's the punch you don't see comin'. There's nothing you can do about it but try your best and recover. That's what you did against Mikey. You did good."

That was my final exam as a boxer. I passed the test and quit the same day. But what I hadn't understood at the time was that Gordo wasn't just talking about the ring. That hammer was waiting for everybody. It came at you in the form of cancer, infidelity, the tax man, or a comet out of the western sky here to annihilate any creature over fifty kilos in weight. The hammer had come down on Norman Fell; it was watching me with two steely eyes.

I SAT BACK from the ledger pages and looked at the palms of my hands. I have big hands with thick, blunt fingers. When Twill was a little kid he'd always be asking to arm wrestle with me. He'd sit down, thump his sharp elbow on the dining table, and try his very best to pin my arm. I'd let him strain for a minute or so and then I'd press down, taking his arm off the table and pushing him all the way to the floor. He'd squeal and laugh and shout *No fair!* He'd always win by default.

I had more strength in one hand than Twill did, even as a teenager, in his entire body.

There was nothing else for me to do about the ledger entries so I called Tiny to see what progress he had made.

"Hey, LT," the young man answered. He didn't even give me a chance to ask the question, just launched into the report. "The girl's name is Mardi Bitterman. She paid for the IP with her father's credit card. His name is Leslie. He's an office manager for Parley and Lowe, a company that buys up debt and liquidates properties."

"Anything on 'em?" were my first words.

"Not even a parking ticket. The girl is a fair student. She has a younger sister, Marlene, but the mother's not on the scene."

"Died?"

"I can't find anything on that. She's just not there."

"Thanks, Bug. Can you dig a little deeper?"

"Are you paying?"

"The going rate."

I CALLED TWILL and he answered on the first ring.

"Hey, Pops. What's happenin'?"

"I wanted to ask—" I began.

"Hold on a minute," he interrupted. And then, to someone else, "It's my father, Teach. Mom's in the hospital and I might have to go help." Another moment passed and he said, "What can I do for you, Dad?"

"You could start by not lying to your teachers."

"It's almost the end of the period," he said. "And you know I wouldn't even be in summer school if it wasn't for my sentence."

"No lying."

"Okay. Done."

"I want to get together with you soon. Make sure you're home tonight. All night."

"Uh . . . I did have some plans."

"For me, junior."

After a momentary pause he said, "You got it, Pops."

GETTING OFF THE PHONE, I took a deep breath, and then another. I had liked the slow breathing in the dream. I tried not to worry about the problems that surrounded me. My mantra, behind the breathing was, *I'm alive and safe, ambulatory and able to think.*

It worked until the landline rang.

"Hello?"

"Hi, Mr. M," Zephyra Ximenez said. "You have a couple of minutes?"

"Sure. What's up?"

"A Mr. Towers called your office and cell seven times yesterday afternoon. I only answered because you said you wanted me to. He was very rude. I hope you tell him that I really don't know how to get in touch with you sometimes."

"Sorry. I'll talk to him."

"He never left a message but there's still the one from the day before that you haven't listened to."

"Thanks, Z," I said. "You're a pal."

"I love it when you talk like the old movies."

"That mean you'll go out with me?"

"Fifty years ago? No problem."

I DIALED THE NUMBER to the answering machine that Zephyra kept at her house. I use a machine because I can be sure when I erase the tape that no one else will be able to retrieve it. The automated voice told me that I had one message.

"Hello, Mr. McGill, this is Ambrose Thurman. I'm afraid that I haven't been completely honest about the investigation you conducted for me. I was trying to protect my client.

"To begin with, my name is not Thurman but Fell, Norman Fell. I do live in Albany. I am a detective. I used a fake name because my client didn't want to be known and didn't want you to trace them through me. I guess that should have warned me that something was wrong but they put so much remuneration on the table I was blinded. You know what it's like in this business.

"But that's all water over the dam now. It has come to my attention that Mr. Frank Tork has been murdered—"

I heard a slight sound in the background of the recording.

"—who are you?" Fell said with a gasp.

There was a stifled yell and a thud, a clattery jumble of hard items, maybe even the smack of a skull against the desktop. There came a sickening gurgle and choking sound and then the hiss and shuffle of something heavy being moved. I pressed the phone so hard against my ear that it hurt.

After a moment the phone was placed gently in its cradle.

I listened to Norman Fell's last words eleven times, moving the receiver from left ear to right. I listened from behind closed eyes, and with my head bowed. Once I even pinched myself. But try as I might I couldn't get any more out of the recording than I did on the first hearing.

Of all the things I'd done wrong I had never been a party to murder, at least not directly. I had killed, but that was in self-defense. So hearing the panic in Fell's voice in those last moments struck a deep chord in me. The killer was brutal and remorseless, he hadn't spoken one word or uttered a sound.

When I put down the phone I realized that my fingertips had gone numb. Looking around the office, I noticed a clump of dust in the corner next to the Swedish couch. There was a solitary cloud hanging in the sky, perfectly framed by my old-fashioned window. I wanted to get up and open the window but my body said that it wasn't moving, that it was going to stay put.

The shade of white of the ceiling, I noticed for the first time, was subtly different than the white of the walls. I wondered if that was because of some kind of electrical or plumbing work they had done above and when it came to repainting they were unable to match the hue; maybe they just didn't care.

I realized how absurd my meandering was, so I decided to pull my mind back to the murder. But instead I conjured up a name somewhat like Norman's. It was the name of a man I'd never actually met: Fellows Scott.

Scott was an investment banker at Bowman Towne Home Security. He was in charge of loans and foreclosures. Fellows had managed to make a loan to a collective town in southeast Alabama named People. He was aware that some years from the date of the loan the property would grow in value exponentially because of a plan he'd been made privy to by one his wealthier Japanese clients.

Fellows Scott gave the people of People a loan with a balloon payment that would have choked a sperm whale. But this odd collective of college professors and farmers had a plan. They were building a dam. With that they could not only power their collective but could also sell the extra electricity, making more than enough money to pay off Bowman Towne.

"Socialists should never put their trust in capitalism." That was something my father said almost every day. "The hot lead of the revolution is far more trustworthy."

When Scott heard about the dam, he offered to make another loan and to find a contractor who would give them the best possible bargain.

It really wasn't such a good deal. The substandard materials used to fabricate the dam gave way in four years. Seven people died. The town was nearly destroyed. And that big red balloon floated all the way from People to lower Manhattan. Sadly, Fellows had no choice but to foreclose and sell to his foreign clients, who built a large car-parts factory in the hole that had once been a dam.

A romantic might tell you that Fellows couldn't help himself. He had a reason to be so greedy. He loved gambling and prostitutes. Almost all of his ill-gotten gains went into these pastimes.

I got this story from Gert Longman, the perennial temp who went from place to place, helping me find patsies who could take the weight on the various jobs I had taken on.

Fellows Scott's employers knew about his wanton ways but they had no desire to fire someone who had brought in so much lucre. So they made him vice president of a bank in Queens.

His luck went bad when Sam Beakman burgled that branch. He had an inside man give him the codes he needed to get next to the vault. Gert had long ago met a reformed working girl who knew the story of the town called People. It seems that Fellows, who was close-mouthed as a rule, was a regular blabbermouth with prostitutes. I guess he'd never heard of the six degrees of separation.

The setup involved two doctored phone records, which Bug was happy to provide, and a key to a safe-deposit box with a little of the stolen money inside.

The police love gamblers who spend their nights with whores; juries hate that kind of guy. Scott's involvement in the fraud, and his malicious intent toward the town of People, came out in the trial. Bowman Towne are still in court over the suit against them.

Beakman died in an armed-robbery attempt before the Scott case ever came before a judge. Fellows died of strangulation the next year in what the newspaper article called a sexual assault.

Gert told me that Fellows deserved what he got.

"Yeah, I know, babe," I said. "But don't we deserve it, too?"

THE PHONE RANG and I answered reflexively.

"Hello?"

"So what's the answer, LT?" Tony the Suit asked.

"To what question?" I replied.

I knew that he'd never speak literally about something so serious over the phone. I guess I was feeling kind of mean and so without a fly to pluck the wings from I decided to torture Tony.

"You know what I'm talking about."

"Sure I do, Tony. You're looking for real estate and I'm looking for a new profession."

"Yeah," he said. "Yeah. I'm looking for a house all right. Can you find it for me?"

"No problem, man. I will do that for you."

Tony was silent a moment, not completely understanding the meaning that underlay my lighthearted demeanor.

"But you gotta do me a favor, Tone," I said.

"What's that?"

"My secretary told me that you were kinda rough with her on the phone."

"That bitch wouldn't put me through."

"If you speak harshly to her again our deal is off. Do you understand that?"

"She's more than just a secretary for you, huh?"

"She means more to me than your whole fucking family," I said, using every ounce of the iron in my jaw.

I wanted to see how serious Tony was about finding A Mann. If it was, as he said, just to have a talk about some old business sheets, he wouldn't have allowed me to speak to him like that.

"Okay, LT," he said. "You don't have to get all upset. I'm sorry. I'll leave the little girl alone. Scout's honor."

It was then that I knew what he had on his mind. Business as usual, in my world.

The best time to kill someone is when they're going through a door. While passing from one place to another most people are a little off guard, distracted by the subtle displacement separating here from there.

He hit me on the upper part of my left temple as I was walking from my outer office into the Art Deco hallway. It was the hardest I'd been struck, by a fist, since Big Pink knocked me out of boxing. This was no weak-sister amateur like back-alley Jonah. No. Whoever hit me had a lot of practice and good muscle to back it up.

As I half-sailed through the atmosphere toward my faux receptionist's desk I passed from the real world into a limbo back over thirty years, when George Foreman bounced Joe Frazier around the ring like a fat kid thumping on a basketball.

I was that basketball, and somewhere Gordo was shouting, "Get up, kid! Get up! You can't let him do that! Get in close! Cut off his power!"

I was in a supine pose and saw no reason to get up and let George hit me like that again. It was comfortable there on my back on the canvas, or maybe it was the floor. Flat on his back is the safest place for a boxer who has met his better.

The referee must have been distracted. Maybe he was trying to get George to go to a neutral corner. I started the count for him so when he got to me he wouldn't have to recite all those numbers.

"One—two—three," I counted but then I heard something slam.

I lost my place and had to start all over at one. By the time I got to four a clawless she-bear had decided to shamble into the ring and caress me by the throat. The problem was that this *Ursus arctos horribilus* didn't understand that she was far too strong. The bear wanted to caress me but she might have choked me to death if she wasn't careful.

I do believe that I would have passed pleasantly into unconsciousness if it wasn't for those paws around my throat. It was an intimate embrace—until I couldn't breathe.

Sparring and working out at Gordo's gym was more than just an exercise regimen for me. It also kept me in touch with a boxer's quick reaction time. Boxers can fight when they're out on their feet; they can feel a blow coming from behind their heads. A boxer, like a chess player, sees many moves ahead. He has physical speed far beyond normal human reflexes. And, most of all, his profession is survival.

That was my job, too.

I brought my fists together on either side of the big bear, George Foreman's head—at least that's what my addled brain told me I was doing.

The man who was on top of me fell back, allowing me to get to my feet. Even squatting down on one knee he was nearly my height. I hit him with everything I had and all he did was stand up straight. I swung again but he took a step back with his long, pillar-like legs, crossing over to the front door, which, in my stupor, I heard slamming.

I had all of two seconds to appraise my white male attacker. He was six five at least, wearing army surplus fatigues from a jungle war, not Iraq. His fists were bigger than Sonny Liston's and his face was both slack and spiteful. The hair was a golden brown, and if someone told me he weighed three hundred pounds I wouldn't have been surprised.

He came at me, quickly and lithe, like a born athlete. Lucky for me his ability was from nature, not training. I sidestepped the lunge and clocked his jaw with a solid right hook. He swung his left arm and nearly knocked me down with the push. I have a low center of gravity, however, so I sidled away like a crab.

My gun was in the inner office. So that was out of the question. The front door was closed, and I wasn't fast enough to open it before he could drag me down and strangle me for good.

He tried to grab me but I ducked under and hit him in the midsection with two perfect uppercuts.

He didn't even grunt.

I backed away and he lunged again. I ducked and punched for all the good it did me. He looked like he was going to jump again so I went low. But he didn't come all the way. He stopped and threw an uppercut of his own. I think I might have discovered a new galaxy at that moment, seeing that my opponent had just ripped a hole in the fabric of my reality.

I went into my shell and he hit both shoulders with two untrained roundhouse blows. Every joint in my body rattled.

Once it was only a suspicion, but now it was a fact: I was too old for this.

I looked up just in time to see him jump at me. I fell to the floor and rolled away, letting him crash into the wall.

Any intelligent creature would have stopped a moment after slamming into a wall. But Big Boy just turned and sought me out with his dull, hateful eyes. He didn't say anything. He wasn't breathing hard. There wasn't even a bruise from my pinpoint punching or on the part of his head that had put a dent in the plaster wall. It was one of those moments when you realize that only a higher power could see you through.

Whenever a door is opened in my office, hidden digital cameras go to work. They take pictures every few seconds for eight minutes, so the whole fight between me and Big Boy was captured in two-and-a-half-second lapses. I've studied the fight more than once, and every time I see it I wonder why I'm not dead.

He hadn't landed more than a few flush punches but he was so strong that that hardly mattered. I hit him maybe a dozen times with absolutely no effect. I tried to kick him in the balls—I wasn't proud—but he was too tall and easily avoided my craven attempt at survival.

At one point I ran behind the receptionist's desk, hoping for just a few seconds' respite. But the guy, with only one hand, slid the desk across the room and into the wall.

That was one of the most disheartening moments of my deeply unsatisfying life. I had never seen such raw power. And I knew that this man had already murdered Roger Brown, Frank Tork, and Norman Fell. His hateful idiot face told me that he would not listen to my entreaties.

Two half-seconds passed. During the first increment I realized that I was very close to the end of my life—that this man was going to slaughter me and there was no way out. I used the rest of my last second deciding that I should go out on a high note.

I screamed like a berserker Viking and grabbed the backrest of the thirty-six-and-three-quarter-pound swivel chair that nobody but me sat in. I swung that chair up using the last of my fear-induced strength. My nemesis took a step back, and I knew I was done for. But then the backrest came off in my hands and the rest of the chair went flying at the big man's head.

It hit him and he went down and out.

I fell to my knees wheezing, a Greco-Roman wrestler at the end of a championship bout. When I tried to rise to make the 911 call I fell flat on my face as I had done in Gordo's Gym a thousand years before.

Some upstanding citizen heard the ruckus and called the cops. That citizen should have been me. Don't get me wrong, I did call the police, but only as my second act of consciousness. That was five minutes later. It took three minutes to get to the phone and two more to call Breland Lewis, my long-time lawyer and sometime friend.

Way before Breland got there I was on my knees, with a plastic tie holding my wrists behind my back. There were eleven cops in the twelve-by-fourteen room, where a good deal of the floor space was taken up by the body of the most powerful man I ever fought.

"This guy's alive," one of the boys in blue shouted.

Alive? A blow like he received could have killed a real bear.

There's a small squad of policemen assigned to the Tesla Building. With so many businesses—and possible crimes—there are always a few cops in the vicinity. Each and every one of them has my name and statistics committed to memory. I was a person of interest to the NYPD. No amount of redemption was going to change that fact.

Sergeant Kenneth Holloway was the officer in charge. He had told me, more than once, always in the exact same words, that "I will see you locked up for forty years, McGill."

He said it to me again when I was on my knees, but I didn't have the strength to care.

"Why did you attack him?" Holloway asked.

I looked up and saw skinny, diminutive Breland Lewis shoulder his way past cops twice his size.

"Out of my way," he peeped like an angry chick. "Mr. McGill is my client and I have every right to see him. Leonid, are you okay?"

"We got your client on attempted murder, Counselor," Holloway said, grinning ugly.

Looking at those two, I had to wonder about the American idea of a white race. Holloway was tall and beefy, pink-skinned with stingy porcine eyes and ears. Lewis, on the other hand, was a flyweight with fine features carved from the ivory of a recent kill. As far as that went, the white man on the floor had brownish-white skin. He was a Caucasian, too, by American standards, but in ancient Europe those three would all have been considered different races.

My mind, I realized, was still wandering. I thought maybe I should go see a doctor soon.

"This man pushed his way into Leonid's office and attacked him," Breland was shouting.

"Then why isn't LT dead on the floor?" Holloway bellowed.

"Release my client!"

"To Attica, for forty years!"

I wondered what the number forty meant in the cop's interpretation of justice.

Just then the paramedics barged in. There were four of them in white and blue, two women and two men. There were now eighteen people in the antechamber of my office and spilling out into the hall. It was like a party.

"What's the combination to your inner office?" Holloway asked me after consulting with the head meat-wagon attendant.

"A secret," I replied.

I was hoping that Holloway would slap me, not to claim police brutality but to snap me out of the malaise that exertion and a beating had brought on.

The paramedics were turning Big Boy over onto a hydraulic gurney that had been lowered to the floor. He didn't look good. There was a gash on the left side of his forehead and his tan skin was wending toward blue. He was breathing, though, and even my ideologue father would have to admit that breath is the only true definition of life.

Holloway and Lewis were arguing: the bulldog and the chicklet. I was still breathing hard, and trying to think of something that would make sense in a situation like that.

"What's goin' on in here?" a familiar voice commanded.

Everyone went silent as Carson Kitteridge entered, parting the sea of blues and white.

"Your boy tried to murder this man," Holloway said, triumph buoying his words.

Big Boy was being rolled from the room on the gurney. Kitteridge glanced at him and then turned back to the fat sergeant.

"What'd he say?" Carson asked, nodding in my direction.

"Who cares what he said? It's obvious what happened. We caught him trying to escape. And I bet ya dollars to doughnuts that when the victim comes to, he's gonna have that story to tell."

Kitteridge tried to stifle his sneer. Instead of responding, he went over to my displaced desk and climbed on top. There in the corner he pressed a panel and a section of the wall gave way. Unplugging the digital camera he found there, he hopped down and returned to Holloway.

I didn't have to look to know what they were seeing. I once had occasion to show Carson pictures taken with the secret camera.

I have to give Holloway credit. He knew when he was beaten.

"Release him," he said to a sandy-haired minion.

After snipping the plastic tie, the young man even helped me to my feet.

"Tell me something, Sergeant Holloway," I said while massaging the blood back into my hands. "Why do you make suspects get down on their knees?"

"Makes 'em easier to control," he said.

If I was an innocent man I might have struck him down. But the truth was, I deserved Holloway. All the years I'd pulled the plug on men who maybe weren't angels. I was Gordo's hammer for more than a score of men. That's why I could be tied up and thrown down on my knees.

That's why someone will kill me one day.

THEY TOOK MY CAMERA but I didn't care. All the photos taken were transmitted to a storage device in my inner office. Even if they *lost* the evidence, I had two other cameras and a backup.

Slowly the cops left my offices. Along with the camera they took the swivel chair. Holloway was the last of the uniforms to depart. Before going through the door, he pointed at me, making his thumb and forefinger like the hammer and barrel of an old-fashioned six-shooter. It wasn't an empty gesture.

"Did they strike you?" Breland asked me.

"No."

"Did they castigate you?"

"What?"

"Curse you, use harsh or foul language?" he said by way of explanation.

"I know what the word means, man. This is cops and killers here. There might have been some cursing, but damn, it would be a miracle if there wasn't."

Breland was an odd guy. A decade older than I, he looked ten years younger. He'd once worked for a lawyer who represented a reputed crime boss and his associates. That's how we met. When the crime boss and his lawyer were brought down, Breland needed work. I liked the guy, so I sent some fairly honest jobs his way. It turned out that he was the loyal sort, and so, even though I might have been a little slow with my payment schedule, he was always there when the chains rattled at my door.

Kitteridge had taken a seat in one of the surviving visitors' chairs.

"Are there more questions, Detective?" Breland asked.

"Not here."

"What do you mean?"

"I'm taking your client to our offices for an interrogation, a prolonged interrogation."

"Mr. McGill needs medical attention."

It occurred to me that the paramedics hadn't even looked at me. Just the fact that I was under arrest meant that they didn't care about my health.

"You want a ride to the Rikers medical facility, LT?" Kitteridge asked.

"What grounds you got to arrest me, man?"

"Have you ever heard the words 'material witness'?"

24

Blood leaked slowly from the split on my temple down onto the lapel of my jacket. Now and then a droplet would splash on the pale-green Formica tabletop in the interrogation room.

"We should get you some first aid," Carson Kitteridge said.

"It'll wait until I get home."

"You're getting blood on my table," the detective complained.

"I didn't ask to be here."

Carson wasn't happy, but neither was I under arrest. He could have taken me to a prison infirmary but he wanted answers and knew from long, hard experience that I wasn't the kind of guy that he could bully. The blood was part of our dialogue—if he wanted to have a conversation, it would be with the wounded man he wouldn't allow to rest after a horrific beating.

"So tell me about Willie Sanderson," Kitteridge said.

"Who?"

"Come on, LT. Don't get me mad now."

"I don't know anyone named Sanderson."

"You nearly kill a guy and you don't even know his name?"

"He's still alive?"

"Who is he?"

"Never met him before. Never heard of him. I doubt that he's even human if he survived that flying chair."

"If he dies it's manslaughter."

"Bullshit. That man was trying to kill me. You saw the pictures."

The cop sat back and did that lacing-his-fingers thing. I've never understood what he intends to communicate with that gesture.

"We got one, maybe two men bludgeoned and strangled, and a third who almost fell in line," he said.

"What men?" I asked.

"Your boy fits the description of the guy who went to see Roger Brown. If you take off the hat and fake whiskers he looks an awful lot like the guy who paid Frank Tork's bail. That's what I call suspicious."

"Yeah," I said. "Suspicious about your boy Sanderson. I'm just a victim here."

"That's one way to look at it."

"What's that supposed to mean?"

"Maybe you were in business with Sanderson," he suggested. "Maybe he decided to take you down and keep the profits for himself."

"What business? What profits? I was walking out of my door and he attacked me. He didn't say a word, and my bankbook's got cobwebs all over it. I was not in business with him, and I never met him."

Kitteridge was watching my eyes. He did that often. He believed, I think, that he could tell when a man was lying by looking into his eyes. I believed that he could also.

After a moment he pulled his fingers apart and made an open-palmed plaintive gesture.

"Help me out with this, LT," he said. "We got some white maniac from Albany killing African-Americans on the street. It has the stink of a hate crime."

"I never even understood the idea of a hate crime," I said, wasting time, trying to digest the fact that my would-be killer was from Albany. Was he the one who hired Fell? No. Fell didn't recognize him when he came in for the kill. "I mean, if you kill somebody with evil intent, it's murder and you should pay for it. That's all, right?"

"I can sit here all night," the cop replied.

I leaned forward and three neat little droplets splashed on the tabletop.

"I'm beat, man," I said. "I been thumped on, handcuffed, dragged down here, and made to wait for hours while you shuffled papers and drank bad coffee. Let me go home and get cleaned up. Let me get some sleep and maybe I'll come up with somethin' for ya."

"I could arrest you."

"For self-defense?"

"This isn't going away," Carson said. "This is murder. If Sanderson pulls through and incriminates you, all bets are off."

"I don't know anything."

TWILL WAS WAITING near the front desk of the Chelsea station. He wore black trousers and a pin-striped blue-and-white dress shirt that was wanting a pair of cuff links. He was sitting there on a wooden bench next to a young blonde in gold hot pants and a blue halter. The young woman was smiling brightly, chattering away at my son. He nodded sagely now and again and spoke in a low voice.

When he saw me Twill stood up, but we didn't embrace. Twill is too cool for kneejerk expressions of fondness; I guess I am, too.

"Hey, boy," I said. "What you doin' here? It's nearly two in the morning."

"Mr. Lewis called," he said. "He told me that you'd been arrested and so I called up to find out what precinct Detective Kitteridge was working out of."

If anyone was an example of having too much on the ball it was my son. He would track down Satan and then try to brace him for a bad debt.

"This is Lonnie," Twill said. "She's waiting for her boyfriend, Juman. They got him in here on a seventy-two-hour thing. I gave her Mr. Lewis's number. I hope that's okay."

Lonnie had the lovely, and somewhat awkward, physical contradiction of skinny legs and big breasts. She stood up and shook my hand like her mother had taught her when she was five.

"Pleased to meet you, Mr. McGill. Your son is great."

"Tell Breland to call me," I said. "If it's just a simple thing, I'll cover the charge."

"Thank you, sir," she said. "He's really not a bad guy at all."

Before we left, Lonnie kissed my son on the cheek and whispered something to him.

"WHAT DID LONNIE say?" I asked Twill. We were walking down the ramp that led to the garage where he had parked my classic car.

"She wants me to call her. Says that Juman is on the way out and she'd like to buy me a coffee or something."

I gave him a doubting stare.

"Don't worry, Pop. She was just thankful to have somebody help her out in there."

He didn't say whether he was going to call her or not.

ON THE WAY home Twill asked me about the interrogation. I told him what happened, then tried to get deeper into him.

"So you didn't really say if you had a steady girl," I ventured.

"Don't worry, Dad. Lonnie's not my type."

"I'm not worried about her. I just wanted to know if you had something going on. You know, a steady, like."

He laughed. I think he might have been a little embarrassed.

"What's funny?" I asked him.

"Here some man you never even met tries to beat you to death and you're asking me about if I have a girlfriend or not?"

"Near-death experience makes a man want to pay attention to the little things. Is it so hard to answer a simple question?"

"I'm not gay, if that's what you're asking."

"You know, son, you're better than I was in that interrogation room."

"What do you mean?"

"Something's going on with you, Twill. I want you to trust me."

"I trust you fine."

"Then talk to me."

"I'm okay, Dad. You don't have to worry about me."

Most parents of teenagers could identify with that banter. There I was, the dedicated fisherman, and he was like a lively trout slipping between my fingers in an icy-cold stream.

The difference between Twill and other young men was that he was planning a hit in New York City with no more trepidation than a teenage girl fixing her lipstick between kisses.

"Tell me somethin', Pop."

"What's that, son?"

"Why'd they let you go? I mean, Mr. Lewis said that he thought they'd keep you all night at least."

"I think they just got tired," I said. Then I yawned.

Oh my God. Oh my God," Katrina chanted again and again, daubing my head with a damp towel. "It's so terrible. Why would a man hit you like that? How could someone be like this?"

It's a disheartening feeling when you can't stand the touch of someone but neither can you push them away. There hadn't been love between Katrina and me for a dozen years at least, and before that the passion was sporadic at best.

It would have been impossible to explain in a court of law, or in a marriage counselor's office, how I believed that every gesture she made, every comment that came from her lips, was considered before its fabrication. Katrina had made herself into the image of a loving wife because she had tried her best to leave and the ground had fallen out from underneath her.

Sometimes I wondered how my life ended up in that sad configuration. How could I be the father to other men's children, the life-partner of a woman who believed that wealth and beauty somehow combined to make up love?

I was like a man, shovel in hand, finding himself standing in a freshly dug grave but with no memory of having dug it. I stayed there because at least if you've hit bottom you had no farther to fall.

"Leonid?" Katrina said in a tone that made me think she'd called to me more than once.

"Yeah?"

"Are you insured?"

Every now and then even my wife could say something to make me laugh.

I AWOKE AT five the next morning, as usual. I've always been a nervous sleeper, an early riser, and prone to naps.

After two cups of extra-strong press-pot French roast I honed my thoughts down to the trouble I was facing. I needed to extricate myself, but before I could do that I had to understand the nature of the mess that I was in.

There were plenty of clues: the four men I had searched out, Norman Fell (aka Ambrose Thurman), and the as-yet-nameless person who hired him. The client's initials, VM or BH, was something—but not much. Even at the moment of his death, when he was confessing to me, Fell had been cagey. The illiterate had made sure not to put a gender on the employer that he was supposedly betraying. I didn't know if it was a man or woman who'd hired him.

There was also Willie Sanderson, and maybe a kid who died named Thom "Smiles" Paxton.

Someone wanted these low-rent young men killed, and then, to cover their tracks, Norman Fell was destined to die. I didn't know if I had always been on the hit list or if maybe Sanderson had heard him talking to me and then had been sent to shut my mouth, too.

Sanderson had to be a hired killer—of that much I was almost certain.

But who would want four low-life young men killed? Who'd pay a man's bail to murder him? The scenario was simple, it just didn't make sense, like a live cat sealed in a glass globe, or the United States declaring peace.

I WENT TO the den and got online, looking for some event that would hold the four targets together at the time Fell's client's son last saw them. That was in early September 1991.

That fall was a very interesting moment in modern American history. The dictatorship of the proletariat was disintegrating in Russia. Gorbachev and Yeltsin made their move to take power from the Soviet congress. The Baltic nations gained their independence and the CIA was looking for a new way to justify its existence.

Out of a thousand executions over the previous fifty years, for the first time a white man was executed for murdering a black man. The Republicans and Democrats were battling over Clarence Thomas's bid for a seat on the Supreme Court. President de Klerk was having a hard time trying to democratize South Africa while holding back power for his white brothers.

Frank Capra died.

The country was in the midst of a recession, and the political and social world was spinning off its axis, though no one knew in what direction it would go.

A lot was happening but nothing about the four teenagers that I had found for Fell.

Thom Paxton had died that year. I found the entry on the ninety-seventh page delivered by my Bug-designed search engine. It was an article in *Newsday* when *Newsday* was a city paper. The young man had died of a broken neck incurred when he fell from a high girder. He and some unnamed friends were trespassing on the site and there was some evidence that the victim was intoxicated.

It was a solid clue, only it would have been better if his last name started with an *M* or an *H* as did Fell's client's. I tried to find out more about young Thom, who, the article said, was seventeen, but there was nothing more to fetch.

AS LONG AS I was online I looked through my e-mails. I got offers to enhance my penis size and to get rich off of diamonds in South Africa, a holler from a girl named Shirl who swore she could get me out of the funk men my age experience, and a missive, replete with attachments, from Tiny "Bug" Bateman.

Mardi Bitterman had published a story in an online teen magazine about a suicide pact between two sisters who lived in Iraq. The fictionalized children were being tortured for some reason, and the only way they could defend themselves was to die. This wouldn't have been so bad if Mardi hadn't also spent many hours browsing sites that claimed to have information on exotic poisons derived from household ingredients.

The father, Leslie, didn't have anything nearly so dramatic in his digital background, but there was a shadow there. He received a regular certified package that was arranged through a website, which he accessed through his office account, some outfit called Phil's Olde Tyme Almanack. Bug couldn't find any other reference to the business, nor could he identify any other customers.

He was sure about the Bitterman address. Which was maybe fifteen blocks from our place.

"I'm drawing a blank on this one, LT," Bug wrote.

I turned off the machine and left the apartment before anyone else was up.

AURA WAS WAITING in the antechamber of my office, a much lovelier sight than Carson Kitteridge or The Suit.

"Hey, babe," I said as nonchalant as I could with a cockroach-sized bump on my left temple.

She put her arms around me and I relented, feeling the air fill my lungs and the full weight of my body evenly distributed on the soles of my feet.

"I wanted to call you," she whispered in my ear.

"I know."

"You've got to take better care of yourself."

"I didn't hit myself in the head."

She leaned back and stared into my face. There was no plan in her heart, no goal she was reaching for. Aura liked being in my presence. She filled my life with a knowledge and a confidence that I'd never known before. And that was because I tried my best not to lie her, and to never misrepresent who I was.

"What are we going to do?" she asked.

"I'm going into my office and you're going up to yours," I said. "For now that's all we can do."

"Theda misses you, and so does Trini."

Trini was a Tibetan spaniel, and Theda was a precocious twelve-year-old whom Aura adopted when her best friend, Nancy, Theda's mother, died. Twill dropped by their house now and again because they'd gotten to know each other while Katrina was off with Banker Zool.

"I miss them, too," I said, disentangling myself.

"Call me?" she said before going out the door.

THE RECEPTION AREA of my office had been cleaned up. Even the holes in the wall were spackled and awaiting a new coat of paint. Aura took care of me as best she could. If I was a good guy I would have told her not to wait, to find a new man who deserved her attention. And I wouldn't have said it because there was no chance of us getting back together. Katrina could leave at any moment. The problem was that I might, one day soon, find myself free and available. But then what? Would she end up murdered just for being my friend, as had Gert Longman? Would she end up snarling at me as she died, like that girl calling herself Karmen Brown had done?

AFTER APPRECIATING THE job well done and castigating myself for not being able to live without hope, I went through to my office and lay down on the sofa. There were fires burning all around me, but I slept long and hard.

I jerked awake at 11:07 when the buzzer from the front entrance went off. It's not a loud sound, but who knew what new assassin might have been pressing that button? I went over to my desk, opening the second drawer on the right side. The small monitor was connected to four concealed electric eyes that covered every possible angle outside my front door.

Lieutenant Kitteridge had the woman he was with stand to the side so that the one camera he knew about wouldn't reveal her. This gave me pause, but not in a doorstopper kind of way. I just wondered who she was and what her presence might portend.

As I have said many times, the honest cop and I had no love lost between us. He despised me and I had a healthy dislike for him. But I understood as I made my way toward the front that he was one of the few people, outside of a handful of intimates, that I trusted implicitly. I knew that he wouldn't bushwhack me, wouldn't set me up just to see me fall. He was the better man and I had to respect him regardless of any other feelings I harbored.

"Who is it?" I called through the outer door.

"Police," Kitteridge said in a false authoritative tone. I remember thinking that he must've been in a good mood.

"Who's that with you?" I asked. I had to. Every

now and then the cop needed to be shown that I was a step ahead.

"Sergeant Bethann Bonilla," he replied evenly, without any show of surprise.

I opened the door. The thirtyish sergeant was a head taller than her colleague. She had half a head on me. She was slender but wore a bulky blue suit to give the illusion of substance. As white as Kitteridge, she had black eyes and hair that whispered the accent of her last name.

"What can I do for you?" I asked.

"Let us in, LT."

WHEN WE WERE all seated in my office there was a moment of silence: those few seconds before the first round of the main event, before the bell rings and all hell breaks loose.

There was a very long cargo ship cruising down the Hudson, under the Statue of Liberty. Its passage gave me ideas that led far away from that room.

"Sergeant Bonilla is the newest addition to midtown Homicide," Carson said. "She's hoping to make you her first collar."

"I don't know," I said. "I got a thick neck."

Bonilla smiled in a way that I didn't quite get. But one thing was for sure—she wasn't intimidated by me.

"You know, that's always how I thought it should be," I opined.

"What's that, Mr. McGill?" Bonilla asked. Her voice was pleasant and throaty.

"A man should always be introduced to his executioner. That way there's nothing shadowy or sinister about the deed. If the government is gonna kill you, everything should be aboveboard and nothing kept secret."

There was that smile again.

"Willie Sanderson's still in a coma," Kitteridge said, throwing my philosophical line of reasoning off track.

"What you should be saying is that he's still dead," I said, "with little hope left for his resurrection."

"This coma might become a permanent condition," Carson said as a retort and in preparation for some other kind of attack.

Bonilla's stare was starting to make me feel uncomfortable.

"We'd like to know what you can give us on Mr. Sanderson," she said.

"The first time I met the man was at the wrong end of his big fist," I told her. "I was a fool not to check the monitor before going out. I'll probably be that same fool again someday soon."

I was going out of my way trying to be witty. Maybe I had a concussion or something.

"Sanderson has a long history of violence," Carson put in. There was a definite competitive tone to his voice. "From assault and battery all the way to intent to commit murder and manslaughter. The doctors say that he has some kind of chemical imbalance. It's a condition that I can't even pronounce which causes a state of mind that the lawyers and scientists say make up a valid claim for insanity. He can't help it if he's off his meds. But our doctors tell us that he's been on the right drug for at least the last thirty days."

It was a nice little speech that didn't seem to require a reply, so I leaned back and nodded.

"Now it's your turn to give," Carson prompted.

I hunched my shoulders and consciously kept from looking in Bonilla's direction.

"We have a record of you flying to Albany recently," she said in spite of my cold shoulder.

The shiver bounced back and went through me.

"So?"

"You know," Kitteridge said.

"How did you find out about my flight?"

"We're not gonna debate the constitutionality of the Patriot Act, LT," Kitteridge instructed. "What were you doing in Albany?"

When your opponent has the edge on you it's best to go on the offensive.

"Excuse me for being cautious," I said, "but I'm the victim of an assault, not a suspect in a murder, as far as I know. I haven't killed anybody but still I'm being interrogated by a homicide detective. So before I answer any questions, please put these pieces together for me."

"Sanderson murdered Roger Brown," Bonilla said. "His skin was found under the slain man's fingernails."

"And a business card with your fingerprint on it," Carson tag-teamed, "with Roger's adolescent nickname scrawled at the bottom, was in Brown's pocket. You visited Frank Tork a few days before he was killed in the same fashion that Brown was. Sanderson then came after you. You see the pattern?"

I was waiting for the three-minute bell but I knew it was not to come.

"Ambrose Thurman," I said.

"Who?" the police said in unison.

"About a month ago a guy named Ambrose Thurman called me. He said he wanted to hire me to find someone and would front me twenty-five hundred dollars for the legwork. He wanted to meet at the Crenshaw. I needed to keep up on my grocery bills and expected him to pay for the drinks."

"Who is he?" Bonilla asked.

I took out my wallet and handed over the fake card Norman Fell had pawned off on me.

"Said he was an Albany detective working for a client up that way."

The sergeant studied the yellow card and handed it over to Carson.

"He was looking for four guys," I said and gave their nicknames. "I asked around the East Village, came up with their names, and turned them over. I visited Frankie in the can just to make sure he was who I thought he was. Same with Brown, only I never got to meet him. I left that card with the receptionist. That's it."

"You went up to meet this Thurman in Albany?" Bonilla asked.

"No, he came down here."

"So what were you doing in Albany?" Her repetition of the city's name set my teeth on edge.

"I saw that Frank Tork had been murdered. That bothered me, so I went up there to ask him what was up."

"Why didn't you call?" Carson asked.

"I did. Phone was disconnected."

"What did he say?"

"There was no Ambrose Thurman in Albany. It was a sham."

The two cops sat there, digesting my story. The card was a good touch. It had worked for Fell, maybe it would do the same for me.

"You think maybe this Sanderson guy was working with Thurman?" I asked after a respectable span of silence.

"I think maybe you know more than you're saying."

"I never heard of Sanderson. I wasn't looking for him. I wanted to get the lowdown from Thurman before coming to you. But when he turned out to be a shadow, I got worried that he'd set me up. I guess I was right, only he was planning to kill me, not get me accused of the crimes."

Carson was looking into my eyes so he knew I was lying, but he couldn't figure out about what exactly.

"Do I know you, Sergeant?" I asked the homicide cop, partly to avoid Carson's stare.

"I used to be in vice," she said, smiling enigmatically. "Had a snitch named Dolores Devine back then."

Dolores Devine, one of my many guilty victims. She'd set up half a dozen prominent men for prostitution stings with the feds and the NYPD. The wife of one of those men wanted revenge and was willing to pay. I found out that Dolores smuggled H for a man in Newark now and again. All I did was drop a dime, or maybe it was a quarter.

"Never heard of her," I said.

"Oh?"

"Friend of yours?"

"We'll check out your story, Mr. McGill," she replied, getting to her feet. "Let's hope that you're more innocent than Dolores was."

27

The police love it when a suspect, or just somebody they don't like, is feeling uncomfortable. It doesn't matter if that person of interest is innocent and doesn't deserve the abuse. They don't drop by and apologize the week after the case is cracked and somebody else is proven guilty. Their job is to make people like me feel nauseous and angst-ridden.

The police deal in ulcers and heart attacks, nonspecific neuroses and straight-out paranoia.

That's why I learned the Buddhist practice of meditation.

After the representatives of the NYPD left my premises I sat me down in the office chair and took in a long slow breath while counting the number "one." I exhaled, considering the numeral "two," and went on in that fashion until I made it to "ten." I started at "one" again, many times, until the counting fell away and all that was left was a kind of bliss that lasted a little more than half an hour.

I could have gone on like that for much longer but the buzzer sounded again. Rather than shock I felt only a mental nudge. I'd become a brightly colored carp resting in a chilly corner of a shallow Japanese pond. I breathed in through my mouth and looked down into my hall monitors.

Ryman Lucas and Hal Pittman were ugly men. Lucas had a nose, ears, and eyes that belonged on a much larger head. Pittman was just scary. He was always in a rage, and his face expressed that fact with brutal clarity. They were both white, the same height—under six feet but still way taller than I. They wore bad suits—one camel, that was Lucas, and the other a dusky orange.

I stretched languorously, putting my whole upper body into the movement, then pulled my .38 out of the top drawer and sauntered up toward the entrance.

The buzzer had sounded twice more by the time I'd reached the front door. I pulled it open slowly, then showed the thugs my pistol and gestured with the barrel for them to take seats in the receptionist's visitors' chairs.

Aura had replaced the confiscated assault chair with a posh brown-leather thing from somewhere in the bowels of the Tesla. It was set to the height I liked, which made me smile as I settled there before my attentive hostages.

"You don't need no gun, LT," Pittman said.

"You, on the other hand, need a new tailor," I replied.

"Com'on, man," Lucas chided. "We just here 'cause the man told us to be here."

"In the beginning," I said, hoping to prime them.

"Huh?" Lucas asked.

"Why are you here?" I felt the air leaving my lungs and the chair holding my weight.

Pittman recited a ten-digit number that began with the primary Chicago area code. A muscle in my left buttock tightened a bit.

I picked up the receiver with my left hand, cradled it against my ear on that side, and entered the numbers spoken.

On the first ring he answered: "Leonid?"

My right butt cheek knew the voice.

"Mr. Vartan."

"I'm down on the first floor, south side of the building, at the Coffee Exchange."

"I'll be right down."

I thanked Buddha for his breath in my lungs. Without that little bit of an edge I might have done something crazy—like murder the men sitting before me.

"You guys can go," I said.

"But—" Pittman began.

I leveled the pistol and pulled back the hammer. That got my unwanted guests to their feet and out the door with no more argument.

This action sounds more deadly than it actually was. It was no more violent than slapping a horse on his belly when he has been acting both willful and lazy.

I WAS SURE that the leg-breakers would be waiting for me at the elevator doors on the first floor. When Harris Vartan tells someone to do something he is bound to be obeyed. That's just the way things work in his world.

I, however, had left that sphere and could think of no better way to articulate that fact than to use the key that Aura had given me to take the utility elevator down to the first floor.

Vartan was sitting at a corner table, sipping his coffee from a porcelain demitasse cup. His lavender suit was somehow understated, while his tie, made from a print of Picasso's *Guernica*, spoke of his sophistication.

With silver hair, olive skin, and eyes that at least appeared to be black, Harris Vartan was either the cream or the scum at the top of the container that is New York City. How you saw him depended on where you stood.

"Hello," I said.

"Leonid," the dapper advisor to evil said, giving me a minimal smile. "I see that you've eluded Tony's men."

This would be the only time that Vartan, known in both police and criminal circles as The Diplomat, would mention The Suit's name.

You had to be on the ball to keep up with Vartan's patter. He spoke in allusions and metaphors that were too vague ever be useful as evidence in a courtroom.

"I'm out, Mr. Vartan," I said. "All the way out."

The fit septuagenarian allowed another hint of mirth to flit across his lips.

No one gets out, his smile said, *unless it's on his back.*

I first met Harris Vartan when I was twelve and he was called Ben Tilly. He and my father worked together as labor organizers, but Ben and my old man went on different paths.

"I'm only asking that you do what you do, Leonid," he said. "After all, a man is defined by his labor."

A cell phone sitting on the table started vibrating. Vartan paid it no attention.

"A man is also defined," I said, "by those who work for him—and those whom he works for."

"Sometimes it's not so clear who is working for whom."

"That may be," I speculated, "except when the individual in question is self-employed."

"No man is an island," Vartan lamented, "no king not a man."

At that point Lucas and Pittman appeared at the open glass doors of the coffee shop. Vartan raised a solitary finger, stopping them in their tracks.

"Do your job, Leonid," Vartan said as he stood up from the table. "That's all anyone expects."

A waiter came up to him, saying, "Did you want your check, sir?"

"My friend is paying."

Vartan departed with Tony's dogs at his heels.

While taking out my wallet I wondered what it was my father's old friend was telling me. Every nuance, including appearing there with Tony's men, meant that whatever I did, it had to be just right.

Or not.

I once had a partner. His name was Bill. Bill was an okay guy and we were, at least from a technical standpoint, an ideal team in a shady kind of way. He was white—a tall, sandy-haired, handsome guy with a couple of years of college, which made him at least literate and able to deal with the concept of two plus two. I was a tree stump of a black man, home-schooled by a dyed-in-the-wool Communist revolutionary, with more books and ideas shoved into my mind than the librarian at Oxford's Bodleian.

We, Bill and I, did things that would not have made us look good in front of a judge and jury but we were slicker than graphite on a block of ice, so the courts might as well have been in heaven while our feet were mired in New York clay.

I trusted Bill.

He trusted me.

I suspected that he'd slept with my wife a time or two, but Katrina and I slept around so much that the word "betrayal," in our private lexicon, had synonyms like "naughty" and "sly."

Bill and I didn't have an office. We'd meet in coffee shops and stand-up pizza joints, planning how to take down *innocents* on behalf of our bent clientele. That was half of our business. The other half entailed the secret resolution of internal disputes.

One time we were hired by Four-fingers John Marr

to pass a document to the police that would incriminate his rival, Hard Joe Tyner. It was a delicate procedure that took half a day of planning. We did it while strolling through the Museum of Modern Art. Pretending to study the paintings of Lichtenstein and Rauschenberg, we hammered out a plan that would hit all the points of the service we provided.

Hard Joe had made one mistake in his otherwise spotless criminal career. He was extorting the president of an insurance company and accepting the money personally through a complex series of money transfers. Marr had gotten a list of the account numbers used. That's all the cops would need. Once they identified the victim, all they had to do was offer him immunity and Tyner would fall, hard.

But Marr didn't want his associates to suspect him and so he came to us—me and Bill.

"I don't see why we can't just put the shit in an envelope and send it to the detective in charge of investigating organized crime," Bill said after we gave the guard our tickets.

"Tyner's people would suspect Marr," I said patiently. "He's the one with the most to gain."

"So?"

"It's not professional, and anyway a good lawyer might be able to get evidence obtained in that fashion thrown out on some obscure technicality. Also, the police would get suspicious. Or worse, they might get stupid and ignore it."

"We could turn it in ourselves," Bill offered then. "Just walk into One Police Plaza and say, 'Hey, look what we found.'"

"And we'd be their bitches from then on. Anytime we said no they'd threaten to turn us out."

Our talks always started out like that. Bill had a good mind but he was lazy. He didn't see our job as a craft, more like a pickup pool hustle, where there was always a chance that you could lose. Luckily he deferred to me when it came to finalizing a plan, so we went on with our museum excursion.

After getting our fill of culture we settled into the restaurant bar for espressos and biscotti. I brought up a friend of Bill's who worked for Tyner. The man's name was Sharp. Sharp was in debt to a bookie who wasn't afraid of Tyner. Tyner didn't like his people gambling and would have come down hard on Sharp if he heard about it. Sharp was also well acquainted with Tyner's accountant, a man named Norman Bly. Bly had a girlfriend, Mae Lynn, who managed to look like Jayne Mansfield while not being much older than Shirley Temple—when Temple was singing "On the Good Ship Lollipop."

The plan followed nature, which was always the best way to go. Why blast a path down a mountain when erosion has already excavated the best route?

First we would take some incriminating pictures of Bly and Mae Lynn, then we would go to Sharp and offer him the cash he needed to call off the leg-breakers; all he'd have to do was put a few papers in Bly's briefcase on a certain day. We'd pretend that the papers were only there to incriminate Bly.

Now it made sense to go to the organized crime unit. We'd have a delivery service hand over the pictures and Mae Lynn's father's address. That very afternoon Bly and Lynn were going to meet in a midtown hotel managed by Tyner's real estate company. We didn't have to worry about the cops ignoring our delivery. They'd be happy to pass around pictures of a mature fourteen-year-old and old fat Norman.

It worked beautifully. The cops busted the couple in the nude. They confiscated the briefcase and found the numbers connecting Tyner to the extortion scheme. They offered Bly a deal that he couldn't refuse and Tyner went to prison.

It all went exactly as planned . . . but there was a problem.

Bill let his college certificate get him in trouble. Since he was better educated than all of his hoodlum friends, he thought he was smarter—than anyone. So he figured if we were getting fifteen thousand out of Marr, then Tyner would pay double. He went to a guy named KC Longerman to pass the plan (without our names attached to it) along to Tyner. But somewhere in Bill's education he skipped the course that would've told him I was the one who introduced him to KC.

I went to Bill's place, with murder in mind, the night after we put the plan in motion. Norman Bly was in police custody and Joe Tyner was soon to be a guest of the state. As far as I was concerned, this was also Bill's last night of life.

His plan wouldn't have worked. Tyner could have easily found out who Four-fingers had contracted with. But Bill thought he was too slick. He didn't mean to get us killed.

I was so angry that murder was only a twitch away. But as I stood over him I realized that Bill's betrayal was my fault. Men like Bill and me should never have been partners, not in the long-term straight-world way of contracts and agreements. We weren't businessmen. We were independent agents out for ourselves by necessity, and by nature. Bill didn't see any problem with getting a little on the side. As long as I didn't know and wasn't hurt, what did I have to complain about?

I left his apartment door ajar, with a hollow-point .45-caliber bullet standing like a soldier on his breakfast table.

We haven't crossed paths since.

I REMEMBERED BILL because even though I have eschewed partnership since that time, I am still, as Harris Vartan noted, not completely self-sufficient. With the police knocking on my door, dead men in my wake, and killers studying my name, I knew that I had to get my butt in gear and head way downtown, where the laws of nature and the laws of man intersect, intertwine, and make up a whole new system of justice.

In spite of my sporadic fantasies about foreign climes, the only city I could live in is New York. Most other American municipalities are segregated by class and culture, education and personal choice. But in New York everybody is jumbled up together and bounced around until you have African princes walking side by side with Appalachian Daughters of the American Revolution, and aspiring starlets making room for hopeful housewives past their prime. Even with real estate costs climbing above the reach of almost everyone, you can still find all the elements of humanity riding the number 1 train down under the West Side of Manhattan.

There were at least a dozen readers in the car I rode on the trek toward Wall Street. They perused novels and textbooks, newspapers and hip-hop magazines. There were displaced housewives going to work because one income didn't pay the rent anymore. Many of these watched their soaps on tiny screens plugged into earphones. That afternoon I saw books by Thomas Mann, Joy King, Edwidge Danticat, and Danielle Steel being read. One dusty fellow kept turning his head suspiciously, looking for enemies that might be sneaking up on him. A chubby white woman smiled at me and even pursed her lips. At one point a troupe of doo-wop singers composed of one Asian and three blacks made their way through our car, crooning "On Broadway" and "Up on the Roof."

There were two middle-aged women sitting across from me, one black and the other white. They were laughing and chatting happily about work. It seemed that a supervisor who had been leaning on them had an affair with a secretary who was also fooling around with the big boss.

"Honey, when he came out of Metcalf's office he was white as marshmallows," the black woman was saying.

She was having such a good time that she didn't notice the little guy in the unremarkable clothes sitting next to her on the bench. He wore tan trousers and a navy shirt. His once completely yellow head of hair now was layered with differing shades of dirty gray. His back was almost fully turned to the black woman but somehow Regular Joe's elbow had jostled her big blue purse so that it fell partly open.

The next step would have been for him to get up when the train came close to a stop. That way, when the brakes were applied, he could pretend to fall off balance and make a fast grab. People in his profession had good hand-eye coordination and great dexterity.

Maybe fifteen seconds before the process was to begin I coughed. In the pickpocket's ear I might as well have yelled, "Stop thief!"

He looked up at me and I shook my head ever so slightly.

He smiled and nodded, got to his feet, and moved on down the line.

"Ma'am," I called across the aisle.

"What?" the chatty black woman said in a markedly unfriendly tone.

"Your bag is open."

Her reaction was completely predictable. First she grabbed her purse and searched it. A red wallet floated near the top. But there was also her cell phone and MP3 player to check out. She cinched the bag shut and glared at me for a second and a half, wondering if somehow I had tricked her. The defiant stare then melted into contrition and she finally, reluctantly, said, "Thank you," as if I were a mischievous child who just pointed out that her underwear was showing.

THE ARCHITECTURAL EQUIVALENT of the nondescript pickpocket was a gray-walled building a few blocks north of where the World Trade Center used to stand. There were no guards or doormen in the lobby, and the man I was looking for didn't have his name or title on the sparse directory.

By way of the stairs I entered into a dull green corridor on the seventh floor and turned right, following the slender hallway past five doors to offices that were permanently locked. It was only the unremarkable sixth door that had any life behind it.

I knocked and waited. A minute went by but I didn't knock again. Another minute passed and I waited patiently. A few seconds later there came a loud click. The portal eased open on its own and I walked in.

THE ANTECHAMBER TO the Important Man's office was as bare as an office can get while still serving a function. There was a maroon metal desk with a no-frills swivel chair behind it and another folding chair set up in the corner. There were no paintings on the light-green walls, no carpeting on the unstained but sealed pine floor. There weren't even any light fixtures, just two high-wattage stand-up lamps set in opposite corners.

Behind the desk was seated, as erect as a high school teacher in a Norman Rockwell painting, an effeminate, forty-something black man wearing gold-rim glasses and no smile. His burgundy necktie was thin enough to qualify as string and the black suit was tight fitting with stingy lapels.

This man was Christian Latour.

As I have said before, this was the year 2008, and race, though still a major player in American culture, had undergone a serious transmogrification. A black man was running for president. There was a legally blind black man in the governor's seat in Albany. White American children and adults had heroes from Snoop Dogg to Tiger Woods. This wasn't the age of being pushed to the back of the bus or excluded from the awareness of the media.

Seeing this arrogant and thin Cerberus before me, I remembered my father once telling me, "There is no greater slave name than Christian. Bill and Robert and Joseph and Dorothy are all equally qualified slave names. Any name that reflects the conqueror is a nod to his superiority. But to take his religion as your appellation is like falling down on your knees before him."

My father had never met Christian Latour. This man was the epitome of defiance. He hadn't so much taken on the name but rather he took it away from the people who once owned it. He sat like a Catholic cardinal in that simple throne, and you would never call him subservient or a victim.

"Mr. McGill," he said, neither in greeting nor as a question. It was just a comment.

"Mr. Latour," I responded.

"You don't have an appointment."

"I didn't have the leisure to make one."

I liked Christian. He was so righteous in his monklike cell. He had one of the most important jobs in the Western Hemisphere and even though no one knew it he was in no way nonplussed by this anonymity. He was satisfied in his own skin, and that was a rare feat for any American.

Even though I liked him, Mr. Latour did not approve of me. I was coarse and gruff, listening to barrelhouse blues while he dreamed in operatic splendor.

There was a black box on Christian's metal desk. There was a small aperture in the top through which light of any of the primary and secondary hues of the color wheel could shine. The hole shone a brilliant blue. Christian glanced at it and let his lip curl slightly.

"Mr. Rinaldo will see you now."

30

Where Christian's cubicle was barren and undersized, his boss's grand hall of an office was a study in opulence. Thick burgundy carpets ran between royal-blue walls upon which hung Renaissance masterpieces lit from the ceiling by spotlights, artwork on loan from the Metropolitan Museum of Art (which has a policy of not lending out its possessions).

Ten steps into the room I passed a fully stocked mahogany bar built into the wall on the right. Across the way, on the left, was an altar carved from a solid block of apple-green-and-white jadeite. This sacred stand was tall as a man and twice as wide. Images of faces and animal forms, gracefully understated, flowed across the priceless sculpture.

There was no window, no portal to the outside world, but a green, red, and blue songbird with long, drooping feathers sang out gloriously as I passed. It was a greeting, or possibly a warning, but regardless the tune subsided before I had taken the final twenty-three steps to Alphonse Rinaldo's desk.

He was standing behind a dining-table-sized piece of furniture made from a single plank of unfamiliar dark wood. He always stood when I entered the room. Maybe he did that with everyone—I don't know.

Alphonse was of medium height (that is to say an inch or three taller than I), with flawless medium-white skin, black hair, and hard dark eyes. To the casual observer he might have seemed to be of a mild temper, but many of the worst monsters I've known were like that: pleasant even in the regrettable act of murder.

His hair, which was neither long nor short, was perfectly coiffed, and his suit would have turned Giorgio Armani's head.

"Have a seat, Mr. McGill." If quicksilver could talk it would sound like him.

The chair I preferred, Alphonse had once told me, was pre-Columbian, carved from a single piece of volcanic rock.

"It was used for sacrifices," he'd said on that day a few years earlier. "There was a tray that led down from the seat to carry the blood to the vessel."

I suppose I must have looked a little uncomfortable, because he added, "Don't worry, Mr. McGill, it was used exclusively on virgins."

I had once asked Rinaldo if he answered directly to the mayor.

"I am the special assistant to the City of New York," he answered as if there were a grim god that lived under the stone and steel, concrete and grime, of the city, a god whose will carried more weight than any politician or generation of voters.

And if Manhattan was an ancient deity set to oversee our island and its neighbors, then Alphonse Rinaldo was an errant angel thrown down among swine. He could buy your soul from a third party and send it twirling like a glass top on the granite stairs of justice. He was without peer, the most dangerous man in New York City. And he almost always knew more than anyone else in the room.

I HAD DONE the special assistant a favor some years before. There was a certain gentleman named Todd who had so much money that he owned a sprawling single-story home set atop a midtown skyscraper and encased in one-way glass. He could see out but the world could not see in.

Todd's daughter was in love with a man the family considered beneath them. I was brought in to incriminate the gentleman in question. They had considered "other means" of dealing with the problem, but in the final analysis Todd didn't want his daughter to suffer distress.

Alphonse asked me to find or manufacture evidence that would convince the daughter of her lover's turpitude (Alphonse's word, not mine). It was a complex job because even though the boyfriend may have been seen as low class by the Todds, he belonged to another kind of family that wielded a great deal of very raw, very physical power.

Alphonse was well aware of the situation and had reasons within reasons for me to be successful, and not . . . but that's another story.

In the end no one was happy, but I had made a connection with the Important Man, and so from time to time I did him favors, and he paid me back in kind.

I hadn't seen Rinaldo since deciding to go from crooked to only slightly bent, so it was a tricky business, me asking for a favor today when I might well have to turn him down tomorrow. But the way I saw it, I had to live through today in order to suffer the ramifications of later on.

"WHAT CAN I do for you, Mr. McGill?" Rinaldo was all about the business. If he had friends, I wasn't one of them. He didn't care about my health or my day.

"I need to find one guy and get to another one."

"People I care about?"

"I doubt it."

"People that matter to the city?"

"Maybe. It might be that I can help your people clean up one mess and get myself out of another one."

I respected his receptionist, Christian, that's a fact. He was one of a kind, a man who lived in his own estimation of the world. People like him were the only real people, in my opinion. I respected Christian but I was, in spite of myself, in awe of Alphonse Rinaldo. The secretly ordained city manager had a preternatural aura around him. He never wasted a movement, or a word. Sometimes he did things that I didn't understand, but I knew there was a good reason behind his every action, or inaction.

He didn't ask me what I meant. He just waited for the evidence to make itself known.

I was good but not on the level of Alphonse. I had made it all the way to his den, but I still had doubts.

"I don't mean to rush you," he said after maybe thirty seconds of my silent second thoughts, "but the attaché to the newly elected president of Russia is due to show up in nine minutes."

He wasn't bragging so much as showing me my place in the scheme of things.

"I need a pass to get into Larchmont State Prison, to get an hour alone with an inmate named William Nilson. His nickname is Toolie. And . . . " I hesitated again. My old life was teeming around my ears, a swarm of killer bees casting a shadow and humming a dirge. ". . . and I want to know the whereabouts of a guy, a man, an accountant named A Mann."

"Are you sure you want to find this man?"

"Yeah. Why? You know something?"

"You just seem a little doubtful."

"Life is uncertain, isn't it, Mr. Rinaldo?"

That got me a three-second smile.

"His first name?"

"The vowel."

He reached under his desk and picked away at something. It took all of a minute. Then he stood up.

That was the drill. I stood up, too. I was supposed to leave then. As with Harris Vartan, it was important in Rinaldo's ether that the people he dealt with picked up on the subtle nuances of his gestures. That's why I was surprised when a quizzical expression crossed his face.

"What?" I asked.

"I was just thinking," he said, sounding almost human.

"'Bout what?"

"You and Christian are the only two black men, American-born black men, that have ever been in this office. Do you find that strange?"

"Only thing strange is that you realize it."

He didn't offer a hand and neither did I. I took the couple of dozen steps back the way I'd come and exited that particular conduit to hell.

By the time I'd reached Christian's cell he had nearly everything I needed. Alphonse must have had a computer under his desk that he used to communicate with his living data engine. Christian was just finishing scribbling down A Mann's pertinent information on the back of a pizza-delivery slip. These included a street address and a website that would be ready later that day.

"And the prison?" I asked after reading the address and dot-com-to-be.

"All you have to do is show up and tell them who you're there to see."

"Should I give them a name?" I asked. "A reference or something?"

His sneer was a thing to behold.

"Okay," I said. "Thank you." And I turned toward the door.

Christian did not wish me a good day.

THREE HOURS LATER I was out near Coney Island sitting in my green-and-white 1957 Pontiac across the street and down the block from a small wooden cottage on Murray Lane. I'd been there for twenty minutes, but that was okay by me. I liked it when I got time alone in my car, playing songs from my youth. I listened to everything from Gordon Lightfoot to B. B. King.

Thanks to MP3 technology I could carry around my entire four-thousand-album collection in my shirt pocket.

I'd hired Twill to copy the collection two summers before, telling him I'd give him two dollars for every hour of music he recorded. That way I figured to keep him out of trouble when he wasn't in school, while maybe getting a thousand or so records transposed in the process.

Three weeks after I hired him he came to me with the MP3 player, saying, "Here you go, Pops."

I hadn't seen him doing a thing. He was out day and night the whole time but there my records were, all of them, cross-referenced by genre, album, artist, and song name. He'd copied nearly forty thousand cuts in just over twenty-one days.

When I asked him how he did it he told me that he had a friend with five MP3-friendly turntables complete with mechanical stalks that could hold up to eight albums at a time.

"I just promised him two thousand to do the collection in three weeks," Twill said, smiling.

It was a good deal, seeing that I owed my son six thousand.

Not having the cash on hand, I paid off his friend in installments over the summer and got Twill to agree to my starting a college account for him. I'm still depositing money on the first of each month, and listening to my favorite songs every day.

"Suppose I don't want to go to college?" he argued when I first brought up the notion.

"You need to go," I told him. "After that you could go into business and become a billionaire."

"Not interested," he replied, holding up a lazy hand intended to short-circuit the capitalist curse.

"Not now," I said with fatherly assurance.

"Not never, Pops. Money makes people weak and stupid. And you know when you're rich nobody ever likes you for you but for what you're worth. I'd rather just make enough to do what I want and keep the electricity on."

He was fourteen years old at the time. I promised him that if he didn't want to go to college by the time he was twenty he could have whatever money was in the account.

"FAT MAN" BY Jethro Tull was playing on the Bose speakers I'd installed in the backseat. Twill wasn't my son by blood but I would save him from himself. He deserved a better life, despite his intelligence and predilections.

As I sat there waiting for the prey to show itself, I turned my attention to Norman Fell.

I wondered what it was like to live a life when you couldn't read a word. How strange the titles of books must seem; even your own name would only be familiar in a symbolic kind of way. To be a man like him out there hiding in plain sight, making a life for himself half swathed in internal darkness.

But literacy didn't make you smart, just like, as Twill had already figured out, money didn't make you rich.

Both Fell and I knew that finding those men was wrong, but we had bills to pay and shoes to replace, pretenses to keep up. Well after the properties had been condemned, we were still trying to build lives.

I used to believe that I was getting somewhere, that with enough experience and enough money in the bank I could become a well-heeled member of some exclusive club. I'd leave the street life to the mooks that lived it. I'd climb to the penthouse all the time knowing that the higher one gets . . .

I kept a storage space in the Bronx that had information on over three hundred *cases* that I had been involved in. I had once counted on those files to be my exit plan. I'd call everyone still alive and sell what I had for five thousand dollars a pop, on average. Or, if I got busted, I could use that information to deal myself out of a prison sentence.

But none of that mattered anymore. I was no longer a moral illiterate. I could read the signs and I knew what they meant.

"BLUE MOON" BY the Marcels was just ramping up on my system when a man came out the front of the yellow-and-blue cottage. A Mann. I knew his face from the temporary website Christian had provided. He was walking an elderly dachshund on a red shoulder leash. The old dog was pulling, halfheartedly, I thought, trying to get out and piss on the streets where he'd squandered his doggie youth.

The twelve-pound pet was a mottled brown, his master was pink and bulbous. If A Mann was thirty pounds overweight, forty of that was flab. He walked like a man who had never exercised a day in his life, a little wobbly on every fourth or fifth step. He wore jeans and a white T-shirt. This ensemble wasn't very fashionable but that wasn't saying much—Mr. Mann would have had to undergo a serious TV makeover to get him looking like he belonged anywhere.

On the other hand, he didn't seem to care about appearances. A muttered to the dog and waited patiently for it to do its business. He was ready with a little plastic bag. It was painful, seeing him lowering to one knee on those weak and rusty pins.

When he was halfway down the block I got out and followed from the other side of the street.

We strolled in our separate worlds down toward the ocean. He was thinking about his dog and I was wondering how to make him my bitch.

With Christian's help I knew that A had no wife or children. His mother lived with a sister in Tampa, and they had fallen completely out of touch. He'd changed his name to Dwight Timmerman and lived a very quiet life on a stipend garnered from a lifetime of careful investments. He lived in a kind of self-imposed, self-generated witness protection program.

Christian's thoughtfully constructed website told me that A, when he realized that he was working for gangsters, had gone to a wealthy friend from high school who had made it rich. This friend, a man simply referred to by Christian as Mr. Jones, helped him change his identity. Jones had done all this with the help of one of Rinaldo's subordinates.

Alphonse Rinaldo threw a broad web over the city of New York. Almost everyone was connected to him, though few knew it. His control over the city was so complete that he might have even pulled the strings of his own employers.

I had suspicions about Fell (aka Ambrose Thurman), but in the case of Tony the Suit there wasn't a shadow of doubt: the moment I turned over Mann's address, he and the dog would be dead. And if I refused to turn the name over, I'd be on Tony's blacklist and someone else would root out the accountant.

The odds between me and Tony were pretty much even but if Harris Vartan decided to weigh in on the gangster's side I wouldn't make it a day.

I didn't have much of a choice, and I had a family that needed me breathing in order for them to stay afloat.

THE STROLL LASTED for about thirty minutes. Mann and dog had to stop four times to catch their breath. One time there the accountant plopped down on a bench with his back toward the ocean. He was breathing through his mouth while the dachshund panted laboriously. The dog was looking up at A while he stared at the clouds. It was a moment of grace in an awkward life. I remember feeling a little jealous.

After that five-minute breather the duo lurched back to the cottage—probably to take an afternoon nap.

After leaving Coney Island I was at sixes and sevens, as my foster aunt Moth used to say. I didn't want to set A up for a hit, but he was a dead man whether I did or didn't. If I was still in the life I might have been able to turn Tony down; I'd've had other clients who could block his demands. But as it was, I had no protection. And I didn't have much room to move in either; there was other pressing work that had to be done.

I dropped by Gordo's Gym to work off some of the frustration.

Gordo gave me that grin again when I came through the door. He shifted his gaze to a lithe young fighter shadowboxing gracefully against the far wall.

Jimmy Punterelle was a handsome white kid with thick brown hair and a dark-blue tattoo of Rocky Marciano on his right shoulder. He was already stripped down and warmed up, so when Gordo introduced us it was the easiest thing in the world to suggest that we have a friendly sparring match. The kid sneered, then became a bit suspicious when Gordo told me that I wouldn't need protective headgear.

Jimmy should have run.

He had a good jab and natural upper-body movement, but, despite my height, I have a long reach, especially when it comes to the ribs.

Jimmy lowered to one knee in the middle of our third round. It took everything I had not to hit him when he was down.

THE NEXT MORNING I drove up to the Larchmont Correctional Facility. Christian was right: I came to the admittance gate and was ushered in like royalty. They didn't even search me.

After offering me really bad coffee, the two guards, whose names, TOMI and PETERS, were stitched over their hearts, took me to a special floor in the infirmary.

"Why's he here?" I asked the younger Tomi.

"Somebody stabbed him," the white kid said. "You can hardly blame 'em. Nilson's a fat fuck."

Peters, a full-figured black man, grunted.

They didn't ask why I was there. I was a VIP whom the warden's betters had sent in for reasons of their own.

They had given Toolie a private room for the interrogation. Peters asked me if I needed someone to stay with us but I said no. Toolie had been stabbed, and even if he hadn't I doubted that the four-hundred-plus-pound convict could have moved fast enough to give me reason to worry.

He was propped up in the double-sized cot with his bulging legs stretched out and his back leaned at an angle against the wall. His dress was festive: bright-yellow pajamas with a few dozen red *X*'s scattered around.

They had lashed two single beds together to accommodate the fat man's size and weight. Toolie was like a big black walrus beached just that many feet too far from the sea. His breathing was labored and his bloodshot eyes suspicious. Toolie was bald and stuffed with fat everywhere: his hands and fingers, jowls and the back of his neck.

I wondered how a man could get so obese on prison fare.

He watched me as I came in, as I pulled a chair up next to his bed.

"Cigarette?" was my first question.

"Can't smoke," he said. "They got sick people all up in here."

"They'll make an exception in our case," I said, proffering him the pack.

He took the whole thing. (That was how I gave up smoking for the sixth time.) I gave him a light.

"Who stabbed you?" I asked.

"What's your name?" he parried.

"Greely. I work for a guy in the city. He needs to know something and thought maybe you could help."

For some reason these words reassured the giant. In reply to my question he pulled open his yellow pajamas at the breast, showing me a thick bandage surrounded by puffy, bloodstained black skin.

"Mothahfuckah tried to kill me," he said.

"Who?"

"I nevah saw him before. White dude. They had to transfer his ass, 'cause my homies woulda killed him daid."

"When did this happen?"

"Day before yesterday."

Damn.

"You didn't do anything to him?" I asked.

"I nevah even seen 'im. He just come outta nowhere and went for my heart. What the fuck you care, anyway?"

Toolie smoked his cigarette in a very particular way. He'd take the smoke into his mouth and then, folding his lower lip over the upper, express the fumes into his nostrils while inhaling.

I asked him about the three friends of his youth.

"B-Brain split when he was still in high school," Toolie said. "His mama an' them thought we was a bad influence. I used to see Jumpah an' Big Jim from time to time, but Big Jim took a shot of pure H and killed his ass."

"Jumper was killed a few days ago," I said. "Roger Brown, too."

"Both of 'em?"

"Yeah."

"Damn."

"And now there's you."

"Me? I ain't daid."

"Come on, Mr. Nilson," I said. "You got some dude you never knew tryin' to cut you open. That's too much of a coincidence."

"Who wanna kill three niggahs like us?" Toolie complained. "I ain't seen Roger in seventeen years at least, and I didn't have nuthin' to do with Jumpah—not really."

"Maybe it was something from back when you all four ran together," I suggested.

"Like what?"

Suspicion was reemerging in the fat convict's eyes. The news I was bearing was tough even for a hardened criminal. The fact that a hit had been arranged in prison made him vulnerable. If the price was high enough even one of his *homies* might stick a knife in his back.

"I could put in a good word to protect you," I said.

"Why you wanna do that?"

"Tell me about Thom Paxton."

"Who?"

"You used to call him Smiles."

The fat around Nilson's eyes contracted down to a puffy squint. He maintained that stare for nearly a minute.

"That was a accident," he said at last. "Even the cops said so."

"What happened?"

Toolie swiveled his head before speaking. He'd lived long enough to know the truth of *Anything you say can and will be used against you.*

"If I walk out of here without the story, someone is gonna kill you," I promised.

"I ain't done nuthin'."

"Neither did the others."

"What I do, man?" he whined.

"What happened to Smiles?"

"Well, you know," Toolie said, unconsciously raising a defensive shoulder. "Me an' them used to go to this construction site to get high."

"Smiles, too?"

"Yeah. Back then that white boy was our nigga. Smiles could hang. But you know, in the summer he'd go upstate to be wit' his father an' them. But then he'd come back down in the fall 'cause he had a scholarship to this private school."

"He lived with his father?"

"Yeah."

"What about his mother?"

"She was sick or sumpin'. Maybe she was daid, I don't know."

"What school?"

"I'on't know, man. But Georgie Girl's brother worked there an' she met Smiles through him."

"You mean Georgiana Pineyman?" I asked.

"Yeah. Yeah."

"Was she there at the construction site?"

"Naw, man. It was just us. Jumpah had some blunts and we was gettin' high. That's all."

"How did Smiles die?"

Toolie gave me a sharp glance. He knew that he couldn't push the truth too far out of shape.

"Can you really help me, like you said?" he asked.

I nodded. "Now tell me what happened."

"That was Big Jim's fault. I mean, it was a accident, but if Big Jim didn't keep on runnin' his mouf it wouldn'ta been no accident."

"What did Jim say?"

"He kep' sayin' how B-Brain was keepin' Georgie Girl company in the summah when Smiles was upstate. He kep' sayin' it an' Smiles got hot. He was white an' all, but that boy was tough. Roger tried to laugh it off but Smiles was high an' wanted a fight. He came at B-Brain but that niggah runned." Toolie laughed at the memory. "He runned up a ladder and climbed out on one'a them—what you call 'em—them girders. Roger could move. But Smiles was mad an' so he went after him. So Roger went higher an' higher an' then when he was about six floors up he jumped on this elevator platform one floor down. Smiles tried to do it, too, but he fell. Broke his neck.

"We tried to run but somebody musta called the cops so they arrested us. We was in jail two days but they called it a accident an' let us go."

"You know his mother's name?" I asked.

"Roger's?"

"Smiles'."

"Naw, man. Smiles lived with his old man, like I said. Upstate."

"Albany?"

"How the fuck I know? So you gonna help me?"

"Do you know his father's name?"

"Naw, man."

"Yeah," I said to the big wheezing convict, "I'll help you."

I was thinking that the best thing I could do for him was to hide his knife and fork.

On the drive back home I called Christian and asked him to tell his boss to put out the word to protect Toolie.

"Tell him that it might come in handy somewhere soon," I added.

Christian hung up when I said these last few words and the phone vibrated in my hand. TTS, standing for Tony the Suit, appeared on the display. I thought about it for two full throbs before pressing the ignore button. I then entered my own number at Zephyra Ximenez's office.

"Hello, Mr. McGill," my telephonic and computer personal assistant answered cheerily. "How are you?"

"I'd trade places with you in a heartbeat."

"How can I help you?"

"Albany," I said, "and this time make me a reservation in a good hotel."

"The Minerva's the best," she said.

"How do you know that?"

"One of my clients is a plastic surgeon who works there two days a week. He always stays at the Minerva."

I WAS GETTING USED to the flight. I just brought along my MP3 player and a blindfold. Norah Jones sang to me in darkness. I think I might have even fallen asleep for a moment there.

THE MINERVA WAS an old-fashioned place with a real desk where you sat down to check in. The young woman receptionist didn't frown at my shoes or knuckles.

There was a wide stairway covered with red-and-blue carpeting that led to the first stage of the upper floors. It was so inviting that I shunned the elevator for the climb.

The room was large, much like a room that an upstate relative might keep for guests. I intended to take a bath but the tub was very close to the design of the one that I found Norman Fell in, so I stripped down and washed at the sink before taking my rental down to Tinker's Bar and Grill in the South End.

It was a pretty empty block in a part of town that might once have had an identity, expressed by old-fashioned dark-brownstone architecture. But now the neighborhood had gotten old and forgetful. Many of the buildings were abandoned. The only life was in the broad and gaudy bar-restaurant. It took up almost half the block, and the whole front was glass so you could see in at the tables filled with people from every race and element of society. There was a long bar at the back of Tinker's and a stage on the north side of the big room.

A group of young black men dressed in bulky suits loitered around the entrance. One of them was making rhymes extolling his fearlessness and sexual prowess. He kicked that bitch and flipped that shit, sent out a something, and then broke it down. His fellows seemed to approve of the words and their brooding execution.

As I approached the front door the largest of these men stood up to block my way. He was wearing a double-breasted cream-colored cashmere suit with a hot-pink dress shirt and at least the chain of a pocket watch. His coloring was a greenish medium brown and he had a round scar on his right cheekbone that might have been made by a small-caliber bullet. There was something wrong with one of his eyes but I tried not to stare.

"How you doin'?" the gangster-child said to me.

As he spoke, his friends moved toward him as if in the pull of a certain kind of magnetism, the kind that draws gawkers to the site of a bloody demise.

I couldn't have fought my way past them. Even if I had a gun, they were probably all armed, too.

"Here to see Big Mouth," I said, smiling falsely.

"So what?" the one-eyed man-child replied.

"Is he here?"

"Are you?" the kid answered, making me wonder if he was an existentialist or a rapping fool.

I'm told that hard exercise keeps up the testosterone levels in men my age. I could feel it right then. The rage growing in my shoulders was in response to this kid's belief that he might be my better. I took a deep breath in through my nostrils.

"My friend Seraphina told me to drop by if I wanted to talk to Jones."

One of the posse, a youngster in a loose-fitting iridescent green suit, broke off from the group and wandered into the restaurant.

"How you know Seraphine?" the kid asked.

"Does it matter?"

"You got a smart mouf, you know that, man?"

"Yeah. That's what they tell me."

"I could stomp yo' ass right here in the street," he promised.

"If I had six dudes backin' me up I wouldn't be scared neither," I responded.

"Say what?"

"You heard me."

"Leave him alone, John-John," a familiar female voice said.

Seraphina, wearing a pink slip, walked into the group of Scarface pretenders.

She came to my side and even took my hand.

"Come on wit' me, Mr. Carter," my slender and dark-skinned savior said.

"YOU SURE DO KNOW how to get in trouble, don't you, Mr. Carter?" Seraphina chided as we came into the bustling establishment.

"I just wanted to see Big Mouth."

"You got to be polite to people like John-John," she said as if she were the elder and I the child.

"I like you, girl."

"You a fool."

"You know many men who aren't?"

The hardest thing I might have done that month was getting Seraphina to grin.

"Why did they give me trouble?" I asked. "I mean, there's all kindsa people here."

"John-John an' them out there to make sure it's safe for the people," she said.

"I'm a people."

"Maybe so," she said. "But you look like trouble. When you meet Big Mouth, don't call him Big Mouth. He don't like that name. His real name is Eddie Jones, but he don't like people callin' him that neither."

"What do *you* call him?"

"Eddie."

"I see."

She brought me to a table fit for six behind a half-wall to the left of the crowded bar. There were eight or nine men gathered there but the only one I was interested in was the dolphin-faced black man sitting against the back wall. That, I was sure, was Big Mouth Jones.

"Hi, Eddie," Seraphina said to Jones. "This here is Mr. Carter. He said he wanted to aks you sumpin'."

"He your friend or customer?" Big Mouth Jones asked, ignoring me.

"Friend."

I wondered if it was the tip or the fact that I didn't want sex that made Seraphina like me. Maybe it was just because I made her almost laugh. My father, for all his left-wing idealism, had often told me, *Leonid, you'll find as you get older that some women are attracted to trouble.* Whatever it was, Jones rapped his knuckles against the shoulder of a skinny walnut-colored man next to him. This fellow, who looked to be about half my age, stood up without a word and moved off. I pressed my way toward the back of the table, taking the vacant position.

"You heavy?" Jones asked when I was seated.

"No." I looked around to see Seraphina walking away.

"How you know Seraphine?"

"We talk from time to time."

Jones's face was ageless and unfathomable. He could have been mistaken for thirty-five but he was closer to fifty-nine. He smelled of a little too much good cologne and stale cigarette smoke.

I was about to start in on my line of questioning when the houselights went down and a spotlight hit the stage.

"Frank," Jones said to a blocky man on the other side of the table.

"Yeah?"

"Walk around with some guys and make sure the people quiet down."

The man nodded and departed into the gloom.

I turned to ask Eddie my question but his attention was glued to the stage.

A brown woman made an entrance. She wore a tight-fitting dress of golden sequins. Her hair was perfect and the body looked as if it had been designed for just that night, just that stage. Without preamble, recorded music came up and she started to sing. It was perfectly good singing, on key, strong, deeply felt. She was singing about a man she'd die for—from the look in his eye, I could tell that Eddie thought that man was him.

"Can I get you something to drink, sir?" a voice whispered from behind my right shoulder.

It was a small white man with a Jimmy Durante nose.

"You got a good brandy?"

"Yes sir. We have a wonderful Armagnac."

"Bring me a triple shot."

THE SINGER BELTED out four love songs before taking her bows; the dress was cut so low that I almost looked away. The whole restaurant broke out in applause. I couldn't help wondering if Big Mouth had anything to do with that.

The lights went up and the woman, who was no more than thirty, came to our table. She moved past me and gave the impresario a deep soul kiss.

"That was beautiful, baby," Jones said.

She beamed in reply.

"This is my girl, the next Whitney Houston," Jones said to me, "Brenda Flash."

I smiled and lied to her. She smiled in my general direction, never asking my name.

Another one of the men left and Ms. Flash settled on the other side of the boss. The table was abuzz for a while about the potential for her career. I listened and sipped.

The waiter was right about the liquor.

"SO WHAT IS IT you wanted to ask me?" Big Mouth said, nearly an hour later.

Brenda had departed, promising to see her man upstairs somewhere when he was through with his business. The restaurant was in full swing.

"I was wondering if you knew a man named Willie Sanderson."

Jones's deceivingly benign features took on a sharp, dangerous aspect, bringing to my mind a knife being drawn from its sheath.

"Why?" he asked.

The other seven men at the table were staring at me.

"He tried to murder me."

"Tried?" Jones asked.

"Yeah. I broke his head for him and so he gave up."

"You a lyin' mothahfuckah," a brutal guy from across the table said. He was bulky from too much weight lifting.

"Would you like me to show you?" I asked the frowning goon.

This man stood up, making a sound that maybe made sense in the hinterlands of Albany. The most memorable things about him were his Caucasian features and coal-black skin.

"Sit down, Sammy," Jones ordered. And then, "I said sit yo ass down."

When Sammy did as Sammy was told, Jones turned his attention back to me.

"Yeah," he said. "I know Willie. White dude likes the darker things in life. He used to hang out here. Even sat at this table once or twice. They say he got a wicked temper, but he was calm around black peoples. What you wanna know about him?"

"Anything I can," I said. "I mean, this Willie tried to slaughter me an' I ain't nevah even met the boy."

Jones looked at me—hard. His smiling dolphin lips seemed to be frowning also.

"Why come to me?"

"You the man."

I could have died at that table never knowing what happened to my father after he went down to Chile. No one had notified us of his death and I'd made a promise to my mother before she died.

While I was having these final thoughts, Eddie Jones came to a decision.

"Willie killed a bus driver that disrespected him," the gangster informed me. "But when they brought him to trial the judge said he was what they call chemically insane. His aunt worked for these rich white people and they send him off to the Sunset Sanatorium. Doctors give him some pills an' say he's cured and can go home, only he likes it there so takes a job as a orderly. It was a good gig until they figured out that he was sellin' prescription drugs from their medicine cabinet and buyin' recreational drugs for the wealthy clients they had."

At the end of this speech he shrugged and gazed into my eyes.

I silently nixed the thought of asking about Fell because, as far as I knew, the body hadn't been discovered yet.

"Thank you, Mr. Jones," I said.

This response surprised him.

"You don't wanna know nuthin' else?"

"No. Why?"

"I'on't know. I thought maybe you heard that Willie was workin' for me when he was up at the loony bin."

"Did you send him down to New York to kill me?" I asked.

"No."

"I just wanted to hear a little about the man tried to kill me. If you don't have anything to do with that, then I don't have any more questions."

Big Mouth's stare was interminable. He was the master of his world because he paid attention to every detail.

"What you thinka Brenda?" he asked at last. "You know, I'm gonna get her a recordin' contract."

"She's a beautiful woman but . . ."

"But what?"

I stood up.

"But," I said, "you got a soul singer on your center stage and all the young muscle outside studyin' how to throw rhymes. And you know the only dis worse than disrespect is the disconnect."

Big Mouth frowned at me, but I was already moving away.

I called Katrina on my way back to the Minerva.

"Are you all right?" she asked me.

"Fine. I'm just up here in Albany looking into a few things."

"Be careful."

"I will."

When I got off the phone I realized that my ire at Katrina was based on events from long ago, events that no longer mattered. I wasn't mad at her, and she was genuinely concerned about my well-being. But like with Baum's Tin Man, the only thing missing was a heart.

I SLEPT LONG and hard in the old bed. It was one of the few times I could remember that I didn't dream about fire or falling. Opaque drapes kept out the summer sunlight, so I didn't rouse until almost seven. I washed, shaved, and dressed in a different suit that looked just like the one I wore the night before. I ate scrambled eggs and bacon while scouring the *Albany Times Union* for any word on Norman Fell. He was yet to be discovered.

After breakfast I got directions from the concierge and drove my rental southeast of the city about twenty-five miles.

The Sunset Sanatorium was set off from the highway behind a forest of maples. The thirty-foot wrought-iron gate was painted violet-pink, and the road leading to the guard's kiosk was paved in real cobblestone. The buildings beyond the sentry's station were made of brick and covered in ivy. It looked more like an Ivy League college campus than a mental institution.

When I pulled up next to the booth a black man in a powder-blue uniform and a dark-blue, black-brimmed cap came out to brace me.

"Can I help you?" he said.

I handed him a business card that said I was Ben Trotter, a private detective working out of Newark.

"Looking for information on a Willie Sanderson," I said while he read.

"Willie doesn't work here anymore," the middle-aged, dark-brown man informed me.

He was short and slight, built for the long haul—the kind of man who could carry half his weight in tobacco or cotton from way out in the fields.

"Yeah," I said. "I know. They got him in a hospital after he tried to kill a man. My client wants to know why."

The guard had descended, like me and many of our brethren, from a long line of suspicion. He pinched a corner of my card, regarding it with unconscious intensity. I believed that I could read that stare. He was thinking that there was something wrong with my brief explanation. But he was looking beyond the lie, to see if I posed a problem or if I was okay. After a moment he came to the conclusion that I was okay enough.

"Make a left at the end of this road," he said. "The second building on your right is number four. That's the human resources office. I don't know what they can tell you, though."

"Thanks," I said and drove on.

I PARKED IN the lot that the guard directed me to but didn't go into the HR offices. Instead I walked around the other side of the building into a large quad where a couple dozen patients and their handlers were taking the sun.

It was like no other mental institution I'd seen. The staff wore gray-and-white clothes that were uniforms only because of their similarity of color, while the patients dressed for leisure. It might have been a Florida retirement community, except many of the residents were middle-aged, and even young.

I walked around, getting a feel for the place, trying to understand something, anything, about the environment that Willie Sanderson had been immersed in. He was my only living link to the murderous conspiracy.

"Hello, young man," a white woman said.

She was older, maybe seventy-five, wrapped in a summer frock of swirling emerald and turquoise and holding a pink parasol up against the sun. She was seated on a violet-pink wrought-iron bench.

"Hello," I said.

"Are you a visitor?"

"I guess so," I answered, sitting down.

"You don't know?" She was small with big eyes and lots of red rubbed into her thin lips.

"Well," I said lightly, "I'm not a patient, and I don't work here, so what's left?"

The older woman smiled and then grinned. Her teeth weren't well maintained but the mirth outshone her bad hygiene.

"Do you know somebody here?" she asked.

"I know somebody who used to be here."

"Who's that?"

"A guy named Willie Sanderson."

"Willie," she said with wistfulness and wonder in her frail voice. "Yes. He didn't want to help me with everything, but he brought me dreams when I needed them. But he's not here anymore. They sent him away. They send all of the good ones away.

"Do you think that an old woman is sick if she wants to be with men?" she asked, changing the subject as if it were a summer's breeze and she Mother Nature.

"Not at all," I replied, tacking my sail to her whim. "A woman is a woman until the day she dies."

"My family doesn't agree with you," she said. "There I was, sixty-seven with a husband limp as a popped party balloon—and I was still young in my heart. And not only there."

Her tone was both suggestive and engaging. I liked her.

"Do you want to get out?" I asked seriously. She seemed sane to me and I was always looking for work, no matter how bad things got.

This question grabbed the old girl's attention. She heard the earnestness in my tone, just as the guard at the front gate had heard the lie.

"No," she said. "I'm getting older, and I find it easier to get what I need right here."

This reply seemed to punctuate the end of something. I took the opportunity of this lull to ask my question.

"Did you know Willie very well?"

"Is he dead?"

"No. But he is in the hospital."

"Oh my. What happened?"

"He got into a fight."

"He liked to fight," she said, nodding. "He was a nice boy but he had a bad temper. No, I didn't know him very well. We weren't the kind of friends that I would have liked. But he was close with Bunny. She and Willie were friends even before he came here. He brought her love. Not in the carnal way, mind you. Willie kind of worshipped Bunny."

"Is Bunny around here somewhere?"

"Oh no. She only stays for a little while. I think she was in for a long time once, but that was years ago. Since then, every once in a while she has a little kind of nervous breakdown. They bring her in, but she can leave whenever she wants to."

"What's this Bunny's last name?"

"Hey, you!" a definitely masculine voice commanded.

The tone frightened my new friend.

I turned to see two well-proportioned staff men coming toward me. One was brown, the other a darker brown. They both had me, and only me, in their sights.

I stood up and, through the miracle of peripheral vision, saw the old pagan woman scuttle off under the portable shadow of her semitransparent pink parasol.

"What you doin' here?" the darker attendant asked.

"It's a beautiful day," I replied as if that were a perfectly acceptable answer.

For a moment the two men were stymied by my easy demeanor.

"This is private property," the other male nurse/enforcer informed me.

"And I'm a private detective," I said, "here trying to get a line on a guy name of Willie Sanderson."

The men looked at each other and then back at me.

"This is private property," the lighter of the two repeated.

"Let me speak to your boss," I said.

Six magic words that roil deep in the bowels of anyone collecting a paycheck on a biweekly basis. It's like winking at a leprechaun: he has to give up his pot of gold, and yet no one knows why.

The two brutes brought me to an office that seemed oddly utilitarian for such an affluent institution. It was at the far corner of the main hall of what I thought must have been the administration building. We walked into the shotgun office without a knock or pardon-me. A middle-aged man in a too-green suit was sitting behind a gray metal desk at the bottom of the long room. Behind him was a big window looking out on the idyllic quad.

The man was leaning over a long and wide ledger page, making small marks here and there, giving me the impression that he was checking details and changing them to fit his needs.

When the man raised his head I was startled. Director Theodore Gorling (which is what his nameplate read) was the only man I ever met who had more throat than he did face. His neck was a great bulging stalk of a thing while his head was like a seedpod that had not yet reached maturity.

"Yes?" he asked the darker guard.

"This guy was hangin' out in the yard. Says he's a detective." The guard handed over the false card that I had given to prove my half lie.

Gorling moved his small head from side to side, taking the few simply printed words in from differing angles. Then he put the card down in the center of the neat desk. His movements were both mechanical and fleshy. He seemed somehow dangerous, like a priest one might find on the wrong side of redemption.

"I'm looking for information on Willie Sanderson," I said when it became obvious that Gorling had no intention of asking why I was there.

"Why?"

"He's been killing people, seemingly at random. He murdered a young man name of Brown in Manhattan and the parents want me to find out why."

"This says that you're from Newark," Gorling said, tapping the card with the middle finger of his left hand.

"So are my clients," I said. "But their son lived on the Upper West Side. He was trying to make it as an actor while working as a model. Was your man Willie Sanderson gay?"

"Why do you ask?"

"The son was making his living as an underwear model," I said, sticking out my lower lip in a knowing way. "I thought maybe the murder could have been a sex thing."

I find in my profession that it behooves one to appear ignorant, or, better yet, stupid, to the people you interrogate. It gives them a feeling of superiority, of having a mental leg up on you, so to speak.

"Have a seat, Mr. Trotter," Gorling said. Then to the men in gray and white, "Wait for us outside."

When the underlings had done his bidding, Gorling turned his throat to me.

"I have no idea what Mr. Sanderson's sexual preferences are," he said of his own volition.

I grimaced. "No? You see, these people hired me to find a reason for their son's death. The cops don't care because they got him on evidence. I thought maybe you guys up here would know something."

Gorling had small hands. He raised them to indicate his helplessness.

"Willie was an employee, not a patient," he lied.

"But the lady outside told me that he had been a patient before he got his job."

"What lady?"

"The one with the pink parasol."

I should have said "umbrella." Better yet, I should have left the sheltering apparatus out completely. Using accurate language always puts people like Gorling on alert. I don't even know if he realized it but his attitude toward me changed. His little face got rigid.

"Oh yes," he said. "I had almost forgotten. That was so long ago, before my time."

"What was his problem?"

"That's a medical matter, Mr. Trotter. We are prohibited by law from giving out that kind of information."

"You can't even tell me if he was here because of the threat of violence?"

"I look at this institution less as a hospital and more like a university for the besotted and bemused," he said with something like a smile. "The people here are learning their various lessons over and over, one step at a time. We coddle them and care for them, and never betray their trust."

The alien hospital administrator blinked at me with smug satisfaction.

"So if I was to go to the Browns and tell them that their son was murdered by a man who had been put in here for manslaughter and then let out without the proper supervision, you wouldn't open up your records like a dirty old man exposing himself to little kids on a crosstown bus?"

That pushed Gorling back into his chair.

"It's not our responsibility to make a man take his medication," he said.

"That, my friend, is for the lawyers to decide."

This aggressive tactic was my second misstep. Gorling looked soft and corrupt but he had the reflexes and instincts of a club fighter. He wasn't going to go down just because I showed him something. He was made from sterner stuff.

"Cedric!" he called out.

The two orderlies came immediately back into the room. They seemed ready to take physical action.

"I think it's time that you leave these premises, Mr. Trotter," Gorling said.

He stood up and, after a moment's hesitation, I followed suit.

I didn't like it but I had lost that particular bout. I had a few grains of knowledge, but without help I couldn't make any sense of them.

GORLING AND HIS HENCHMEN walked me through the hall toward the front of the administration building. There were no patients and few employees there.

"You'll find that threats don't work on us out here, Mr. Trotter," Gorling instructed as we went through the double doors out into the beautiful summer's day. "This is a place where we help people. That given, we aren't responsible for them after they leave our care.

"By the way, how did you get in here?"

"Told the guard that I was applyin' for a job where I get to wear a gray T-shirt and cotton pants."

"I'll have to instruct him to keep a stack of application forms at the gate. Is your car in the lot next to the personnel building?"

"Sure is. Should I give one of your boys here my key so he can run and get it for me?"

I hated myself for underestimating Gorling. Sometimes being a New Yorker brought on a feeling of false superiority that made me slip up badly.

"That won't be necessary," Gorling said. "They will escort you to your car."

I took a step down to the path, turned, and held out a hand like a good sport. Gorling didn't want to touch me but that didn't matter. When I looked up into his Adam's apple I saw the dedication chiseled into the wall over the door: BRYANT HULL HALL.

On the way to the car my lighter-skinned brother put his hand on my shoulder. I stopped walking and he took a step to the side.

"Keep on movin'," his partner commanded.

"Let's get this straight, friends," I said. "I'm leavin' just like you want me to. But you don't put your hands on me, understand? If you want me arrested, then call the cops. If you wanna throw down we can do it here and now. I might not beat the both of you but I swear that you'll feel it for months."

Maybe I sounded a little crazy, but this was damage control. I didn't want them to get pushy with me, forcing a fight. Because I would have fought them, but what I really wanted was to make a beeline for the person who could help me decipher the clue.

SHE WAS A septuagenarian named Poppy Pollis who had once been the head of the whole library system but who now volunteered her time going through rare volumes and collections that were inherited from or donated by wealthy patrons.

I didn't know Poppy's name when I drove away from the sanatorium but a quick call to the information line of the local public library was all I needed. I identified myself, with the deft elocution of a university professor, as Jonah Rhinehart of Manhattan, explaining that I needed to speak with someone who had worked for many years in the system and who knew its history. The helpful librarian I spoke with said that there were three such individuals, though my best chance was with Ms. Pollis, who was working at the main branch on Washington Avenue.

Librarians are wonderful people, partly because they are, on the whole, unaware of how dangerous knowledge is. Karl Marx upended the political landscape of the twentieth century sitting at a library table. Still, modern librarians are more afraid of ignorance than they are of the potential devastation that knowledge can bring.

I went to the information desk on the first floor of the downtown branch and came upon a young black man wearing big round-lensed glasses and reading a small blue-gray book entitled *Why Is There Something Rather Than Nothing?* written by someone named Leszek Kolakowski.

"Good book?" I asked.

"Very good," the young man replied, nodding sagely. "Very good."

"I'm looking for Poppy Pollis," I said, now that the quality of the philosophical monograph had been decided.

"Third floor," he said.

I thanked him and went to look for the stairs.

POPPY WAS SEATED at a huge table piled high with musty old books. She was thin, probably tall, sporting short silvery hair and wearing a blue sweater that was buttoned to the throat. The air-conditioning was up too high.

"Are you Ms. Pollis?" I asked.

"Yes I am, young man."

"Hi," I said, taking the seat across from her. "My name is Peter

Lomax. I'm a graduate student from New York and I'm doing a project, a master's thesis at Brooklyn College on philanthropy."

"How very interesting." She didn't question the fact that I was rather long in the tooth to be a graduate student. In 2008 the baby boomers, both black and white, were looking for an edge.

"Thank you. I think so, too. You know, our cities' most valuable institutions are so dependent upon donations and yet there is so little work done understanding this infrastructure, this very personal, what should I call it . . . webbing of relationships."

"Exactly so," the elder exclaimed in a soft voice modulated by decades spent in silent reflection and examination. "Without entrepreneurship the libraries and other cultural institutions, such as museums and opera houses, would be lost."

"That's what I was thinking," I said, matching her enthusiasm with my own. "I know that every relationship developed in a system such as this one is personal, but I wanted to look at the different kinds of giving."

Poppy took off her glasses to underscore her interest.

"Like you, for example," I said. "You must have had to develop all kinds of relationships in order to keep the doors of this system open."

She nodded, maybe even misted up a little.

"It was hard work but I loved every moment of it."

"Yes. I know it must have been both difficult and rewarding. I'm also aware that you can't reduce a lifetime of experience into some equation to be passed on but . . . I was thinking of approaching the problem by looking at philanthropy and separating what they call old money from the nouveau riche." I figured that my target was most likely the former.

"How interesting," Poppy Pollis said. "That really is the major concern, you know. People just coming into their wealth are looking for a place among the wealthy, for recognition, whereas the old families have a traditional format that allows them to maintain their names, as it were . . ."

She went on to tell me that there were twelve important families in Albany's history. Really there were only eleven but the society page had added the Sampson clan. Poppy considered the Sampsons a Johnny-come-lately bunch of car salesmen, but the newspaper people liked the idea of an even dozen so the Sampsons were included.

I had to sit through a lot of useless information, asking questions that I didn't care about. I had my notebook, though, and took very complete notes. It was maybe forty minutes later when we came upon the Hull family.

According to Poppy, the Hull clan was, on the whole, a dynasty of debauchery. Maxim Hull was the great-grandfather. He helped to build the infrastructure of the modern Albany library system. It was said that he made his fortune as a bootlegger and smuggler along with Joe Kennedy back in the era of Prohibition. He also built the second-largest Protestant church in the city.

Maxim's son, Roman, had always felt that he lived in the shadow of his father and tried to outdo him in every way that he could. At the age of fifty-eight he shot and killed an up-and-coming young race car driver, was deemed insane, spent four years at the Sunset Sanatorium, got out, and proceeded to marry the driver's young widow. The marriage didn't last but the memory of the scandal certainly did.

Bryant, Roman's son by a previous marriage, was presented as the current head of the family. As far as anyone knew he was an upstanding citizen. He built the administration building at the Sunset Sanatorium, married an older woman named Axel or Jackson or something, and had raised two beautiful children—Hannah and Fritz.

"Was the wife's maiden name Paxton?" I asked, pretending to be looking up a note.

“I don’t remember exactly what it was, but I’m sure it wasn’t Paxton,” she said. “Why do you ask?”

“Of course I knew about the Hull family,” I said. “I thought that Bryant had married a woman named Paxton. I guess I was mistaken.”

There was a bank of public-access computers on the first floor of the library. It was easy for me to look up society page newspaper articles, which finally gave me the location of the Hull residence. The family mansion was on a private road, Road Royale, thirty-five minutes north of the city.

Getting to the entrance of the road took forty minutes from the library parking lot.

I told the guard that I was delivering an envelope for Mr. Hull from a man named Jacobi, one of The Twelve, as Poppy Pollis called them.

The guard wasn't very concerned, and I saw why when I had driven about three miles down the pastoral country road. The Hull home was protected by a fourteen-foot-high electrified black iron gate that was topped with razor wire. It looked like the domain of a wealthy Third World oppressor, not the second cousins of the tyrant but the thing itself.

I stopped at the front gate and pressed a coral-colored button.

It was a beautiful day. Birds were chattering and the clouds hung around gracefully appreciating the deep wood as they basked in the rising heat.

"Yes?" a young voice asked over the intercom.

"Leonid McGill for Bryant Hull," I shouted. I always shout when speaking into intercoms.

I was expecting another question but instead the

gate rolled to the side as if my coming were prophesied in one of Poppy Pollis's old books of Albany lore.

The house was a letdown. I was expecting a Russian battleship replete with cannon and high metal buttresses but it was just a house; a big house, a very big house—a mansion in fact. It was four stories and took up the space of half a city block but my imagination had led me to expect so much more.

It was an old structure built from gray stone—intended to last. The front door was set back on a large green porch that was lined with twelve-foot pillars of white marble. Walking toward that door, it felt as if I were walking into the maw of a great gray and toothed toad.

I RANG THE BELL and waited for a while. The front door was at least fourteen feet high and eight wide. A big brass doorknob was in the lower center spacc. I had been standing there for maybe three minutes when the huge plank finally swung open.

"Yes?" the fair-skinned, russet-haired girl-child said. I knew her face from the articles I had perused at the library, which her great-grandfather had helped to build. From my reading I knew that she was twenty years old. Hannah could have passed for fifteen but she had none of the awkwardness of an adolescent.

When she looked at me she caught sight of something that was a part of her imagination. She smiled at the phantom I represented as I grinned at her beauty.

"Leonid McGill," I said.

"May I help you?"

"I wanted to see your father, Hannah," I said.

"Have we met?"

"No."

"Oh."

"Is he here?"

"My father?"

"Yes."

"No."

"When do you expect him?"

"What is your business with my father, Mr. McGill?" This phrase I believed came from the instinctual caution of the wealthy.

"It's a private matter."

"Oh," she said, pouting over the words. "Well . . . what do you do for a living?"

"Many things," I said with gravity. "I work for myself, but always on someone else's behalf."

"That's cryptic," her college education said.

"We've just met," I replied.

That got her to smile.

"Come on in." She made a jaunty turn and led the way into the gray mausoleum.

Hannah traipsed down the entrance hall. She was wearing a tawny shift with an uneven hem that showed a lot of her powerful and slender legs. There was a city girl's sway to her hips.

The hallway was lined with family portraits and pastel-colored doors.

We came to a room that was kidney-shaped and small. There was a burgundy couch and a matching chair arranged around a fireplace.

The girl gestured toward the chair.

"Please have a seat," she said, or, rather, her breeding said with reflexive grace.

She flopped down on the sofa, pulling one foot up on the cushion.

I sat, taking care not to stare at her hamstrings.

"I want to be a pilot," she said. This childish bravado I thought might be the real Hannah Hull. "What do you think about that, Mr. McGill?"

I hunched my shoulders and poked out my lower lip. "The sky's the limit as far as I'm concerned."

"That's pretty brave of you."

"What's brave about telling a young person that they can do something?"

"My father might be mad at you," she said speculatively.

"I don't owe him a thing."

This answer so surprised Hannah that she sat upright and stared.

"Why are you here?"

"Do you know a Thom Paxton or a Willie Sanderson?"

"I never heard of Thom Paxton. I don't know a Willie, either, but once we had a woman work for us, a cleaning lady named Sanderson. Lita Sanderson. I don't remember her having a family. Who are these people?"

"One of them died seventeen years ago," I said. "The other, Sanderson, tried to kill me maybe seventy-two hours back."

"He really tried to kill you?" She moved to the edge of her seat.

"Really, really."

"And you think my father knows something about it?"

"I think he might know something about Paxton or Sanderson."

"Murder is the worst crime man can commit," she said.

"It's very high on the list," I agreed.

"I want to be a pilot," she said again, "but I'm studying philosophy."

"At Wellesley."

"Yes. How do you know that?"

"The rich can't hide much from the people," I replied, thinking that I had heard the same words from my father, though intending something very different.

"I'm doing a summer paper on anarchism," she went on, shrugging off my insincere Marxist patter. "It's about people who believe that they are morally required to share the fates of their victims. In other words, the murderer must murder himself to keep his intentions pure. What do you think about that?"

I felt as if someone had stabbed me in the liver. This pain didn't start with Karmen Brown, it was something from a long time ago, a cloud that hung over the length of my entire life. It was rare that I was ever touched so deeply by a stranger. I looked up at the girl. Her expression was inscrutable but nonetheless intent.

"I need to speak to your father," I said, automaton-like. "When will he be home?"

"They're at our house in the city," she said. "Two blocks north and half a block west of Gracie Mansion. It's a big, ugly house."

I stood up abruptly, feeling that knife shift in my gut.

Hannah stood up, too.

She reached out, maybe intending to stay me by touching my hand. But she didn't touch me.

I have a daughter—sort of. I'm over half a century in age but I felt something very natural about this aborted invitation. There was a momentary connection between us.

"Who the hell are you?" someone shouted.

Standing in the doorway of the kidney-shaped den was a very skinny and tall young man with wiry red hair that stood up here and there. His eyes were bluish and his expression one of indignation that teetered upon madness.

This, I knew, was Fritz, Hannah's slightly older brother. There seemed to me something natural about this wild intrusion, like the comic relief in a bloody slasher film.

Fritz wore a dark-green jacket, brown trousers, a buff-colored shirt, and a red-and-black bow tie. He wasn't wearing glasses but should have been—to make the geek image complete.

"Who the hell are you?" he asked again, a little louder this time.

"You don't have to shout, Fritzie," Hannah said. "This is Mr. McGill. He's looking for Daddy."

"Why is he in my house?"

"It's my house, too," the princess said to the nerd.

"What are you doing with my sister?" Fritz asked me.

I couldn't help but feel a little bit exposed, a masher in the sudden light of a passing car.

"What are you doing to my sister?" he said again, this time looking at Hannah.

"He's not doing anything. He was just telling me about why he's here."

"He might be stealing from us," Fritz said. His agitation was definitely escalating.

"I've been with him the whole time," Hannah argued. "How can he steal anything when we're sitting down, looking at each other?"

"He has pockets," the boy pointed out as if having discovered a new continent in the distant ocean. "I have to search him. He could have taken something when you weren't looking."

I began to think that Bryant Hull's endowment of the Sunset Sanatorium might have been a wise long-term investment.

"You wouldn't want to do that," I said to Fritz in a detached, objective tone.

"I sure the hell do."

"No you don't."

"Why not?" he screamed.

"Because I'm a trained fighter and if you touch me I'll knock you unconscious. And when you're out cold, imagine how much I could steal before you came to."

"Why did you let him in here?" Fritz yelled, turning on his sister.

The girl's response was to look at me. She didn't want me to do anything. Hannah just asked me silently, with her eyes, to bear witness to something she lived through every day, or maybe every other day, making the span in between one of dread.

I thought, *Of course she wants me to stay*. And of course she couldn't ask. I understood the impulse in an instant. I wanted to protect her but didn't know how.

So I turned my attention to Fritz, worried that in his agitation he might try something foolish.

The boy was standing in place, shivering—no, shaking. The tremors were increasing. His eyes lost their focus. Pretty soon his balance was affected. As he fell, I stepped forward and caught him. His was an awkward weight because he'd gone rigid. I lowered him to the couch as his sister fled the room.

I wanted to run myself but there were flecks of foam coming from the boy's mouth. He was shuddering. I looked around the room searching for a wedge that I could put between his teeth to keep him from biting his tongue. His blue eyes were wide, staring right at me, indicting me as a dead man accuses his murderer.

For a brief moment I felt the urge to kill him, to wrap my hands around his throat the way Willie Sanderson had done to me.

I squelched the impulse before Hannah scurried back into the room. She was carrying an alligator case that she unzippered while running to her brother's side. She took out a disposable syringe that was already filled with an amber fluid.

"Help me!"

"What?" I asked.

"Pull off his jacket."

It wasn't easy but I turned the boy on his side, yanking against his jacket collar, pressing down on his rigid arms. When I got it down to the middle of his forearms Hannah moved in between us. He was wearing a short-sleeved shirt and so she easily found the vein just below the biceps and then expertly injected the medicine.

Maybe twelve seconds later Fritz relaxed and fell into a deep sleep.

Hannah sat down on the floor and sighed.

It was the family photograph that would never be taken: a sister who had just saved her brother, exhausted by the lifelong task of having to be there when the emergency arose. Why didn't he have a nurse? Why wasn't he on a regular regimen of drugs? Because Hannah was there to save him and to bear the brunt of his imbalance and frenzy.

She stood up and began pulling on her brother's arm.

"Help me take him upstairs," she said.

"Shouldn't you call a doctor?"

"No. This happens all the time. He'll be fine."

"Don't you have any servants that can help?"

"They'd tell my parents and then Fritzie would be hospitalized. He can't stand that. He'll kill himself if they commit him again."

I bent down and lifted the skinny boy in my arms.

"Where?"

She led me further down the hall, away from the front of the house. After a little way we came to a staircase leading up. I carried the kid to the second floor and, under Hannah's direction, brought him to a small room filled with various kinds of science tools: a microscope and telescope, a rock collection and butterfly pinboard. There were no posters, not even any music players. Here was a young man born to one of the wealthiest families in America and he didn't even have a TV set.

I put him down on the single bed and stood back while Hannah undressed him. She took off all of his clothes and threw a sheet over him. Then she folded his shirt and pants, placing them on a walnut table in the corner.

Fritz looked very different in his sleep: older and defeated. I watched him for a while before Hannah touched my arm and we walked out into the hall.

I hadn't registered the surroundings before as I was straining under Fritz's deadweight. The white carpets were of thick virgin wool and the paintings on the hall walls were originals by Chagall, Picasso, and the like.

"Thank you," Hannah said, attempting to express some deeper feeling.

I remembered the young woman who had made love to me in her small apartment. A little tingle in my chest was the hope that I could actually make up for some of the wrong that I'd done.

"It was nothing," I said.

"You didn't have to stay and help," she said. "You don't even know us."

"It's okay," I replied, placing two fingers on the crook of her elbow.

It wasn't anything sexual or suggestive. She folded her arm, hugging my fingers in that fashion to show how much the little I'd done had meant. And I understood. Unconscious, casual kindness is sometimes felt most deeply.

"I like you," she said, and my heart, despite all intentions, quailed.

"I have to go."

The rest of that day consisted of the drive back to Albany, a bottle of Wild Turkey, and a dreamless sprawl on the big bed at the Minerva; that and a midnight call from Katrina.

"Huh?" I said into the cell phone, so eloquently articulating my state of mind.

"Leonid?"

"I'm in Albany, Katrina. I need to sleep." These words bumped around in my head, reminding me of my eldest, my only blood child.

"I just wanted to tell you that we can work something out," she said.

"I'll talk to you later."

The next thing I knew it was morning and I wasn't sure what my wife had meant or if she had called at all.

I DECIDED TO TAKE the train back to New York. I couldn't face the notion of flitting around in the sky after the emotional chaos of the Hulls' house.

When I was a kid, living in enforced poverty because of my father's commitment to being working class, I used to pray that I would be adopted by a family of rich capitalists. In the fantasy, my father went away, never to return, and Mr. and Mrs. Moneybags decided to take me in, feeling sorry for the poor, black, red-diaper orphan.

My father did go away, and my mother died for good measure, but I never got adopted. Looking at Fritz and Hannah, I couldn't help but feel that maybe I got off lucky.

AS THE LOCAL TRAIN wended its way down toward Manhattan I sifted through the various newspapers and books I carried in my bag. But after a while I realized reading was beyond me.

At first this was because I couldn't get my bourbon-soaked mind off of Hannah Hull. Most people I get a read on pretty quickly; it's a requirement in my line of work. But Hannah was indecipherable to me. She could have been a psychotic child with depraved tendencies, though I didn't want to believe that. I wanted to believe that she was the victim of a family that had veered off course, that she saw in me a man who could be relied upon—a jutting rock in a stormy sea.

That was the role I fantasized myself in since relinquishing my underhanded ways. I wanted to be seen as I hoped Hannah had seen me.

It was almost funny, the way I was buffeted around by these mercurial emotions. A step or two more, I thought, and I might have turned into Fritz. This realization brought a smile to my lips.

"What you grinnin' at?" a man said derisively. "Life is hard out there. You see me smilin'? I ain't got time to be silly. I got to pay the rent an' put shoes on your feet. Life is serious, not no playtime."

This voice came from across the aisle. The speaker was the male head of a young black family, which included a mother and child. The boy was no more than four years old and could have been younger. His father hadn't been in his twenties very long. The mother, a gentle and plain-looking woman, glanced in my direction and smiled apologetically. The boy's head was bowed under the heavy criticism of his father.

They were all the same dark-brown color.

"Are you listenin' to me?" the father asked his son.

I picked up my newspaper, looking for an article to distract me. The main story was about some midwestern governor arrested by the FBI for paying prostitutes to cross state lines. It was hard for me to concentrate on the article, partly because it reminded me so much of the kind of work I had once done to bring down otherwise good men, and partly due to the fact that a nearby article said that the Left was claiming that the death toll in Iraq was nearing a million while, by some calculations, we would end up spending a trillion dollars on the effort. That meant, by the end of our Middle Eastern folly, that we would have spent a million dollars for each death. The front page was a kind of triple obscenity . . .

The boy mumbled something to his mother.

"Why you askin' her for water?" the father said. "Does she look like she have water for you? Sometimes you just got to be thirsty. I'm thirsty. Do you see me goin' around askin' people for water?"

I gathered my things together and stood up. The man's idea of pedagogy was too much for me to bear.

I guess my body language betrayed my feelings.

"Where you think you goin'?" the young father asked me as I lugged my bag toward the door between cars.

"I need quiet in order to think."

"What's so important you got to think about?"

I should have just moved on.

"I think about a lot of things," I said. "Just now I was thinking that a child needs to laugh and have mother-love in his life, otherwise he'll turn out to be a little man pushin' children around to make himself feel like he knows somethin' smart."

That said, I went through the door and into the next car.

THERE WAS NOTHING to distract me in that section. One guy was yakking on his cell phone, but I wasn't bothered by that.

The release of anger had put me into a free-floating state of mind. I stopped obsessing about the girl's unbidden, unconscious forgiveness and started wondering about the connection between the Hulls, Willie Sanderson, and the murders that I was implicated in. Certainly there was some connection. And beyond that I had Tony the Suit to answer to, and Twill to save from his own dark heroism.

Everything was flowing together and so I began coming up with ideas that might fit anything. I considered talking to Twill, telling him that I knew what he was up to and offering another way out. I seriously entertained the idea of telling Tony where A Mann lived. The guy was dead anyway. Was that what Harris Vartan was asking me to do?

I had just begun wondering about the Hulls' cleaning lady when a voice sounded at the other end of the car.

"Hey, you!" the young father from another lifetime shouted.

For a brief moment everything had made perfect sense: I wasn't confused or worried at all. It was the kind of moment that never lasts, but it feels permanent for the few seconds it's there.

I stood up as the young father rushed down the aisle. I could see in his face that he'd been stewing over my words.

The guy on his cell phone said, "I'll have to call you back."

My nemesis was in no mood for talking, either. As soon as he came within range he threw a punch. I caught it like a seasoned coach catching a Little Leaguer's first toss, pushing the fist back at its pitcher. He wasn't daunted by my obvious superiority and threw another. This time I backed away to let the punch go wild. A woman yelped and I pushed against the man's chest with both hands. He fell on his butt. I could see by the look on his face that he had finally understood my strength.

The young father jumped to his feet, but he was no longer sure what to do. I had already blocked one blow, slipped a punch, and dropped him on his ass. He knew that the next response would be even stronger.

He hated me, wanted to beat me down into submission, but that was not to be and we both knew it.

"Fuck you!" he yelled, clenching his fists and hopping an inch or so off the floor.

When I didn't flinch he turned around and stormed back to his poor, unsuspecting family.

I felt bad about humiliating the father. He couldn't help what he was, and I hadn't helped, either. At least his son wasn't there to witness his defeat. At least that.

I gathered my things again and moved down a few cars more. That way if he found more courage, or a weapon, I'd be somewhere else and he'd have a few extra moments to think about consequences.

In my new seat I wondered about what kind of father Fritz would make. Then I thought about my own father, who indoctrinated and then abandoned me. It seemed that there was a whole world of wounded, half-conscious sires picking fights and losing them.

When you have no answers, ask different questions," my father once said to me. He was quoting a man who had been a minor official on the fringe of Joseph Stalin's inner circle toward the end of the madman's reign.

I had rejected all of my father's ideology, but his logic remained with me. So about fifteen miles out from Manhattan I called a man I knew in the electricians' union. His name was Duffy and he'd had a hard time of it for a while there when one of his rivals wanted to unseat him from a plum position. I balanced the scales, so to speak. I did such a good job that Duffy and his rival became good friends.

"HELLO," A YOUNG woman answered.

"Let me talk to Duffy."

"He's in a meeting."

"He's always in a meeting. Tell him it's Leonid McGill."

He was on the line ten seconds later.

"What's up, mutt?" He gave the same line to everyone, so it was no insult.

I explained that I needed to root around a building. I didn't say why.

"Sure," Duffy said. "What name you usin'?"

"Richard Siles."

"You need keys?"

"No. I got my own."

He gave me a line to give the super and I committed it to memory.

"What time?" Duffy asked.

"One today."

"Done."

"See ya later," I said.

"Not if I see you first."

I WENT TO my office, changed into a pair of coveralls I kept in a closet, and loaded up my toolbox with a few gadgets, a jumbo ring of master keys, and some electrician's tools. I also grabbed a coat in spite of the fact that it was eighty-five degrees outside. Then I took a cab up to a big gray apartment building about fifteen blocks from my apartment, a block off Broadway.

The building was twenty-eight stories high and dominant among its peers.

"What can I do for you?" the blue-jacketed doorman asked.

"Richard Siles," I said, holding out a hand. "I'm the electrical contractor they called about."

"Oh, yeah," the chubby, pink-skinned guardian replied, "Joseph said you might be around."

He was a big man, in his sixties. When he was young he must have been ready with his fists. You could see the pale ghosts of scars on his face and knuckles.

"Peter Green," he said, introducing himself. "What's this all about, Dick?"

"Layoffs on Wall Street. City revenues are down this year," I said. "At least they're worried they might be. They're checking all the big Manhattan buildings for violations. Wanna make up some of their losses on fines. So a couple'a guys are doing some early checks to maybe save you guys some fines and get us some work on the side."

I asked Peter if I could hang my coat in his doorman's closet and he pointed to a hopper room behind the desk. After that he showed me to a door that led to the basement and I went down to pretend for a while.

I found the nexus for the phone and fiber-optic lines and connected a little box that Bug had sold me for a previous job. Then I wandered, looking for doors that I might use if I needed, for any reason, to make a late-night entry.

I had hung up the coat because I wanted to get behind the desk to see what video monitors the doorman had. They only covered the front door, entrances from the outside, and the interior of the elevators.

So I took in a deep breath and made my way up one of the stairwells to apartment G on the twenty-first floor. I didn't have to make the climb but you pick up exercise where you can in my line of work.

Breathing harder than I would have liked, I knocked and buzzed and knocked again. Three minutes later I pulled out the appropriate master key from the keychain in my toolbox.

People rarely burglarize doorman apartment buildings in Manhattan, so the locks are usually old, and often there's only one.

I KNEW FROM Bug's report that Leslie Bitterman was at work every day. He had no wife. Mardi was taking afternoon summer-school classes and her sister was in day camp. It's amazing what you can find online if you know what you're doing.

The place was like a dollhouse for adults. In the small entrance there was a maple stand with a vase containing two dozen silk roses. The flowers had never been dusted. This was the only sign of faulty housekeeping.

The rest of the apartment was immaculate. There was no mess in the dining room, kitchen, or living room. The girls' bedrooms were also spotless. Leslie's sleeping quarters were definitely masculine, but not too much so. Woolen blankets and one pillow. The window shades, all through the house, were pulled down.

The office was the most amazing of all the rooms. It was almost as bare as Christian's office downtown. The only concession Mr. Bitterman had made to comfort was to put a worn and stained red rug under his desk and chair. He had a desktop computer and a phone line that he used for his archaic Internet connection.

I turned on the computer but couldn't gain access because it was password protected. I connected a specially designed transmitter to a USB port and called Tiny "the Bug" Bateman.

"I see you got a setup for me," the ultra-geek said upon answering. "Gimme a minute."

The screen went black and then a stream of data, all in green characters, began to scroll down. This went on for about sixty seconds and then Bug said, "You're in. Call me if you have any problem."

"Is he online?"

"He is now."

"Much activity?"

"No. He doesn't have much of a footprint. Looks like a couple of online newspapers and his office e-mail account."

"Can you download what he's got on here?"

"He's an old-fashioned kind of guy. Did you connect my crossbox on the phone lines and fiber-optic cable?"

"Uh-huh."

"It'll take a while but no problem," he said and then he hung up.

PERUSING HIS ELECTRONIC folders, I saw nothing unusual. He had downloaded files from his work but this seemed to be legitimate. It just looked like he worked from home sometimes. There were plenty of documents in his word-processor files: letters to a few relatives and complaints to businesses that he believed had not made good on their promises. There were hundreds of word-processor files. One of these was named JOURNAL01. I hoped that this would give me some inkling about why my son and his daughter were plotting his murder. But it didn't. I've never read such a boring rendition of life. He wrote about the breakfast he'd just had, and about some work-related issues—in excruciating detail. The only thing odd about his children is that he never mentioned them.

After an hour of browsing through his computer I had found absolutely nothing. His only pastime, it seemed, was taking color-drenched photographs of zoo animals. He had zebras, monkeys, tigers, and fanciful sea horses in literally hundreds of files.

I scrolled through all the documents and came upon one thing odd. Every file name that he had was a full word or two describing the contents. One file, however, was merely named TI. I tried to read it but only got machine-language garbage. I switched over to his program files and found a program with the same name.

AFTER TEN MINUTES of paging through the digital photographs I wanted to go out and find the angry father on that southbound train. I wanted to apologize to him. He at least loved his son, even if he was overzealous in the expression of that love. But what Leslie Bitterman had done was unforgivable.

There were well over a thousand photographs of a naked man and child in the most depraved positions. The girl in the photographs ranged in age from eight to about twelve, before puberty began to rear its hormones. Sometimes she was smiling, sometimes she cried, openmouthed and in despair. The man had a stern look and was always erect. She was a pale-haired, gray-eyed girl. When she wasn't in despair her expression was resigned, as unreadable as that of Leslie Bitterman.

I knew that it was Bitterman because the photographs had been taken in that very room. He had raped and molested that child on the selfsame red rug.

I made it through maybe thirty percent of the pictures; after that I lost heart. If I hadn't incriminated myself by calling Duffy I probably would have waited and killed Bitterman myself. But the feeling passed and I went into the hall and down the stairs. I retrieved Bug's cross-box from the basement and then came up to thank Peter. I told the doorman that everything looked good.

"You sure you're an electrician?" he asked, eyeing me suspiciously.

"Yeah. Why?"

"I don't know," Peter said, leavening his tone. "I never known one'a you guys not to come up with some kinda five-thousand-dollar job."

"Duffy likes Joe," I said. "He told me to go easy."

I don't even remember how I got back to the Tesla Building.

Twill, I thought while unlocking the many bolts on my outer office door, was a perfect person. Maybe not a model citizen or a particularly productive member of society, not a law-abiding churchgoer with God always on his mind; but in spite of all his social failings, Twill was capable of making flawless decisions about what he would do and why. His resolution to kill Leslie Bitterman was one of absolute sensibleness. I wanted to kill the man myself, but I wasn't perfect like my son. I worried about consequences even if I knew the act in front of me was correct.

Whether you killed the finance expert for past acts or to stem future threats, there were few people who would condemn or even question the act itself. The problem was that those few worked for the state of New York and wore black robes.

But Twill's perfection didn't matter. Once I was in possession of the facts, making a plan to save my son would be easy. I had resolved that problem and so was feeling good. There were other knots in the cord of my life, but they would unravel, too—I was pretty sure.

I was sitting in the new chair behind my receptionist's desk, something I often did while reading the mail.

I was hardly even worried when there came a jiggle on the doorknob followed by the sound of the buzzer.

I considered going back to my office to consult the monitors, but then I said to myself that I couldn't live my life worrying about what awaited me every time I heard a knock or ring. That path led to madness.

HE WAS ON the short side and smelled of a thin layer of lilac spread over an acre of sour sweat. In his left hand he held a battered black briefcase. My visitor was dressed in a well-cut dark-blue suit, but his wiry frame undermined the effect. Who knows what genetic background stamped out his oddly long but, then again, flat white face?

"Mr. McGill?" he asked, his lips approximating a smile.

"Who are you?"

"Timothy Moore."

"Can I help you?"

"Are you Leonid McGill?"

I hesitated. So many things were going on that I wasn't even certain about answering this simplest of questions. I didn't like the way Moore smelled but maybe he had some kind of glandular problem. I was busy but no one was paying me, except if I set up a constitutionally innocent man for a mob hit.

"Yes, I am," I said. "Come on in, Mr. Moore. Have a seat."

I backed away, letting him into the front office. I decided to meet with him out there. That way I didn't have to turn my back to enter the codes for the inner sanctum.

I sat down behind the desk and gave Tim Moore my blandest expression.

"Nice office," he said, lowering tentatively across from me. "Great building."

He was nervous but that didn't necessarily portend anything sinister. Unfaithful wives made men uncomfortable; thieving employees sometimes did, too.

"What's your business, Mr. Moore?"

"I'm an office manager," he said. "I work for Crow and Williams."

"I mean, what is your business with me?"

A smile flitted across the little man's sensuous mouth. This wan grin soon became a grimace.

"Excuse me," he said. "I'm not used to these things."

"You're here now," I said. "Just say it—one word after the other."

"I'm being blackmailed," he said at half-capacity.

He took out a cigarette.

"No smoking in here," I informed him. After all, I hadn't had one since visiting Toolie in the prison infirmary.

He looked at the white paper roll in his hand and then returned it to the pack, put the pack in his jacket pocket, and inhaled deeply as if he were smoking anyway.

On the exhale he said, "I'm married to a wonderful woman, Mr. McGill. I've been in love with her for sixteen years."

I almost believed him.

"You got a photograph?"

He leaned over on one buttock, lifting the other in the armless ash chair. He could have been going for a gun, but since my debacle with Willie Sanderson I had moved a pistol to the outer-office desk; it was in my hand at that very moment.

But all he came out with was a wallet. He flipped it open to the picture of a mousy-looking brunette with big eyes and a painted-on smile. She was in her thirties when the picture was taken. I didn't believe that he would have gone this far to prepare a lie.

I nodded and he put the wallet away.

"Eighteen months ago I strayed with a little Asian girl named Annie," Tim said. "It didn't last long. It was like a forty-eight-hour bug. I was in Atlantic City for a seminar and she was staying in the hotel.

"She came up to see me in the city a few times but I was over her by then and looking for a way to cut it off. Finally I just told her that I loved my wife and that was it."

"How'd she take it?"

"Pretty good." He nodded. "Pretty okay. She looked sad but said that she understood. She had a serious boyfriend and was feeling guilty herself."

"Is this Annie the one blackmailing you?"

"It's a man that called. But she might be putting him up to it. He says that he's got pictures. He knows where we stayed and specific details about things we, we did." Moore hesitated a moment, remembering. "You see, I got this rich aunt that died—Mona Lester. I got a little cash out of it."

"Did Annie know about the aunt?"

Tim squinted the way some inexperienced boxers do when you hit them with a solid body shot.

"In that first couple'a days I told her almost everything. I thought it was love. I didn't know."

"How much they want?"

"Twenty-five thousand."

"How much you inherit?"

"Two hundred eighty-six thousand, but I thought it was gonna be closer to a million."

"Doesn't make sense," I said. "Seems like they should have asked for more."

"I don't know," Timothy Moore replied. "The guy on the phone said that he just needed enough to settle a debt he had. He wants me to bring the money to this condemned building on West Twenty-fourth tomorrow night."

"Why don't you go to the police? They could grab this guy, twist his arm, and go after the girl. That would be easy and legal."

"Yeah." He looked up at me with miserable eyes. "But then there might be an investigation and a trial. Margot would find out. All she'd care about was the affair. I don't wanna lose my wife, brother."

It's always odd when a white man calls me brother, makes me wonder if he's trying to put one over on me.

But he sounded honestly upset. There was pain there, but still . . . that stench of lilac and sweat.

"So what do want from me, Mr. Moore?"

"I'll give you five thousand dollars," he said, as if that was an answer to my question.

"For what?"

"You go to the meeting and get the lowdown on this guy. You tell him that you're a witness and if he ever shows his face again you'll go to the cops. Then give him some of the money, and you, you keep the rest. That way I'll have paid for what I did wrong and, and I can go back to my life with Margot."

He was near tears.

"How'd you hear about me?"

"Luke Nye," he said. "Luke Nye said that you might agree to do a job like this."

"How you know him?"

"Prescott Mimer. I used to tend bar for a friend of Prescott's on the weekends—for some extra cash."

"Who's the friend?"

"What does all this have to do with what I'm asking for, Mr. McGill?"

"Answer my questions, all of my questions," I said, "or walk out the same way you came in."

"Karl Zebriski," he said. "His bar used to be at Fortieth and Second, but now he has a place in the Lamont Towers near Columbus Circle."

I was nervous listening to the poorly put-together man. On the one hand, he seemed to have real feelings, but on the other someone had tried to kill me once already that week.

Everything he said was reasonable. It could have well been the truth.

My life was on the line, more than one line, but that wasn't going to give me a break on the rent; only prison did that, because even in death your plot is only leased.

"Give me a number where I can reach you," I said, pushing a notepad across the desk. "I'll call you in a few hours."

"But I've got the money right here," he said, holding up the briefcase.

"Keep it. I'll call you later and we will see what we shall see at that time."

There was an argument in his eyes but he could see that there was a brick wall behind mine. He scribbled down a number, nodded, and rose to his feet.

"I really need the help, brother," he said.

"And I really will call you," I replied.

Crow and Williams," a young man answered. "How can I help you?"

"I'd like to speak to Timothy Moore, please."

"Mr. Moore is out on personal business. Do you want to leave a message?"

I hung up.

I'd met Prescott Mimer before. He was a construction foreman who liked to hang out in wise-guy bars. I doubted that he'd recognize my voice, so I called him saying that I was a headhunter for office managers and was considering doing some work setting Timothy Moore up with a position.

"He's all right," Mimer told me. "I never worked with him or anything. But he seems like a good guy. Did he give you my number for a reference?"

"No. Your name came up in a discussion with a gentleman named Luke Nye. I'm sorry to bother you."

"That's okay. It's just that I can't help you with his work habits or anything."

"Is he married?"

"What's that got to do with a job?"

"It's an organic grain and cereal company from the Midwest," I said. "Family business. They like a wholesome picture."

"Yeah," Mimer said. "He's crazy over that woman. Margaret, I think her name is . . ."

I skipped Zebriski and went straight to Luke Nye. Nye was a pool hustler who played in private tournaments around the city and up and down the East Coast. If you gave a moray eel a couple of hundred million years he would evolve into Luke Nye.

"Hey, LT," Nye said over the line. "Haven't heard from you in a while."

"Tryin' to clean up my act."

"You callin' about Tim?"

"Yeah. How'd you guess?"

"He came to me yesterday and asked if I knew a detective could help him with somethin' that wasn't quite on the up and up. I heard you weren't in the life anymore, but then I figured you could always say no."

"Was my name the only one you gave him?"

"You're one of a kind, LT."

I COULDN'T SEE a flaw, only smell one. And the smell was all physical.

"Hello?" Tim Moore said through the phone.

"How many numbers in the lock on your briefcase?"

"Three."

"There's a variety store a block or so north of Bleecker on the east side of Hudson," I said. "It's called Iko's. Set the lock to six-six-seven and leave it there for a Joan Ligget."

"Should I put your money in it, too?"

"Yeah. Do that," I said. "Now give me what you got."

Fifteen minutes later I was entering Zephyra Ximenez's number.

"Yes, Mr. McGill?"

"Have somebody pick up a briefcase at Iko's and leave it with the guys at the front desk of my office building, ASAP."

SHELLY AND DIMITRI were sitting down to dinner with their mother when I came in. I had called again, and so Katrina made the service coincide with my ETA. I was carrying the briefcase, less my five-thousand-dollar fee.

"Hi, Daddy," my daughter said just a bit too loudly.

Dimitri grunted and I nodded to him.

Katrina is the best cook I've ever met—bar none. She can make anything. That night she'd prepared red beans and rice with a spicy tomato sauce and filled with andouille and chorizo sausage. In little dishes arranged in the middle of the dining table she had set out grated white cheese, chopped Bermuda onions, green olives, and diced jalapeños—seeds and all.

I pulled up my chair at the head of the table, setting the briefcase beside me. I like a good meal. Katrina beamed from the opposite end and for a brief span I forgot our differences and disconnections.

"Smells great, honey," I said. "How you doin', D?"

"Okay, I guess," Dimitri mumbled.

"How's school?"

"Fine."

"You need anything there?"

He shook his head. That meant that he wasn't going to talk anymore.

But I didn't care. I was thinking about the young woman of Scandinavian descent whom I had loved passionately for nine months, with sporadic recurrences for a year or two after.

What had Tim compared it to? A forty-eight-hour bug. Our love was more like a couple of years of consumption on Thomas Mann's Magic Mountain. It took us that long to recover. Though the symptoms were gone, I was often reminded of them at dinner.

"I'm going to take a special course in African-American history,

Dad," Shelly said happily, still a bit too loud. "I met with Professor Hill about an independent study he suggested for the fall. We'll be covering the black relationship to communism . . ."

She went on to regale me about the political commitment and supposed naïveté of Paul Robeson. It seemed that everything Shelly did was intended to make me happy. Sometimes I wondered if it might be a mercy to tell her that I wasn't her real father.

She was still talking when Twill entered the dining room. Accompanying him was a skinny, teenaged, white waif-child with ash-blond hair and the saddest pale eyes. I had only seen pictures of her as a prepubescent girl but I would have recognized Mardi Bitterman if she were retirement age.

"Mom, Pop," Twill said brightly. "Sis, Bulldog," he said to his siblings. "This is Mardi, a friend of mine from school."

"Hi," the girl said. Her voice was so soft that it was almost inaudible.

"Late for dinner," Katrina chided. "Now sit, both of you."

I could tell by her expression that Katrina wasn't happy with an unannounced guest. But she knew from past experience that if she complained Twill would leave—which would turn my mood sour.

Twill sat Mardi next to Shelly, knowing that his sister would immediately take the child under her wing. My daughter engaged the wounded wraith of a girl. After a few minutes they were gabbing, newfound friends. Shelly talking loudly with broad facial gestures, and Mardi whispering, sometimes even partially covering her mouth.

Katrina had lost her Mona Lisa smile with a stranger at her table. I doubt if Dimitri's mood would have changed if we were in the middle of a nuclear war. The girls seemed to be getting along, and Twill, as usual, was ebullient and lively.

"So what's happenin', Pop?"

"Lookin' for a guy in Brooklyn, and a client came in today to get me to talk to somebody givin' him grief." I didn't mind talking about work in broad swaths. This made my job seem mundane and served to lessen any interest my family might have shown.

"You readin' anything good?" he asked me.

Twill never read a book unless he absolutely had to.

"Picked up this little book on the history of Western philosophy," I said.

"Like who?" my son asked.

"What is it, son?"

"What do you mean?" Even at his most disingenuous, Twill was charming.

"What do you want?"

His grin was perfect.

"Well, you know, Pop," he said and paused. "You know . . . Mardi here is havin' a problem at home and I told her she could stay here a night or two."

"Absolutely not," Katrina commanded from her end.

Twill didn't look at her. He was no longer smiling, either.

Even if I hadn't known about the girl and her father I would have taken the boy's side.

"You have to learn, Twilliam," my wife was saying, "that you cannot just waltz in here and make—"

"Kat," I said.

My wife hates the feline contraction of her name.

"I am not an animal," she would tell anyone who dared use that appellation.

I told her I would never use the term unless I needed her to pay close attention to what I had to say.

She stopped mid-sentence and glared at me.

"Shall we go to the kitchen?" I suggested.

"WHY DID YOU embarrass me in front of our children?" she asked when we'd reached her bastion.

It was the first time she'd shown anger since coming back home.

"Because I have it on good authority that this girl's father has been raping her since she was a small child."

Katrina's lower jaw fell open. She had been ready to unleash one of her fiery tantrums but my words doused that flame.

"What?"

"You can't let on to her or Twill that you know anything about it. You know our son. You know what he's capable of. I need to defuse the situation before it gets out hand. Do you hear me?"

She nodded.

"The girl can stay with you or Shelly. Shell seems to like her, so maybe that would be good. I'll bunk with Twill. I'll tell him that you asked me to so that he doesn't get with the girl, but really I just want to keep my eye on him until I know why he needs her to stay here."

"Her father?"

I nodded.

"That's terrible. We should call the police."

"We will," I said. "But not until I'm sure that the cops'll do something."

I turned toward the door, expecting Katrina to come along with me, but instead she placed a feathery touch upon my wrist. I stopped but could not bring myself to turn and face her. Just as with my contraction of her name, Katrina could do small things that spoke volumes down the corridors of our history.

"Leonid."

"Yeah?" I said to the door in front of me.

"Look at me."

I faced her but could not look directly in her eyes.

"You know that I'm trying my best," she said. "I'm here and I want to be a good wife to you."

I took in a deep breath and counted one in my mind.

"The past is over," she said. "I'm here with you now."

I exhaled and counted.

"Zool went bust," I said. "I asked a pal of mine to see what happened to him. They say he flew to Argentina an hour before the feds issued a warrant."

She took it well: no tears or tremors.

"I learned from that, Leonid. I missed my children. I missed my life with you."

"I'm here, am I not?"

"With one foot out the door and the other one raised to go."

"What do you want from me, Katrina?"

"I want you to try. I want a life together and to be forgiven for whatever I've done wrong."

I had counted up to ten and started over.

"I don't know how to do that." The words came to voice from the empty chamber of my mind.

"Talk to me," she said. "Tell me what happened to you two years ago that made you so much more distant."

The shock of her knowledge of me was muted by the walking meditation. Maybe even the discipline helped me to see what was right there in front of me. I could see that no matter what Katrina would do, given a way out, that she had made up her mind to try and make the marriage work while she was there. She wasn't pretending or lying. My wife wanted, maybe for the first time ever, to make a bridge between her heart and my life. All I had to do was open the way.

I got as far as opening my mouth. An unintelligible sound came out.

"What?" she asked.

That single-syllable question hit my ear like the soft concussion of a far-off explosion. It was little more than a pop, but the seasoned soldier knew that it might very well signify injury or death.

I knew my wife too well to trust that she would never use my words against me. I knew myself too well to pretend to share my life in some guarded, limited way. It was all or nothing for both of us.

That was one of those rare moments that have true meaning in human discourse. Katrina and I had never been closer; our hearts, even if mine was secret, had never been more honest.

But neither of us could break down the decades of detritus that composed our marriage. I could never trust that Katrina would not one day rouse from this feeling. I had seen love turn to hatred too often not to read the portents and signs.

"I'm gonna have to think about this, baby," I said. "You know I'm the oldest mutt in the kennel and they comin' out with new breeds and new tricks every day."

Katrina's blue eyes, at that moment, were omniscient as far as Leonid Trotter McGill was concerned. She saw my every thought and hesitation. I lost the count of my breathing and she held me with that gaze.

"I will still be here trying to make it work," she said.

After a moment more of this special torture, my wife of decades made her way from the room.

A sober-minded Katrina apologized to Twill and Mardi. She told them that she'd had a hard day and was getting too upset over little things.

"You are welcome to stay for a day or so," she said to the girl.

Shelly was so happy that she kissed her new friend on the cheek.

"Can she stay in my room, Mama?"

"Of course."

Twill was looking at me but I managed to keep my eyes on Katrina.

Later on, after the dishes were done, I told Twill about Katrina wanting me to bunk with him.

"Why'd you get on her like that, Pops?" was his reply.

"Because when you looked in my eye I saw that there was something wrong," I said. "I knew that you had a good reason for bringing Mardi here and so I talked your mother into it."

For a moment Twill's eyes tightened, but then he broke into a smile.

"You all right, Mr. McGill."

I don't think I will ever receive higher praise.

LATER ON I went down to Twill's room. He was sitting at his desk, dressed only in dark-blue boxers while surfing the Net for arcane bits of information. When I walked in he signed off and stood up. There was a sleeping bag on the floor at the foot of his queen-sized bed.

"I got the floor," he said.

The sleeping bag was state-of-the-art. The top was dull-green nylon stuffed with goose down, and the bottom was a cushion of a slightly darker hue. There was even a two-ply netting for the face, to keep out mosquitoes while allowing the sleeper to breathe comfortably.

I had given up asking Twill where he got things like that or what he used them for. When he was younger I tried reasoning with him. From the age of five he'd countered my efforts with that winning smile, along with his patented perplexed stare. As the years progressed I tried rewards, punishments, even a child psychiatrist. The presents he shared with his siblings. The punishments he bore without tears or anger. It's anyone's guess what the therapist thought. She was an honest woman named Powell; after seventeen sessions she called it quits.

Nothing could deter Twill from the trouble he was drawn to. But he had a cockeyed code of honor, too. Even as a child he never stole from or hurt family or friends. After the age of eleven, when he'd gained a measure of mobility, this truce spread out to include our neighbors. Smiles and schemes came to him as naturally as breath. I couldn't stop him from being what he was. My only job was to keep him alive and free long enough to become a man.

"SO?" I SAID a few minutes after we were both in our beddings and the lights were out.

It was a very comfortable bed. The thread count of Twill's bright-yellow sheets was at least twelve hundred.

"So what, Dad?"

"What kind of trouble are you in, son?"

"It's not like that, Pop," he said softly. "Mardi and me just friends. She needed to get away, and I knew Shell would be good to her. There's no problem."

"You're wrong about that, Twill," I said. "The problem is that among your peers you are the best, by far. But that doesn't mean that there aren't people out there that are better than you. What I'm saying is that you've got to rely on somebody, sometime."

"I don't know what you mean," his voice came from out of the darkness, dripping with innocence.

"Tell me why you feel that you have to protect Mardi."

"I'm just doin' her a favor, Pops. That's all."

I hadn't expected him to tell me anything. This charade of a conversation was designed to get him to believe that I was suspicious about the girl so that later on, when I took action, he wouldn't suspect that I had his primary e-mail address tapped.

THERE WAS FIRE all around me. My clothes were smoldering and I could hardly catch a breath because I was running hard and inhaling smoke. I ran down a long metal corridor until coming to a huge iron door. I took off my burning jacket, wrapped my hands with it, and tried to turn the knob . . . but it wouldn't give. I slammed into the door with my shoulder but it was locked. I turned to see which other way I could run but Timothy Moore was standing there, blocking the way. He was holding a long-barreled pistol, pointing it at my forehead.

In that moment, time came to a complete stop. I was looking into the killer's dark eyes for an answer.

Why did you make me sign over the money? Why do you want me dead? I wanted to ask, but the act of bringing the questions to my lips started time moving again, and then he fired.

I sat up in the posh bedding, gasping for air. My heart was beating like a pneumatic hammer. It took more than a minute for me to catch my breath.

I crawled on hands and knees to the foot of the bed. Twill was sound asleep in his portable body bag. He'd unzippered the face net and the front was open down to his waist. I could just make out the peaceful face of his repose.

I MADE MY way to the small dining table off of Katrina's near-professional kitchen. I brought my jacket with me, but search as I might I couldn't find the cigarettes. Then I remembered that I had quit again and so went to the cupboard for the bottle of brandy Katrina kept there.

Three shots later I calmed down enough so that my pulse was near normal and my mind was working in a fairly linear fashion. Timothy Moore, no matter how good his story was, didn't make sense. The dominoes were just too perfect. There was a slim chance that he was on the up-and-up, but I'd have been a fool to play it like that.

I took out my personal cell phone and entered the code "666."

And even though it was 3:17 in the morning, he answered on the first ring.

"LT?"

"Hush."

"What do you need?"

"Some assistance."

"When and where?"

THERE WAS NO going to sleep for hours after that dream.

I went to the dining room and reflected on the wilderness of my mind.

I had always been the runt since as far back as I can remember. After the age of twelve I was fatherless and poor for real—not for the Movement. My mother died when I had just turned fourteen. She just gave up. I never blamed her, though. I was alone in the world and rarely took a backward step in the ring of life. I was what Gordo called a banger. I moved forward, took my lumps, and gave just as good. If a bigger kid picked on me he better know how many teeth he could afford to lose. And if the principal or some foster parent thought that I was there to take orders—they learned.

I can count on one hand the number of people who have ever truly frightened me. Hush is at the top of that list.

As far as I know I'm one of only three people who know his real name, and I would never say it out loud, much less write it down.

For nearly two decades he was the man the professionals went to when they wanted somebody dead. He would kill anyone, anywhere. If you needed it to look like an accident, there was a heart attack or a car accident in the offing. If the body needed to disappear, it would never be found. He was so good that even the head men of foreign mobs thought twice before uttering his code name—and no one ever refused to pay.

Few people had ever seen him for who and what he was. When he showed up as a delivery boy or trash collector, all and sundry were unimpressed. He was a pale white guy, five-ten with close-cut brown hair. He was powerful but not particularly well built. The only thing that marked him was a deep voice that rumbled rather than spoke.

He could kill an armed man with only a mouthful of water.

No one wanted to hear that Hush was after them. He was the walking, breathing personification of pancreatic cancer.

When people found out that Hush was after them, their reactions were many but predictable. Some ran. Others bought life insurance and settled up their affairs. A few went to the police and sought witness protection, but in the end they all died. I know this because I know Hush.

People responded in all kinds of ways when they were tipped to Hush's intentions, but of them Carter Brown of East New York was unique. When Carter heard that his uptown rival had paid a hundred large for Hush's services, he laughed. He was the one man who wasn't afraid of the excellent assassin. He wasn't afraid because he knew about the hit man's Achilles' heel: a young black woman named Tamara and a toddler that was Hush's child.

It had taken at least twenty-five moving pieces for Hush to get in touch with me. The meet was set for one of those big glass-and-chrome salad bars in midtown Manhattan at 2:15, when the lunch crowd was winnowing down but still pretty busy. He was seated at a table for two by a window looking out on Forty-eighth Street.

I knew he was the killer when I looked into his eyes.

He laid out the whole problem right there in the open, with a hundred masticating clerks and secretaries jabbering around us about their bosses and sex lives and children.

Tamara and the boy, Thackery, had been kidnapped and Brown was demanding the execution of his rival.

It was hard for me to concentrate at first. After all, in my profession, Hush was like royalty.

"So?" he said after explaining his dilemma.

"Why not just kill Big Joe?" I asked, pretending that there was some equality between us.

"I would if I felt that Brown would keep his word. But he knows that I have to kill him for doing what he's done. He has to get rid of me, and then who would protect my family?"

"Okay," I said. "I'll do it."

"How much?"

"On the house."

That set the killer three inches back in his seat.

"Why?"

"Professional courtesy," I said and then I stood up on legs that have had easier times in the ring, sparring with heavyweights.

IT TOOK ONLY five hours for me to locate and liberate Tamara and Thackery. Carter could hide them from white eyes but it was easy for me to see beyond his blind of race. I called a guy I knew, the brother of one of Carter's ex-girlfriends. He told me of a safe house that Carter kept for "visiting dignitaries" like Colombian drug lords and Russian mobsters, Chinese slavers and Mexican cartel bosses who dealt in protection rackets for a broad spectrum of illegal labor.

I didn't feel guilty about betraying a brother. He had kidnapped a black woman and her child, after all. And Carter was a very bad man, worse than I ever was, so I didn't mind taking his living shields away.

Carter disappeared that very evening and Hush took his services off the market. He got a job working for an elite limo service and now chauffeurs around high-profile clients who might need protecting.

I crawled back into my son's bed at dawn and fell into a deep sleep with no fires or hidden assassins dogging my dreams. When I finally awoke it was a little after nine and the house was empty. I walked through the prewar rooms but no one was there. The kids were in summer school and Katrina was at the gym.

I went to work.

In a little cubbyhole that Twill had cut along the baseboard at the back of his closet I found a .22 pistol in a slightly battered cherry-wood box. The gun was unloaded, but there was a box of ammunition next to it. I considered confiscating the piece but thought better of it. Twill was too cunning for that to stop him for long, and, anyway, I had more than a week before he planned to commit his capital crime.

I MET HUSH in the gentrified meatpacking district just south of Fourteenth Street at 10:45. He usually drove the company Rolls but that day he was behind the wheel of a standard black Lincoln sedan. No need to call attention to ourselves when there might be mischief afoot.

I climbed in the backseat and he glanced up in the rearview mirror and into my eyes. I don't know what he was looking for but he seemed satisfied.

"What's the plan?" he asked.

"Moore says that the blackmailer wants him to bring the money to room C on the third floor at ten tonight. I want to bug the place and see what there is to be seen before that time."

The killer gave a short nod and turned the key in the ignition.

"I'm just the insurance," he said as we pulled away from the curb.

I saw no reason to corroborate a fact and so remained silent.

THE CONDEMNED APARTMENT house was a couple of buildings east of the West Side Highway, on the north side of the street. We parked at the far end of the block. I was told that there was a key behind a loose brick just above the mailbox, but Hush and I went around the back and broke in through the cellar door.

He was armed and so was I. The guns were in our hands. I used a penlight to guide us. The door to the studio apartment was open. A few errant beams of sunlight shot through the cracks in a boarded-up window. We glided in, scanned the room, and then I nailed a small block of wood on the sill of a window that looked out into darkness.

"Good place to kill somebody," Hush commented.

Those words sent a chill through my shoulders.

The dented and dirty block of unpainted wood had a transmitter embedded in it with a tiny fiber-optic lens peeking out like the tip of a nail. It was the kind of little addition that you'd never notice unless you were in the room every day.

WE MADE IT back to Hush's car and turned on the laptop that received the transmissions from Tiny's very special bug. The image of the dark room appeared and all we had to do was wait. If any motion was detected, a red light would start flickering at the bottom of the screen.

I sat in the backseat with the computer beside me. Hush stayed up front, as silent as dust.

There were little red flashes now and then, triggered by passing rats, but that was all.

At a little after one I started getting bored.

"How's it going, Hush?" I asked to cut the monotony.

He only turned his profile to me, but I could see the mild astonishment on his face. Nobody who knew Hush made small talk with him. After a moment he turned far enough to face me. At first his brows were knitted, but then he gave me a weak smile.

"I joined a monastery," he said.

While I was trying to figure out if this was an attempt at humor, he added, "I remembered when you told me about that meditation stuff and connected with a bunch of Zen Buddhists off the Grand Concourse in the Bronx. Black guys mostly."

Hush had once commented on my cool demeanor in rough situations. I told him about Zazen sitting.

"Does it help?" I didn't feel afraid but my pulse had quickened.

"Keeps me straight," he said. "Keeps me focused. They teach you how to sit for hours with your mind in another place. It takes some of the edge off."

I could only imagine what *edge* he was talking about.

Five minutes must have passed. He was still sitting with his back to the driver's-side door.

"I got my girl and son down on an island off the Carolina coast," he said, continuing our conversation. "Everything you need to know about them is in an envelope that I gave that lawyer of yours—that Breland Lewis. Don't worry, though, he won't know you know me until he opens the letter."

I hadn't given him Breland's name, never told him that I had a lawyer.

"I want you to look in on them from time to time if I'm incapacitated or dead," he added. "You'll have access to the funds they'll need. Tamara has to cosign, of course."

"Of course," I said, just to make it a conversation.

I suppose that was Hush's way of saying that he considered me a friend. It felt like having a king cobra slither up on the barstool next to you: you didn't necessarily like the company, but then again, you had second thoughts about any sudden motions, much less getting up and walking away.

At 2:18 my cell phone made the sound of yipping hyenas.

"Hello?"

"Sanderson's awake," Carson Kitteridge said in my ear.

HUSH TOOK THE laptop in the front seat and I walked over to Tenth Avenue, where I hailed a cab.

The hospital they had Sanderson in was up in the Sixties on the East Side.

The man who should have been dead was on the fifth floor, with two strapping police guards on the door.

As I approached they got to their feet, forming a very effective blockade. I might have been nervous if I hadn't already fought and won against the monster that they were guarding.

"Off limits," the cop closest to me said. He had copper hair and skin so white it seemed to be turning green.

He put a hand on my shoulder.

"Get yer fuckin' hand off me, son," I said. Don't ask me why. Maybe it was all the tension from being in such close quarters with a commercial serial killer for the better part of four hours.

"What?" the bright penny said in warning.

"It's okay, Landis," Carson Kitteridge said. He was coming out from the hospital room. "LT here has a thin skin. Breathe on him hard and he feels it."

Landis was six feet tall, so he had to look down to peer into my eyes. He didn't like me. Maybe I should have given him a number and asked him to stand on line.

"Shall we?" Kitteridge said, indicating the room behind with a twist of his head.

"I wanna talk to him alone," I said.

This time he shook his head.

"Nice talkin' to you, then." When I moved my shoulder in preparation to leave, Landis spoke again.

"Stay right where you are."

"Say what?"

"You heard me."

"Tell me something, boy," I said slowly and clearly. "Didn't your mother ever tell you that children should be seen and not heard?"

The green undershade of the cop's complexion was turning pink.

"Stand down, Landis," Carson said. And then to me, "Okay, LT. But I wanna know what you get."

THERE WERE LIFE-SUPPORT machines in the private hospital room but they weren't hooked up or turned on. Sanderson had two IVs dripping medicine and sustenance into his veins and two strawlike oxygen tubes that he'd pulled away from his nose. He was sitting up against a few pillows, staring at me. His left hand was shackled to the metal bed frame. I remember wondering if that short span of chain was enough to hold the monster.

The gash on his forehead was already closing up. It was the first time that I got a good look at what I like to call *the face of the man's personality*.

It was the bloated visage of a petulant boy but I wasn't fooled; I had felt that boy's strength and murderous intent.

Rather than slaughter, there was now wariness in Willie's eyes.

He was looking for the thirty-odd-pound chair upside his head. I could see that, just in our fight, I had only one chance with him.

"They got you on the Roger Brown killing," I said before sitting in the chair next to his mechanical bed. I noted that Kitteridge had placed the seat out of the killer's reach. "They also know about Norman Fell."

Only the quick darting of his eyes told me that he was surprised at the mention of the Albany detective.

"I went up to see Bunny at the sanitarium," I added.

"He put her back in there?" he said.

I must have reacted in some way, shown an eagerness or something, because he clamped down after uttering those few words and nothing I could do would open him up again.

I told him that turning against the people that hired him would lessen his sentence by half a lifetime and that the law would otherwise likely go heavy on him because he'd already committed one murder and gotten away with it. I made a dozen threats and suggestions but he remained mute.

You don't have to be smart to be tough-minded. As a matter of fact, the combination of stupidity and silence might be the greatest weapon in the history of our species.

"WHAT'D HE SAY?" Kitteridge asked when I exited Sanderson's hospital room twenty minutes later.

"Not a damn thing."

"How do you read it, LT?"

"It has to have something to do with the two men getting killed," I said. "Thurman is the key, that's for sure."

I let those last words hang in the air because it occurred to me that the cop should have identified the illiterate PI by then. And if Kitteridge knew who he was, then he also knew he was dead.

"Yeah," the detective said. "You got any more on him?"

"He hasn't called me, if that's what you're asking."

"Anything else you remember about him?"

"No."

"No," Kitteridge said, echoing me ominously.

"I guess I better be going," I said.

"Where to?"

"A case."

"Connected?"

"I sure hope not."

"Okay, then," Kitteridge said. "I'll be seeing you soon."

I wasn't looking forward to that, either.

It was a nice day and I was loath to go back into the close atmosphere with Hush. So I went to a deli on Seventh Avenue and had pastrami on rye with raw onions and hot French mustard. I didn't order fries, but as long as they came with the meal I felt an obligation to eat them.

I got back to the Lincoln just before four. My knock on the darkened glass of the limo was answered by the click of the locks releasing.

I climbed into the backseat and Hush handed me the laptop.

"I had to power it up with the cigarette lighter," he said. "It should have a few hours now."

And so we sat, the semi-reformed hit man and me.

"IT COSTS EIGHTEEN thousand dollars to make a body disappear in Manhattan or most of the boroughs," Hush said a little over an hour later. "Some parts of New Jersey, too. There's a discount for Staten Island. You kill somebody in Staten Island and it's only fifteen thousand. Guy named Digger can be anywhere in the city in two hours or less."

"Why are you telling me this?" I asked.

"I thought maybe you'd like to know," he replied dispassionately. "You've got to be in some serious trouble if you called on me. Serious trouble might need serious help. With somebody like me on the case, Digger just naturally jumps to mind."

"I don't need him," I said with as much certainty as I could muster.

AT A QUARTER to five I took a small briefcase and made my way toward the back of the building, where I was supposed to meet Timothy Moore's blackmailer.

I went to apartment C on the fifth floor and turned on my second computer. I tuned in to the boring transmissions from two floors below and settled in.

"I'm in," I said into the Bluetooth phone hooked around my left ear.

"I hear you," Hush replied.

And for the next hour or so nothing happened. I sat in the darkened room with my screen focused on another, even darker, room.

It was eerily peaceful sitting there in the gloom, staring at an image of darkness. There was no sound to distract me and no image to divert my attention. I was wide awake, fully aware, but in a stasis of sorts. I wasn't thinking about anything, and that was a continual relief, like the monotonous beauty of a cascading waterfall.

"THERE'S THIS BIG guy who looks kinda familiar and the one you showed me the picture of walking up the stairs," Hush said at seven minutes past six.

"Timothy Moore?"

"If that's the picture you showed me."

A few minutes passed and a bright flare burned its way into the room on my computer screen. Two murky figures were revealed by the backwash of radiance from the big utility flashlight. One of the figures closed the door, turned on a portable fluorescent lantern, and then doused the flashlight. There was Timothy Moore in a black, long-sleeved T-shirt and black pants, along with a bigger guy, also in dark clothes. They looked around the room, seemed satisfied at what they didn't find, and then set up little aluminum-and-nylon stools facing the door. The big guy then took a black sack from a shoulder strap hanging on his left side and began to assemble a stripped-down rifle. I couldn't tell the caliber because the fiber-optic lens wasn't that clear. It was like watching an old-time TV show that had been captured on ancient decaying videotape.

The men were speaking, but my bug didn't come with a microphone. I didn't need sound to gauge their intent, however.

"What's happening in there, LT?" Hush asked.

I told him.

"You got thirty-six thousand dollars?"

"No."

"Wanna borrow it?"

"No."

"Well, come on down," he said. "Let's go get us some steaks."

"I want to wait and follow 'em," I said.

"No need. I remember the big guy. His name is LouBob Georgias. He used to do work with the unions."

"You know where to find him?"

"If he's in the life, I can find him any hour of the day or night."

"Okay. I'm comin' down."

ON SEVENTY-SEVENTH near Columbus there was a steakhouse called Riff's that I'd never heard of. They had bone-in rib eyes that were aged for forty-five days. I ordered a scotch and soda to wash it down. Hush had plain water with no ice to accompany his steak and baked potato.

We hadn't talked much on the way up, nor did we speak through most of the meal.

"So tell me about this LouBob," I said after we'd both refused dessert.

"A brawler," Hush said. "Made his way in by getting into fights. I never took him for a pro."

"How do you know him?"

"He was a bodyguard for a guy I had paper on once. Later on we met when I was introduced to his boss's boss's boss. He was standing at the outside gate upstate somewhere." Hush said. "While you were coming down I called a guy I know and he told me where you can find LouBob most nights."

"They were going to kill me," I said.

"Yeah. Sure were."

The check came and I paid.

FROM THE RESTAURANT we went to a place called Little Ron's Piano Bar on the ground floor of an apartment building looking out on Central Park West. Hush got us seats in a corner against the wall where we had a good look at the bar.

The piano man was practicing his Fats Waller so I was happy with my scotch.

Hush then engaged me in unexpected small talk. He knew I liked boxing and so asked me what odds I gave the light heavyweight Antonio Tarver against the man who currently held the title, Chad Dawson.

"Tarver's almost forty," I said, "past his prime. Dawson is younger and fast, but he's also a natural middleweight. It's a toss-up."

Hush and I had to maintain a conversation so as not to look suspicious. I kept it up but it felt spurious, like trying to concentrate on a leopard's spots when he's leering down at you from an overhead branch.

Relief from this torture came when LouBob Georgias walked

in at a little after eleven. He was wearing a green suit and a black hat with a yellow feather in it. He was very big, as broad and as tall as Willie Sanderson. He had a friendly face and smile. He joked with the bartender and the waitress who had served us.

"Want to brace him outside?" I asked.

"Just wait," Hush said.

Maybe a quarter of an hour later a voluptuous brunette came through the front door. In her late twenties, she had a figure that certain men and most twelve-year-old boys dream of. Her dress, what there was of it, seemed to be made from multicolored confetti, and her tanned skin glowed like rose gold.

LouBob put his hand at the small of her back and lifted her off the ground to give her a sloppy kiss. Every eye in the bar was on them. Even the piano man missed a note or two.

Our conversation had ended with the entrance of the woman. Hush was watching them like a cat. I sat back and studied my friend, hoping to learn something beyond my ken.

LouBob and the woman settled at the bar and ordered drinks.

They were on their third round when Hush said, "Come up on the other side of him after the girl leaves."

He got to his feet and walked toward the bar.

Once again I had the picture with no sound. Hush walked up behind LouBob. For a moment I was afraid that he was going to come out with his pistol and shoot the guy behind the ear. It was an irrational panic that subsided after he tapped the big man's shoulder.

The fright moved from me to LouBob when he saw Hush standing there in his medium-black suit and thin green tie. My would-be killer's spine seemed to freeze, and the brunette became curious.

LouBob said something to the woman and she reacted angrily. Hush didn't seem to notice and LouBob turned away. A moment later the woman stormed out of the bar. Hush gave her the briefest glance as she left. It struck me that the ex-assassin got some sort of sadistic pleasure out of humiliating the big man in front of his woman. I filed that little bit of information away and then went over to flank LouBob Georgias.

"Hey, Hush, LouBob," I said when I rolled up on the other side of my would-be killer.

Georgias gawped at me openmouthed but didn't say anything.

"This is my friend Leonid McGill," Hush said and the fear in LouBob's eyes deepened.

The big man was still looking at me while he addressed Hush. "I didn't know he was your friend, man."

"Sit down," Hush said and we all three perched on gilt-and-red-vinyl barstools.

"Can I get you guys something?" the bartender asked from somewhere off to my right. He'd come up from the other end of the bar when he noticed our approach.

"Three black Russians," Hush told him. I think he meant that as some kind of joke about my name.

The bartender, a white man who was maybe sixty and had spent some time in the sun earlier in life, moved back a bit when he observed the deadness in Hush's eyes.

"You got it," he said.

"What's Timothy Moore's real name?" I asked LouBob.

"Far as I know that is his real name."

"Tell us about him," Hush said.

"He, he did a nickel in Attica for bein' stupid, and since then he's worked for this rich guy now and then, doin' odd jobs. He's got a straight job somewhere too, in an office, I think."

"What's the rich guy's name?" I asked.

"I dunno. He never said. We met over this union beef his boss had. It was a strike gonna come down with the hotels before a big convention. We was supposed to talk this guy into puttin' it off. I never knew who hired him. He just said he did work for a rich guy. A rich guy. I don't know his name."

LouBob was sweating but I didn't feel any contempt for him—Hush's stare would open the pores of anyone who had sense.

The bartender came up and put the three drinks down and left without a word.

When he was gone I asked, "How much?"

"For what?" LouBob stammered.

"How much they pay for you to kill me?"

"Six, sixty-five hundred."

"Dollars? Not even euros? You'd end a man's life for pocket change?"

LouBob swallowed hard but stayed silent.

"Where does Tim live?" Hush asked then.

LouBob rattled off an address about a hundred and fifty blocks to the north.

"You got a house on the beach north of Miami, don't you, Lou?" the assassin said.

"Yeah?"

"You look pale. I think you should fly down there—tonight. And listen, don't make any phone calls. None. You hear me?"

"Yeah. I hear ya, Hush."

It was very quiet up in Washington Heights at that time of night. We drove past the address that Lou-Bob had given us, then parked a few blocks away. We sat there for some time, waiting for the night to deepen.

At half past one we sauntered down the street like strollers on a Sunday afternoon. We were both armed, but that was okay. Even if the cops stopped us we had licenses for our guns.

The only sound on Moore's street was somebody laughing in a park down near the water.

No cars passed by.

Tim had a pied-à-terre on Loquat Street, on the third floor of a turquoise monolith that stood over the Hudson.

People like Moore were chameleons: they hid in plain sight. He didn't have extra locks on his door or go under a pseudonym. He was the one that sought you out, put a black mark on your mailbox or gave you a suitcase full of cash, and then had someone else shoot you when you walked into the room. He lived so close to the line of respectability that he made the mistake of thinking that he was a civilian: safe in his own home, under his own name.

I PRESSED HIS BUZZER, 3A, and waited. Hush stood away from the front of the building just in case there was an electric eye that we hadn't seen.

"Who is it?" Timothy asked a minute or so later.

"McGill."

"Do you know what time it is?"

"I got a problem, Mr. Moore."

"Can't it wait?"

"No. I been mugged."

"How'd you get my address?"

"Cop I know let me use his official browser. They had it because of your prison sentence."

"You went to the police?" Tim Moore said.

"I got mugged, man. They stole all the money. Don't worry about it, though. The cops just think I was doing a business deal for you."

"What do you want?" he asked again.

"Let me up."

There was a hesitation. I had given him a lot of information. I'd lost his seed money and talked to the cops, mentioning his name. I already knew where he lived and so had a way of getting to him.

While he was thinking over his options I saw a small wooden wedge on the concrete outside the outer door of the double-doored entrance. People must have used that little hardwood triangle from time to time when they were moving in their furniture and large appliances.

I picked it up.

"Okay," Tim said. "Come on, then."

He buzzed the outer and inner doors only long enough for me to go through one and race the eight feet to grab the other. Hush stayed outside so as not to be seen. He couldn't make it to the outer door in time but that was okay. I just walked halfway down the hall toward the elevator and doubled back to prop the inner door open with the mover's wedge, and then opened the outer door for Hush.

We took the stairs at a quick pace. At the third floor, I made my way down toward 3A while Hush stood just inside the stairwell.

I knocked on the door and it opened immediately. Now there were only four inches of chain separating me from my killer.

"What do you want?" he asked.

"Open up, Tim," I said. "I need some answers."

"Answers about what?"

"Who did you tell about the money?"

"No one. Why?" The wiry little guy wore an emerald-green robe over purple pajamas. He was nervous, and also confused, trying desperately to work out what my being at his door meant. I noticed that his right hand was hidden from view.

"Somebody knew. He came up behind me on my way to the meet, slammed me in the back of the head, and stole the briefcase."

While I spoke Hush moved in accordance with his name. When he was a foot to my right I slammed my shoulder against that door. The chain broke and the door swung open—fast. Moore didn't have time to yelp. He was knocked senseless, sprawled out on the floor while Hush and I rushed in, me retrieving the pistol the point man had dropped and Hush securing the door.

I picked Tim up by his shoulders and threw him into a big yellow chair. Hush moved through a doorway to our right and I checked out the space we were in.

The sofa chair was the only seat in the room. It was placed in front of a seventy-two-inch plasma TV with a small table on the side. The floor was made from wide, dark slats of wood and was heavily sealed.

Moore moaned in the chair and slid down. I let him slump onto the floor. I wasn't concerned about posture or propriety.

The assassin came back in, telling me with a quick gesture of his head that there was no one else in the apartment.

I was somewhat troubled that we worked so well together.

Hush squatted down in front of our target and pinched his cheek until the skin was bright red.

Moore's eyes came open and fear filled them to the brows.

Hush showed him his pistol.

"We are going to talk," he said. "Understand?"

Moore nodded.

"Get in the chair," I ordered, partly to wrest control of the interrogation from Hush.

Tim was a little unsteady getting up but he made it.

"You were trying to have me killed," I said in a markedly pleasant tone. "Why?"

"I wasn't—"

"Don't finish that sentence. Don't lie. I am all out of patience. Just answer my question and maybe you'll see another day."

Moore burped loudly. It had a wet sound to it.

I could see a dozen lies forming and dissipating behind his eyes.

Hush settled on the arm of the big chair, holding his pistol almost carelessly. This pose might have seemed unprofessional, but I could see the ever-growing concern in Moore's eyes. Something about Hush reeked of finality.

Mr. Hush's wasn't the only scent. Moore's sweat was, if anything, even stronger than it had been in my office.

I noticed a small picture frame standing on the little table. It was a photograph of the woman that Moore had in his wallet.

"Hull," Tim said and then he burped again. "Roman Hull."

Finally . . . something that made sense.

"How's that work?" I asked.

"He, he called me and said to be ready."

"And?"

"A delivery service dropped off a box about fifteen minutes later. There was this cell phone in it. Maybe fifteen minutes more and I got a call."

"From Roman?"

"I don't know. I don't think so. It was another voice. They offered me a whole lot of money. A whole lot." He emphasized the last words as a kind of explanation. After all, wouldn't I kill him for the kind of money he was suggesting?

"How do you know Hull?" I asked.

"A long time ago I used to be his driver sometimes. He kept in touch with me when I was in Attica. After I got out he'd give me jobs now and then."

"Where's the cell phone?"

"Same guy came and picked it up an hour later. He left me the briefcase, too."

Hush sat up and Timothy flinched.

"Just to get this straight," I said. "The money was to kill me."

The frightened man nodded.

"How do you get in touch with him?"

"I don't."

Hush stood up.

"Go on down to the car, LT," he said.

"Hey, wait!" Timothy pleaded. He cut off in mid-screech when Hush showed him a single finger.

"No," I said.

"Just step outside the door then," Hush offered.

"We're not here to kill anybody."

"But you heard him."

"I'm turning over a new leaf," I said. It sounds comical to me now, but I was deadly serious at the time.

"Me too," Hush replied, "but this man here tried to murder you. That's a death sentence."

"It's over now."

Maybe for me. But murder had been unleashed in Hush's nervous system and he needed time to let it work its way out. I stood very still while the slender merchant of death allowed the demon to sink back into his bones.

I don't think that Timothy Moore drew a breath.

"Call your friend LouBob," Hush said to Tim. "Ask him what he thinks you should do now that you're living when you should be dead.

"I'll meet you downstairs." These last words were from Hush to me.

He went out the door. I waited for a few beats and was about to follow when a thought occurred to me.

"Hey, Tim."

"What? What?"

"That picture on your table."

"What about it?" he said with the barest sliver of steel in his voice.

"That's Margot for real?"

"Yeah."

"She left you, huh?"

He nodded.

"Was it over an Asian girl named Annie?"

"Yeah."

The truth is always the best way to lie.

47

This time I sat in the front seat as Hush drove down toward Manhattan. Most of the way we rode in silence, but a few blocks from my door he began to speak in a voice so deep it seemed to be coming up from out of the ground.

"That was very unprofessional."

"Yeah. I know."

"Why didn't you let me kill him?"

"I don't kill people," I said. "I mean, I've done a lot of things . . . and some of them have ended up with people dying. But I steer clear of anything like that nowadays."

"Found religion?"

"No," I said. "It's just one day I realized something."

"What's that?"

"It's hard to explain. I mean, it's not a thing, it's a feeling."

"Like what?"

He pulled to the curb in front of my building.

"It's like you walk up behind somebody that you intend to kill," I said, trying to speak his language, I guess. "There you are with your gun pointed to the back of the man's head. You feel cold inside. It's just a job. And all of a sudden you aren't the man holding the gun but the one about to be shot. And you don't have any idea that there's somebody behind you, and all the days of your life have led you to this moment."

"So it's like you're killing yourself," the assassin intoned.

It felt as if I were instructing a newborn deity who was moments away from ascension.

Hush was staring at me. His eyes tightened.

"So, then, it felt like you were saving my life in there?" he asked.

"And mine."

Hush's laugh was a friendly thing, boyish and almost silly.

"I'll be seein' you, I.T.," he said.

I GOT OUT of the Lincoln and it rolled on its way.

I stopped at the door to my building, imagining going up to the eleventh floor, opening the door, taking off my pants before climbing into bed. Then I saw myself wide-eyed in the dark bedroom next to a woman who never understood me; a woman I could not trust. I think I must have stood there for some time before turning away and walking toward Broadway and the parking garage.

I RANG THE BELL multiple times and still had to wait fifteen minutes for the nighttime attendant to rouse himself from sleep in somebody's backseat.

ON THE WAY OUT to Coney Island I tried thinking about Roman Hull. He was the patriarch of the clan but, according to Poppy Pollis, Bryant ran the family business. Why would the old man order my murder? Had he been behind all the killings? And if so, why?

It was obvious that he'd done this kind of work before. The setup was almost seamless. Moore couldn't prove that Hull had called him, and after that he only spoke to a subordinate. The phone and the cash were probably untraceable.

The cash. I'd offered to split it with Hush but he turned it down. Now the money was mine. Like the gun that the me of my imagination used to commit murder-suicide, Roman Hull had thrown the money at his own backside.

AT 6:00 A.M. SHARP, A Mann walked out his front door with the dachshund on a different-color leash. In the pale morning the accountant was more pink than white, more a citizen than an individual. He waited at the red light at the end of his block, even though there wasn't a car on the road as far as you could see.

The accountant ambled down the street as steady as a toddler but with dignity and purpose.

I was beginning to like the man.

I watched him until he'd turned a corner and then I began thinking about how to go against a billionaire who had links to the unions and, at least to a degree, to the mob.

Maybe I should have let Hush kill Moore. That would have sent a clear message to Roman.

My right eye started blinking. There was no itch or irritation, just a repetitious wink that got faster. The left eye joined in with the beat and before I knew it I had drifted off into a light, semiconscious doze.

The sun shone on my face, and so the darkness of my closed eyes was lightened by solar radiance. This crimson glare seemed almost to have a sound, a humming that caught the syncopation of a kind of buzzing. It felt like I could almost count the beats.

My head nodded and then lifted up abruptly.

It was seventeen minutes later and A Mann was waddling back toward his front door.

Could I let him die?

My phone let out a cry of gibbering monkeys.

"Hey, Tone," I said after the third repetition of my ancestors' chattering.

"Where's my accountant?"

"I caught a glimpse of him yesterday afternoon."

"Where?"

"Saratoga. He was betting on a nag."

"Where is he now?"

"I don't know. He knew somebody who worked there and they took him into the offices. He was with this blonde that would set you back twenty-five hundred dollars a night."

"You lost him?"

"Yeah. But that doesn't matter. I know his tastes and I got a line on the blonde. It might cost me twenty-five hundred but I think I can get to him through her."

"I don't care how much you have to spend," The Suit said. "I need to get to A Mann."

"No more than a couple'a days, Tony," I said.

"He spend a lotta time at the track?"

"He was there yesterday."

"That's funny. 'Cause, you know, Mann didn't seem like the gambling type."

"Maybe it's the blonde pullin' him by the nose."

"Maybe. What's her name?"

"She called herself Amelia but that was just a dodge," I said, biting my lip so as not to trip on it. "I'll have something for you in a couple'a days."

"All right. But stay in touch."

"Tony."

"What?"

"You ever heard of a guy named Roman Hull?"

"No. He have something to do with Mann?"

"Uh-uh," I grunted. It was worth a try. "It's this other thing. Don't worry, though. Mann is number one on my list."

"With a bullet," the gangster added.

I WAS HALF the way back to Manhattan when the phone gibbered again.

"Yeah?"

"Hello, Leonid," Harris Vartan said pleasantly.

"Mr. V," I said, wondering if it was my phone or Tony's that was bugged.

"How's it going with your searches?"

"What do you want from me?" Maybe I sounded a bit testy.

"You should never lose your composure, Leonid. Even when you've lost your temper you should not let it show. The boxer lives by such a creed, does he not?"

"Sometimes they carry him out on a stretcher."

"In the end we all go out that way."

No news there. I waited for further information.

"I'll be checking in on you, Leonid," Vartan said and the connection was broken.

48

My next stop was two blocks north and half a block west of Gracie Mansion: the directions Hannah had given me to her parents' New York City home.

It was a six-story red brick manor looming from behind a twelve-foot coral-painted stone wall that was quite thick and imposing. The gate was electric and there was no hiding from the rotating cameras that perched over it like mechanical birds of prey.

I stood across the street, trying to appraise my chances of making some headway. I was still armed and wide awake in spite of only having had a single fifteen-minute catnap in the previous thirty hours.

I didn't know who was in the house at the time. If Bryant was there I could tell him that his father tried to kill me, or maybe I should say that Norman Fell recommended me. I could tell him that I was a private detective looking into the deaths of three young men, including an old case concerning a certain Thom Paxton.

If Roman was there I could say that I was a friend of Timothy Moore and that I had an urgent message from him.

If the river were whiskey and I was a diving duck . . .

It never hurts to bide your time when there's an opportunity to do so.

Standing out there in the shadow of Hull's house, making peace with the fact that I had no idea what to say or why the crimes had been committed, I was still better off knowing that I didn't know than I would have been otherwise.

Understanding my ignorance, I crossed the street and pressed the cracked plastic button to the rich man's home.

I smiled up at the camera that watched me from a lens hole in the white, cast-iron gate. I was ready to argue, wrangle, wheedle, and whine at whoever challenged my admittance.

Instead a buzzer sounded and a voice ejaculated, "Come on in! I've been waiting for you for two days!"

I pushed and the heavy gate swung in on well-oiled hinges. After taking three steps I heard the portal slam shut behind me.

Inside I found a surprisingly large bright-green lawn that grew around a few dozen well-manicured rosebushes. The flowering shrubs had big generous blossoms of every color imaginable. Soon-to-be-extinct honeybees drifted lazily from one bloom to another, narcotized by the heavy aromas and rich pollen.

The stone pathway passed thirty feet or so through the unlikely Manhattan yard, bringing me to a marble stairway. This ascended eighteen steps to a very old, coffin-lid-like door.

I was looking for the dark barrier's buzzer when it swung open, with Hannah hanging on the doorknob, laughing for me.

"I bet you didn't expect me," she said.

Today she was barefoot in tight blue jeans and a dark-blue halter, with bits of glitter here and there, covering her small breasts.

"No," I agreed.

"But I knew that you'd be coming."

"Did you tell your father I'd be here?"

"No."

"Did you tell anyone?"

"Are you going to come in, Mr. McGill?" The multiple personalities of her upbringing and education were gone. She was just a sweet young girl, both vulnerable and fearless. I could see in her eyes that she now saw us as good friends that had passed through the gauntlet of her brother's episode.

She had marked my hesitation correctly. There was something about the ebullience exuding from Hannah that made me want to hang back, or maybe leave. Most guys when they see a damsel in her lonely tower want to ride up and save her—but I knew better. My kind of help shorted out the circuit board, or stripped the gears in your transmission.

She grabbed a couple of my fingers and pulled.

"Come on."

I allowed her to drag me into the palatial entrance hall. You couldn't call it an antechamber or foyer. It was a circular room, twenty feet in diameter, with a wide staircase that crawled up the walls for all six floors, ending at a skylight that sprinkled diffuse sunbeams down on this otherworld. The continuous banister made the spiral seem like the lofty box seats of a theater, with the floor as the stage.

In the center of the room was a round mahogany table with a magnificent bouquet of at least a hundred freshly cut flowers arranged in a way that made you feel you were peering into a rain forest or jungle. The florist had to be some kind of genius.

My awe surpassed itself when a huge, pure-yellow parrot of some kind shrieked and flew out from the tangle of foliage. The bird flew up to the sixth floor and perched on the rail under the glass roof.

"That's Bernard," Hannah said, using proper English pronunciation. "He's my mother's pet. Daddy wants him in a cage but she says that he has to fly free. The staff is always cleaning up after him."

Bernard screamed again and then flew somewhere else in his private multimillion-dollar aviary.

"Come on," the woman-child said.

She led me down a wide hallway that was more like a gallery in an art museum. The paintings here were Impressionist and Post-impressionist masterpieces. There was a Cézanne that I had never seen before, also a Modigliani that was new to me.

I'd spent a lot of my adolescence in art museums—there and the boxing gym with Gordo. I couldn't draw to save my life but I appreciated the stylized chaos that artists of the late nineteenth and early twentieth century wrought.

At the end of the hall, in a little recessed area on the left, was a very small painting by Paul Klee. It was composed of red and yellow and gold boxes, with defining lines of cobalt here and there. On the right side, in the lower corner, there was a scribble done in a slightly lighter blue that might have been a squiggle becoming a man, or vice versa, and on the upper-left-hand side there was an oval, bisected face that maybe the squiggle-man had lost, or maybe it was the sun. It was the most arresting painting I had ever seen. While I stopped and stared, Hannah waited patiently.

"It's beautiful, huh?" she said after a minute or so of appreciative silence.

"Yes, it is."

"Do you want it?"

Yes, I did, but I didn't say so.

"You can have it," she offered in an offhanded way.

"It's priceless."

"No. My mother bought it for me for my twelfth birthday. I'd be happy to give it to you."

I believe that her slamming me in the head with a Louisville Slugger would have made less of an impact.

Material things never mattered much to me. My Communist father had made sure of that. Even though I was not a Marxist or an adherent of anarcho-syndicalism, I simply never gave much thought to possessions. Money paid the rent but it didn't drive my desires like it did for so many other property-hungry people in the West. I didn't have a favorite ring or watch. There was nothing that I saved up for that didn't have a practical use. I had been like that my entire life, but there I was in that hallway, on the outskirts of old age, and Hannah's offer made me feel like a child who still had everything to learn.

"Wow," I said. "You know, that might be the best offer I've ever had."

"So you want it?"

"Can we go sit down now, Hannah?"

"Sure," she said, shrugging lightly as if her responsibilities and that mausoleum of a house did not weigh on her at all.

Three Hispanic women in black-and-white maid uniforms were working in the big kitchen that we traveled through. The women were different shades of brown and of various ages, heights, and sizes. The only thing that they had in common was that they all spoke Spanish. If I were more sensitive to foreign intonations I might have discerned different accents among them because they certainly were not all from the same country.

The ladies shot worried glances at us, obviously wondering if I was some kind of threat to the child or them. I have that effect on people often.

Hannah was oblivious to the servants' concerns. She brought us to a swinging aluminum door and ushered me through. This led to a short hallway, which ended at a small, lavender-colored oval room that had a bay window looking out over a small vegetable garden, another anomaly for a Manhattan home.

The room was furnished with two stuffed chairs covered in well-worn and cracked brown leather. The floor was pine, pitted, and somehow fitting for a room where the masters were never meant to be. I sat in one chair while Hannah settled across from me, in half-lotus.

It took me a moment or two to get my head back into the investigation. I had taken the past few minutes for myself. I was very happy in the presence of the child bearing precious gifts, in that small room, under the only sun that any one of my ancestors had ever known.

"How's Fritz?" I asked.

"He stayed upstate."

"Did he recover okay from that spell?"

"He's walking and talking again, if that's what you mean. He didn't remember what happened. He didn't remember you. And no, I didn't tell anyone that you had been to the house. I thought that you wanted to talk to my father and I didn't want to get in the way. Though I would like to know more about what it is that you want."

"Do you really own that painting?" I asked.

"Yes."

"Have you ever offered to give away anything like that before?"

"You mean something so valuable?"

I nodded.

Hannah's face was long and pretty in its youth, but when she concentrated, it took on a more handsome cast. I liked her in spite of all my upbringing.

"No," she said finally. "Never. But what does that have to do with my question?"

"A guy from Albany hired me to find four men," I said. "I found them. One was dead, another one was in prison, one was awaiting trial for burglary, and the last guy was living the life of an honest citizen. I turned over the information and the three survivors were attacked. Two are dead and the other might be soon. After that, somebody, or maybe two different somebodies, tried to kill me.

"I don't want to be used in that manner. I don't want people to die because of me, and I myself do not wish to be killed. And so I have been investigating, trying to find out who was using me. The detective who hired me doesn't seem to exist, but I'm good at what I do, and I came up with a name."

"What name?" Hannah asked.

"Roman Hull."

"My grandfather?"

I nodded again.

"I'm telling you this because you offered me that painting, and also because it's true. I may have left out a detail or two but you have the gist of why I'm here."

Hannah brought her fingers to her temples and traced little circles there.

"Are you going to kill my grandfather?"

"People like me don't kill people like him," I said. "I just want to get to the truth. I want to know what happened and I want it to stop."

"Grandfather Roman used to pinch me and Fritzie when we wouldn't do what he told us to," she said. "It got so bad that Dad wouldn't let him see us until we were teenagers.

"They say he murdered this race car driver a long time ago and then he married the driver's widow. They didn't stay together long, though."

"I've heard the stories."

"He's upstairs," she said.

"Right now?"

It was her turn to nod.

"Can I go see him?"

"I will take you," she said solemnly, as if the words were a vow.

WE MADE OUR way back through the kitchen. The domestics were gone.

I glanced at the painting I coveted as we passed through the hall of masterpieces. The yellow parrot screeched somewhere when we came into the grand entrance hall but I didn't see it.

"He's on the third floor," Hannah told me as we mounted the stairs.

Upon reaching the second floor we had to walk around the outer hall to get to the next stairway up. There were doors and other entrances along the hallway leading into rooms and down corridors. At the door closest to the next set of stairs a woman wandered out.

"Wandered" is the right word. She stepped from the doorway, moving at an odd angle with her head turned as if she were looking behind. It seemed as though she had gotten lost in her own home.

"Mother," Hannah said.

Startled, the woman turned to regard us. She was a creature of exceptional beauty. From the form of her face to the deep blue in her eyes this woman, who was my age, would always be plagued by the petty desires and jealousies of others. Her form was slender and graceful. The pastel violet of her diaphanous robe struggled to match such beauty. Her hair was blond, becoming ethereally light with the white that had begun its encroachment there. When she gazed into my eyes I felt the need to swallow.

"This is Mr. McGill," Hannah was saying. "He's here to see Granddad."

Hannah's mother rested three fingers on the back of my left hand.

"Are you a friend of Roman's?"

"No, ma'am. A guy I know said he wanted to talk to me. A guy named Timothy Moore. Do you know him?"

"I don't think so," she replied.

Hers was the only smile I'd ever seen that I would call resplendent.

"I hear you once had a servant named Sanderson," I said, looking for answers haphazardly like a child searching for seashells by the shore.

"Yes. Lita was her name."

"Did she have a son named Willie?"

"She had children," Mrs. Hull said. "I never met them, though. Bryant didn't like it when the staff used our house for day care."

"But didn't your husband help Lita's son get into the Sunset Sanatorium?"

All those words seemed to confuse the lady. She sniffed at the air but didn't answer.

"I met Mr. McGill up at the house in Albany, Mom," Hannah said to break the silence.

"Oh?" She had a mild interest. "Did you also meet my son, Mr. Mac? Mick?"

"McGill," I said, wondering when she would remove her fingers. "And yes, I did meet him."

"What did you think?"

"Nice young man. Serious."

"He's sullen and ungrateful," she said, her lightness suddenly shot through with storm. "But blood is blood."

"I have a son like that," I said. "He doesn't know how to talk to people even though he's twenty-one. I figure it's just because his feelings are so deep down inside him."

My words seemed to have an impact on her. Her face organized itself so that she almost saw me.

"Deep inside," she echoed. "Yes, yes. You're right about that. Bryant says that there are debts to be paid, but all debt comes down to blood, don't you think?"

I didn't know the answer to her question.

"Blood debt," she continued, "is the curse of mankind."

"We have to go, Mother," Hannah said.

Mrs. Bryant's fingers were still on the back of my hand.

"Yes," she said, looking deeply into me. "It was so nice meeting you."

I moved my hand and took a step back.

"Come on," Hannah said.

Halfway up the stairs I looked back and saw that Hannah's mother was watching us as if in a terrible rapture.

We made our way to the third floor without any more interruptions or a word spoken between us. Hannah's natural élan seemed dampened by her mother's beauty and peculiar ways.

We came to a black door with a small wreath of dried yellow sweetheart roses hung from it. Hannah gave me a sickly smile.

"My grandfather's room," she said. "He told Fritzie that a black door and yellow roses will keep any curses away."

I nodded and we both looked at the door.

"Your mother seems distracted."

"This is one of her good days."

I smiled.

"You think it's funny," she said with no emotion that I could discern.

"My whole childhood I dreamed about living in a house like this," I replied.

"What do you think now?"

The parrot cried out and flew over our heads just then and we both laughed.

Hannah took a step forward and knocked on the ritualistic portal.

One of the maids from the kitchen opened the door a crack and stared out nervously.

"This is Mr. McGill, Rosa. He's here to see my grandfather."

"I don't know, Miss Hannah," Rosa said with very little accent. "Your grandfather is resting."

"Who is it?" a man's voice bellowed from beyond the olive-and-gold-skinned woman.

"Miss Hannah," Rosa said, turning her head back to the room.

"What she want?"

"She brought a man to see you."

"Show him in, then, girl," the unpleasant and very masculine voice commanded.

I became aware of recorded piano music. The composition had no style to it. It wasn't jazz or classical or even elevator covers of pop tunes—just notes strung together in tight mathematical patterns with no heart.

Rosa stepped away, giving me the room to enter. At the same moment, Hannah took a step backward.

I looked at my young friend with the question on my face.

"I never go into Grandpa's room," she said.

I've gotten less information out of month-long investigations.

IT WAS DIM and hot in Roman Hull's cavernous room. There was a cloying sweet smell in the humid air, accompanied by that relentless, soulless music. When the door shut behind me an irrational flash of panic pulsed in my chest. I saw no windows. The space was set up like a studio apartment cut into quarters. The area to my immediate right was a hot-plate kitchen with shelves and a small table set for one. To the left was an office with an oak desk and a plush red chair. Deeper in, there was a den or library on the left and a sleeping space on the right.

Only the makeshift bedroom was inhabited. There before the bed sat an old man in an ornate electric wheelchair. He would have been tall if he stood up. His face was cadaverous and sunken. He might have once been a white man but now he was gray with all the inferences that came with that color.

Next to him, sitting in a pine folding chair, was a small hard-eyed woman definitely from below Mexico. She wore clothes that were neither made nor sold on this continent, fruit blues and blood reds made from coarse cloth and a purple scarf that wrapped around her head and chin. Her Indian blood had not yet been conquered by the Spanish invaders, and if you had asked me what she was doing there I would have said, without hesitation, "Waiting for death."

Golden-hued Rosa stood behind his chair.

"You here to see Bryant?" the gray man asked.

He wore bright-yellow pajamas that reminded me of the wild bird shitting in the hallway, and fat Toolie sweating in prison. There was a maroon blanket across his lap.

"No," I said, covering the seven steps that separated us. "I came to see you."

"What business could a Negro in a bad suit have with a man like me?" he asked. He squinted and smiled when he spoke. His teeth were gray also.

Regardless of these facial expressions, the only life left in Roman's body was in his eyes. They were a standard brown with a feral, hateful light burning brightly from behind. If I was a superstitious man I'd have thought I was in the presence of Beelzebub's consigliere.

"Timothy Moore," I answered, now standing over him. "My name is Leonid McGill."

I expected at least a little fear behind those satanic eyes. But Roman wasn't going to crumple that easily.

"Rosa, Margarita," he said while staring up at me, "give me and Mr. McGill a few minutes alone."

The women moved without hesitation or complaint. Fifteen

seconds after his request they were gone, leaving the menfolk behind to play their ridiculous games.

"Sit, Mr. McGill," Roman said, gesturing toward the chair that Margarita had vacated. "That was the right word, right?"

"Sit?"

"Negro. You people still call yourselves that sometimes, don't you?"

"I'm here about your interest in my well-being," I said, "not terminology."

"Oh? Educated, are you? No pullin' the wool over your woolly eyes."

If we were in Missouri sometime before 1980 he might have riled me some.

I smiled.

"Why did you ask Timothy to kill me?"

"I used to know a man named Timmy but not any Moore, Moor," he said and then laughed.

"It's not funny, Roman. It's not funny and it takes more than bad puns to make me angry. What makes me mad is a man trying to kill me and I don't even know why."

The octogenarian shook his head and smiled.

"I can't help you, Moor," he said. "I never leave this floor."

I understood then. Roman was dying and he knew it. His life had been limited to that room, with strangers looking after him. His own granddaughter wouldn't come to visit him even when she lived under the same roof. My presence there represented a lifeline.

I shrugged and stood up.

"Where you going?" he asked.

I turned my back to him and took a couple of steps toward the door.

"Don't you want to know about Timothy Moore?" he called after me.

"You don't know anything," I said, not turning. "It must've been Bryant who made the call."

"Bryant doesn't have the balls to kill a man," Roman said in his strongest, most masculine voice. "I'm the one who gave him the thirty thousand to give you, and promised him a hundred more if he did the deed."

That bought him half a turn.

"Why?" I asked.

"Come back over here and sit your nigger ass down," was his reply.

I knew the cautionary rhyme of sticks and stones, but Roman was getting under my skin. I found myself wondering what my most excellent son Twill would have done in this situation.

Thinking of Twill brought a smile to my face. The anger dissipated and I returned to the servant's chair.

"Why do you want me dead, Mr. Hull? I never did anything to you."

"It was just business."

"What business?"

"The most important kind," he said. "Family business."

"Do I represent a danger to someone in your family?"

He was just about to tell me; I was finally going to get an answer to the reason for the murders my investigation had made possible.

"It—" Roman managed to say before the door to the room slammed opened.

"Dad," a man called.

Looking toward the light, I saw him coming. He wore a gray suit with a burgundy tie and hard-soled, oxblood shoes.

"Who are you?" he asked.

I stood up to meet the visitor because his demeanor was less than friendly.

He was taller than I, and white the way old paintings of American presidents are white. His hair was black and gray and his eyes tended toward brown. Behind him stood Rosa, behind her Margarita—Hannah brought up the rear. Her "never," I supposed, became "hardly ever" when her father preceded her into her grandfather's room.

"Leonid McGill," I said, holding out a friendly hand. "I was just asking your father a couple of questions, Mr. Hull."

"Get out of here," he said, not taking up my offer of greeting.

The women behind him were silent.

"Don't you want to know why I'm here?"

Roman was sniggering behind me. The piano music played like razor blades chipping away at my spine.

"No," Bryant Hull said.

I looked up at him, thinking that everybody I met seemed to be taller than I.

"It might be worth your while to hear me out."

"Leave my house or I will call the police."

I didn't have the time to go to jail right then, so I nodded and held my hands open at shoulder level in a sign of surrender. I was playing for time. Maybe he would ask a question in anger that would allow me the verbal foothold of a reply.

"Bryant," a familiar voice said. "Bryant, what's wrong? You sound angry."

Coming into the dark and masculine room was the impossibly feminine form of Hannah's mother. She glided up next to her husband.

They didn't seem to fit together—he a prefabricated manikin dressed and groomed to look like a billionaire, and she the Nordic interpretation of a Mediterranean goddess.

She placed her fingers on the back of his hand.

"Hannah," Bryant said.

"Yes, Dad?"

"Take your mother back to her room."

"But, Bryant," his wife said.

"Bunny, please just go with Hannah."

Bunny.

Roman had begun a rolling, heavy cough.

Margarita went to him.

Bryant turned to me and I was feeling as if Willie Sanderson had just unloaded one of his haymakers on the back of my head.

"Are you leaving?" the rich man asked.

"Oh, yeah," I said. "Absolutely."

I once read a monograph, written by a man named Harlan Victorious Lowe, called *Creativity and Quirks of the Mind.* The author claimed, among other things, that creative thought often happens in the mind's *peripheral vision*, when that metaphorical sight is jogged by obvious mainstream thinking. In other words—when one thing comes to light, the illumination often floods the dark corners with brightness.

Bunny was a blazing sun in the rabbit warren of my mind.

I jumped into a taxi two blocks from the Hull mansion and sat in the backseat, almost catatonic from the realizations as they bombarded me.

On the street in front of the Tesla Building I called Tiny the Bug.

"Yes, LT?"

"I want you to create me a website in somebody else's name," I said. "How many minutes will that take?"

"Five thousand dollars."

"That's money, not minutes."

"Thousand dollars an hour starting twenty seconds ago."

"Sold."

I gave him the details. He grunted twice, asked four questions, and then disconnected the line.

ONE OF MY REALIZATIONS was that I had no choice but to give Tony the Suit A Mann's address.

Back at my desk I placed the call.

"Yeah," a man, not Tony, answered.

"Lucas?"

"Who's this?"

"Leonid McGill."

"Oh," he said. The circumspection evinced by that single syllable told me that Tony was out of the loop as far as Vartan was concerned.

"What do you want?" Lucas asked softly.

"Peace in the Middle East and a brown-skinned president in the Oval Office. And, oh yeah, to talk to your boss about A Mann."

"What man?"

Somebody asked a question in the background and Lucas, the leg-breaker, covered the mouthpiece to answer.

Various muffled sounds ensured, and then Tony was on the line.

"This job is just between us, LT," were his first words, then, "What you got for me?"

"A man's neck size and address."

"Where do we meet?"

"You got my money?"

"You know I'm good for it."

"And you know how I work, Tony. After the job is done I get paid. Job is done and you haven't given me a dime. We haven't even agreed on a price."

"I thought you'd do it for a favor."

"No."

"You don't want to mess with me, McGill."

"Mess with you? I don't even wanna talk to you. But if we do talk I expect to get paid. Fifteen thousand dollars."

"Are you crazy?"

I broke the connection with my middle finger.

Sitting there, staring out the window at New Jersey, I wondered how many times I could get away with a move like that without getting myself killed. That brought a smile to my heart. I was alive, damn it, and that felt very, very good.

A colony of monkeys gibbered in my breast pocket.

"Yeah, Tone?"

"Okay," he said.

"Good. I'm real busy right at the moment. I'll call you tomorrow and tell you where you can give me the cash."

"Today."

"Tomorrow I'll call with a time and place. You bring the cash and I'll give you what you need."

I pressed the red button before he could complain.

INTUITION GUIDED MY next call.

The first number I called put me directly into voice mail telling me that that particular cell phone had been turned off.

Then I dialed the oldest number I know.

"Hello?" a tremulous voice answered.

"Mardi?"

"Hi, Mr. McGill."

"Let me speak to Twill, honey."

"Um . . ."

"It's important."

"He's not, he's not here."

"Not there? Where is he?"

"I don't know," she stammered.

I didn't need any peripheral creativity to worry about where he might be.

"Listen closely to me, Mardi," I said. "I know about your father, what he's done to you, and that you're worried about your sister. I know what Twill plans to do to him. But you don't have to worry about any of that anymore. I can take him down without you and my son going to prison. But you have to tell me where Twill is right now."

Silence.

"Mardi," I said. "Twill will spend the next twenty years in prison. You will, too. Who's going to take care of your sister if that happens?"

"He's . . ."

"Yes?"

"There's a street fair on our block this afternoon."

"I thought that was next week."

"Daddy got it wrong. He has to rush down to the Village to get the photographs he's selling. He should be back by now . . ."

I RACED DOWN to the street and caught a cab on Sixth. I gave the Pakistani driver a fifty-dollar bill and promised him another hundred if he could get me to the Bitterman block in under ten minutes.

We were maybe four minutes into the drive when I realized that I'd left my gun at the office. I considered turning around to get it but I couldn't see any reason for going after my son armed.

Hyenas yipped in my hand as we were crossing Seventy-ninth Street.

"Where are you?" I asked Carson Kitteridge.

"Downtown," he answered. "Why?"

"I gotta call you back."

"Sanderson's escaped," he said before I could switch him off.

"How could a man with a fractured skull stand up, much less escape?"

"Desperation."

We were nearing the Bitterman block.

"I gotta go, Carson," I said. I don't ever remember calling him by his first name before.

The street was blocked off, so I threw the hundred in the front seat and bolted from the cab. My foot hit the curb at an awkward angle and I went down, twisting my left ankle badly. But I got up and walked through the pain, just like Gordo taught me when I was a kid.

It was a bright sunny day and there were a thousand people milling and meandering down the center of the blocked-off street. I limped along, looking this way and that for my son.

My son.

I looked for him through racks of cheap jewelry, past the steam rising from a sausage vendor's kiosk, and across a cell-phone seller's cart. I bobbed up and down, moving in an erratic line past stacks of old *Life* magazines and piles of vintage vinyl albums.

I was bumping into people because of my awkward gait, handing out "Excuse me's" like a politician pressing palms and saying, "Glad to meet ya." I didn't want to call out Twill's name, just in case he shot the child molester before I got to him.

"Hey, watch out!" a man shouted. I think I might have stepped on his foot.

He pushed me as I was bringing weight down on my sore ankle and I fell. But that wasn't punishment enough for whatever insult I had inflicted. He reached down to grab me by my lapels. I concentrated on him for the moment. He was a white guy, in his early forties, with various tattoos on his muscular forearms and that part of his chest that was exposed by an open dark-blue shirt. I remember seeing a skull with a serpent coming out of its eye socket.

I clamped onto his decorated forearms and pushed with my good foot. When I was standing again, and he was understanding the strength of the hands crushing his arms, I saw a slender figure in a dark-green hoodie off to my left.

"Motherfucker!" my tattooed antagonist hissed.

I swiveled my hips, throwing him to the ground as I lunged toward the overdressed figure sporting the form and grace of my son.

"Twill, stop!"

When he swiveled his head to look at me the hood fell away. He had on a fabric skullcap, which threw me for an instant. Also, I had never seen that look on Twill's face—but I recognized it. He was a man but seconds away from a desperate and final act. I looked a little farther to the left and saw, behind a large flat folding table, the man I had heretofore only seen buggering little Mardi Bitterman on a computer monitor. Behind him was a canvas screen hung with colorful photographs of panda bears, zebras, and other creatures reminiscent of childish wonder.

Adrenaline is a miracle compound. It ramped through my system like Popeye's spinach or Captain Marvel's "Shazam!" This internal elixir reached my ankle, temporarily curing me and setting my feet in motion. I reached Twill in an impossibly short span, grabbing him by both arms because, among other gifts, my son is ambidextrous. He tried to pull away but one thing I had on him was strength.

"It's over, boy," I said.

A familiar smile twitched across Twilliam's lips.

"Hey, Pops," he said.

"Are you Twill McGill?" a man asked. Not just a man, but Leslie Bitterman. "Where's my daughter? I know that she's with you."

I don't know what he planned to do next but it didn't matter because I let go of my son and slapped Leslie hard enough to knock him on his ass. He was sitting on the curb, shaking his head to clear out the stars and cobwebs.

"Hey!" the white man who had pushed me down said.

He was coming right at me.

With my slap-hand I brought together his dark-blue shirt collar and pulled his face close to mine.

"I got a gun in my pocket and nothing to keep me from shooting you dead right here, right now."

I don't know if it was the words or the tone of my voice that convinced the guy but he fell back and melted away into the mass of unsuspecting humanity.

I took Twill by his right wrist and dragged him away from the street fair like an angry nanny might do with a naughty five-year-old. We didn't stop moving for six blocks.

"Dad. Dad!"

I realized that my mind had been racing ahead without me.

"What?"

"What's wrong with your foot?"

"My what?"

"You're limping."

His words, it seemed, brought the pain back into my ankle.

We were standing on the western sidewalk of the Natural History Museum. Twill led me to a bench there.

Willie Sanderson was on my mind. Where was he? Who would the monster kill next?

"Dad?"

"You don't have to worry about Mardi's father anymore," I said. "I know what he did to her and I'll take care of him. But you should have come to me, son. You should always come to me when you have a problem."

"Mardi didn't want anybody to know."

"There's no secrets between us, Twill. I would no more betray that girl than you would. Don't you know that?"

"I guess."

"And what kind of fool are you, planning to walk up to somebody and shoot him in broad daylight in front of a thousand people?"

"How'd you know I planned to shoot him?"

"Don't you think I know your hiding places, boy? And I'd have to be blind not to see what was goin' on with that girl. What I couldn't see was how making yourself a martyr in front of a street full of people was going to help."

"No, man," he said to me as if I were one of his school friends. "I had this." He pulled the fabric hat from his head. In his hand the woolen skullcap opened into a ski mask. "That way nobody could see my face and . . ."

Twill stood up and pulled the sweatshirt-hoodie up over his head. Underneath he was wearing an ugly but bright orange-red Hawaiian shirt festooned with images of pelicans and pineapples.

My irrepressible son grinned.

"I woulda walked away with the gun at my side and then pulled off the hoodie in an alley two blocks away. Then I'da made it into Central Park, where there's a rock I'd put the gun under."

It wasn't a half-bad plan. You'd have to be focused to pull it off, but Twill never had an attention deficit.

"Listen, son," I said in spite of how impressed I was. "You're smart and fearless. But you don't know everything. That man deserves anything he gets but not by you taking the law in your own hands. Killing is wrong and I don't want you involved with anything like that." Sometimes I marvel at the simplicity of communication between people who share closeness. I was raised on the Hegelian dialectic, but there is no love in that language.

"That's why you ran out there after me?" Twill asked, but I felt that there was another question on his mind.

"I'd die to protect you," I replied to the unspoken interrogative.

Twill sat there on the public bench, staring into my eyes. I have rarely felt closer to another human being.

After a moment he nodded.

"I'm sorry, Pops," he said.

I held out a twenty-dollar bill and said, "Grab a cab home and put the pistol in my office, in the desk."

"All right. But put that away. I got my own money."

It was going to be a long haul making sure that my son survived his own dark brilliance.

AFTER TWILL WAS GONE I caught a taxi of my own. I gave the Jamaican driver an address near Gracie Mansion and sat back. Now that Sanderson was free I thought I might be able to leverage some information out of BH. I closed my eyes and drifted for a minute or two. My telephone let out a loud bleep, telling me that it was nearing the end of its power.

I nodded a bit more and the hyenas began to yip.

"What?" I said into the invisible mouthpiece.

"We can't find Sanderson," Kitteridge said.

"What were the guards doing while he was escaping?"

"Knocked both of them out before they ever even knew he was there. Hit 'em in the head with some kind of bludgeon. I'm impressed that you laid him low when he was at full power."

"I'm just glad he didn't kill me."

"I wouldn't worry about Willie anymore."

"Why not?"

"Because once we catch him, and I promise you we *will* catch him, we've got all we need to send him to prison for life—or death."

"What do you have?"

My phone made another bleeping sound, telling me that the juice was almost gone.

"That's police business, LT."

"Come on, man. Yesterday you were telling me I was going to prison over Sanderson."

"Somebody had his lawyer call and tell us that Sanderson was trying to shake down his wife. Said that Sanderson had admitted to killing Brown and Tork. He also said that he'd called in a debt to make a hit on a Theodore Nilson in prison and that he murdered a guy named Norman Fell in Albany. This guy Fell is the one who said he was Ambrose Thurman."

Once again my heart was racing. Once again the phone bleeped.

"Was the guy who the lawyer was calling for Bryant Hull?" I asked.

Silence.

"Carson!"

"What do you know about this, LT?"

"Did you tell Sanderson about the charges?"

"Why do you care?"

That was the moment my battery chose to die. There was a clicking sound and then deadness.

I was thinking about Hannah's mother. If Sanderson thought that his Bunny had betrayed him he'd go straight for her.

"Driver."

"Yeah, mon?"

"I need to use your phone."

"The driver's phone is not for public use," he said. He probably said the same words a dozen times a day.

"This is an emergency."

"It always is."

"But this is a case of life and death."

"There's a phone booth on the corner. I can stop if you want me to."

There was no time for the pay phone, and if I got in a fight with the driver I would lose precious minutes. The only thing I could do was to keep on moving.

"I'll give you a hundred dollars, and you can make the call yourself."

"Keep your money, brothah. We'll be where you're goin' in a minute."

My father would have applauded such an upstanding working-class individual. I wonder what he would have thought of me.

THE FRONT GATE'S BUZZER was going when I got there. I found out later that when the home-emergency button is pushed, the gate stays open for the cops to come in.

My adrenaline supply was plentiful that day. I made it up the stone stairway with no difficulty. The door was connected to the security system, too.

Two of the maids were unconscious on the floor. A big black man in a dark cranberry suit looked like he was dead at the foot of the bouquet table. And Willie Sanderson was leaning over a woman's body, choking her, halfway up to the second floor.

Once again I was in motion. After three staggery bounds I leaped upon the killer's back and rained down fists upon his head and shoulders.

At first it felt as if I'd jumped on the back of one of Rodin's bronze masterpieces. Willie's body didn't even sag under the weight. But the accumulation of blows finally got to him. He stood up, throwing me off with the motion. I thought that he was going to come after me but instead he wobbled and then sat down, his back against the railing.

He was staring at me with disbelief on his face. I agreed with him. It made no sense that I could have beaten him even one time.

Sanderson closed his eyes as a thick trickle of blood snaked out from his left nostril.

I looked over at the body of Hannah Hull and made a sound that I didn't know lived inside me.

An overpowering exhaustion spread out from my chest all the way to my fingers and toes. The yellow bird fluttered up and landed between Hannah's lifeless form and her killer. My last conscious thought was that if Willie got up I was a dead man.

I don't remember the journey to the dimly lit and gray interrogation room. I just opened my eyes and found myself sitting there with elbows on the table and pain coming awake at various points in my body. My left foot felt tight in its shoe, and I had pulled an upper-back muscle somewhere along the way.

Willie Sanderson came into my mind and I had the fear of a boxer who connects with his best punches but his opponent keeps on coming, round after round. But the fright didn't last long. Sanderson was a reminder of the girl-child who had offered me a treasure. She was rich, but she had suffered, too. I was too late to save her. I caused less damage when I'd done piecework for killers and thieves.

I don't know how long I sat there or if those thoughts came quickly or slow.

The door to the room opened, allowing Bethann Bonilla and Carson Kitteridge to enter. She was wearing a buff-colored dress suit and he was clad in a shabby green, single-button two-piece that he had owned for at least the last five years.

The homicide sergeant's face was mostly impassive. She seemed distant and maybe just a touch confused. Carson's attempt at a poker face, on the other hand, could not mask the fact that he expected to win the pot.

They pulled up chairs opposite me and settled in.

I wondered if I could walk.

"Lana Hull," Kitteridge said. "Her first name is Veronica but I guess she prefers her middle name."

"That supposed to mean something to me?"

"Her maiden name was Maxwell, but she lived with a guy named Paxton for a while. Her son was Thom Paxton."

I didn't care. My face, I was sure, revealed that fact.

"We know that she hired a detective named Norman Fell to find the men who she blamed for her son's death." Carson could not repress the smile.

"That doesn't make any sense," I said.

"Why do you say that, Mr. McGill?" Bonilla asked.

"Kid died seventeen years ago. How come all of a sudden outta nowhere she's gonna start looking for those men?"

"She didn't know until recently," Carson said. "When Thom was young, just a boy, she was committed to a mental institution by her parents and the father of her child. They say she's a schizophrenic. Her boyfriend, Lloyd, moved away and kept the boy. Later on, when Thom died, the father, through Lana's mother, let her know that he'd succumbed to pneumonia. But when the father died, six months ago, he left a letter for Lana. In the letter he told her what he remembered about the boy's death. There was a letter of explanation from the detective in charge of the investigation.

"It wasn't much. But I guess it was enough for you to find them after Fell fed you the nicknames. How did you manage to get into sealed records, anyway?"

I wasn't going to incriminate his disgraced partner but I'm sure he suspected.

"Fell gave the names to Lana Hull and she told Willie," Carson continued. "They had become very close when she was at the nuthouse after a relapse.

"Willie killed three of the men outright and had his cousin pay somebody to knife the one they call Toolie in prison. Toolie's dead, by the bye, he had a heart attack. They're calling it homicide anyway."

"Mr. McGill?" Bonilla said tentatively. There was a hesitance in her tone, as if she hoped that her question would go unanswered.

"Yeah?"

"Why?"

"That's a big question."

"Why risk your life like that?"

I opened my mouth but that was as far as I could get.

"He might not say it," Carson interjected, "but you better believe that old LT has an angle."

I could see that Kitteridge was smitten with the homicide sergeant. She, on the other hand, was not convinced by his cavalier indictment.

"Why am I here," I asked, "instead of at home, in my bed?"

"You know," Kitteridge said.

"No, I don't."

I gazed into Sergeant Bonilla's eyes and she glanced away.

"Fell," Kittridge said.

"I know a guy named Thurman."

"Three other dead bodies, four if you include Willie."

"Sanderson's dead?" I asked.

"Brain hemorrhage. You finally got him, LT."

I only had a high school diploma but I knew my numbers. There should have been five corpses even if the security guard under the flower arrangement had not died.

I looked up at Carson and his eyebrows rose an eighth of an inch.

"Am I under arrest?" I asked. I was feeling better.

"No. The DA is concentrating on Lana Hull, but he can't get to her."

"Why not?"

"She's up in Albany, institutionalized again. Her father-in-law, too. You know the old man was knee-deep in gangsters since he was in his teens. We think he might have helped the wife but they got more lawyers than a teenager's got pimples. If it ever comes to trial, you will be asked to testify."

"I'll keep my calendar open," I said, grabbing on to the table and hoisting myself up.

I put some weight on my left foot and almost fell back into the chair.

"Should I get you a crutch?" Bethann asked.

"No need," I said.

I took a step and stopped, took another step. The pain didn't ease but I was coming to understand it. I limped to the door, grateful for the knob, and then lurched out into the brightly lit, light-green hallway. I had taken half a dozen steps when Carson called to me. Gratefully, I rested my hand against the wall and waited for him.

"Thanks for the save," he said. "You did a good job out there. I should've sent a squad car up to the Hulls' place. I wasn't that worried because I figured they were rich and had some kind of security system."

"They had a good gate," I said. "How did Sanderson get in?"

"It wasn't clear but he probably had the combination to the keypad."

"Lana would have given it to him—if they were friends."

"Probably. Anyway, LT, you saved my butt there. If it had gone wrong, I'd probably be out of a job or writing parking tickets on Staten Island."

He held out his hand.

I accepted the capitulation.

"My son was surfing the Net the other day," I said, "looking for porn, I guess. Anyway, he came upon this site called zebramanonthehunt517.com. You should take a look at it. I think that it'll get you some brownie points with the brass."

Carson frowned.

"What?" I asked him.

"This doesn't let you off the hook, LT," he said. "I still plan to put your ass in stir."

"What's a little jail time between friends?"

I took a cab straight from the police station to the Hulls' house.

The two brawny guards in size fifty-six suit jackets didn't surprise me one bit. They were both white guys, but the coming conflict between us would have nothing to do with race.

I hobbled up to the space between them and smiled.

"Move on," the one on the right said. He had a shaved head and crystalline blue eyes.

"Can't," I replied brightly. "Here to see Bryant Hull."

"Not in," the darker-hued titan on the left said.

"Tell him it's Leonid McGill."

"You better be moving on, little brother," Blue Eyes warned.

"Call him," was my reply.

I wasn't afraid of them. They had too much confidence, and I fought dirty. And anyway, I had defeated Willie Sanderson, the Frankenstein monster of the twenty-first century.

The darker guy pressed a button on his earpiece and said a word or two.

A few moments passed before the release for the gate made its noise. The titans parted and I limped through, feeling like Odysseus at the end of his trials.

THE MAN WHO let me in wore a black suit. He was slender but more deadly than the bruisers at the door. The only muscle you could see was in his hands. I was glad that I wasn't planning any mayhem. He saw what I was in just a glance.

"Hurt your foot, Mr. McGill?"

"Yes sir."

"There's an elevator to Mr. Hull's office at the end of this hall. Let me show you."

We walked in silence and waited for the elevator, both of us mum and without expression. The car arrived and we both got in. It was another posh elevator, carpeted, and with a seat in the corner. It reminded me of the Crenshaw when I'd taken a ride with the two party girls, Tru and Frankee, and Norman Fell, who was now deceased.

The door opened and we entered into a dark-wood library with a big desk off in a corner.

"Mr. McGill," Bryant Hull said as he rose from behind the desk and made his way around to see me. "I'm surprised that you're up and around so soon. They said you collapsed after your fight with Sanderson."

"Did Hannah survive?" I asked.

Bryant turned to his man.

"You can go, Mr. Jacobs."

The security chief hesitated.

"I think it would be better if I stayed, sir."

"No."

"You don't know this man."

"I've been around men like this since before I could walk," he said.

I believed it. I'd met his father.

Jacobs stalled for a beat or two more, but in the end he was just hired help. He fixed me with a warning stare and went back to the elevator. Hull didn't speak again until the security expert was gone.

"Let's go over here, where we can talk, Mr. McGill," the billionaire said.

He guided me to an L-shaped piece of furniture in a corner. Where the seats met there was a table with a lamp on it. Hull turned on the lamp and I eased my backside onto one of the seats.

"Hurt your foot?" he asked.

"Hannah," I replied.

"She's fine. I have her in a private hospital on Forty-ninth, but it's just for observation. The doctors assure me that she will live."

I let out a breath that I had been holding for a very long time.

After a second exhalation I had a question.

"How could that be?"

"You saved my daughter's life."

"You're not following me," I said. "I met Sanderson before. He could break that child's neck with no exertion whatsoever. He had more than enough time to kill her while I was running up the stairs."

"You don't understand me, Mr. McGill. The first time you went up against Sanderson you hit him in the head with a heavy chair. That's what the DA said."

"Uh-huh?"

"Apparently you caused some kind of brain damage. The doctors think that he wasn't able to use his full strength to close his hands as a result. He was choking Hannah but did not have his full range of motion. He could hit and kick, but choking was beyond him."

"Damn."

"I love my daughter, Mr. McGill. She is the one good thing in my life." I wondered where that left Fritz. "I can never repay you."

"Where were you when Sanderson busted in?" I asked.

"On the way to Albany. I had to commit my wife and father to an institution up there."

"They confessed to you?"

His left shoulder rose an inch or two.

"Lana told me what she had done after you left today. She said that when she found out that her son might have been murdered while she was living her life, making no effort to get in touch, well, she lost her mind and hired Sanderson to do those terrible things. She's getting help."

"How does your father fit into this, Mr. Hull? You know he tried to have me killed."

"When Sanderson overheard Fell talking to your answering machine he went after you. After he was arrested, Lana confided in my father. They knew each other from the sanatorium, too. He still had his old contacts, and access to money. That's over now. I have receivership over all his assets, and he will not be allowed to contact anyone outside of Sunset."

"So your wife has four people murdered, and your father tries to kill me, and all they get is a ticket to the country."

"They're my family, Mr. McGill. I met Lana at the sanatorium when my father was first there. She was—she is the most beautiful being I have ever known. What would you do if you were me?"

The same thing. Only I didn't have millions to burn.

We sat there together in silence, both of us slumming in different ways.

"What can I do for you, Mr. McGill?"

"I don't need anything," I said. "Your father's man gave me a briefcase full of cash already."

"I want to do something *for* you," he said, "not buy you."

I pretended to think for a moment but I already knew what I was going to say.

"There's a little red-and-gold painting by Paul Klee you have in a hall downstairs," I said.

"Yes?"
"Hannah says that it belongs to her."
"It does."
"She said I could have it."
"It's priceless."
"And yet, I'm told, your wife bought it."

Mrs. Selma Guttman was in San Francisco visiting with her daughter for three weeks. Through a website advertising temporary rentals that Zephyra kept tabs on I was able to get her a place for that time. It cost two thousand dollars but it was worth it.

The place was ideal. She had a window that looked out on the street with a table set before it, and even a rocking chair.

At 3:03 a.m. on a Tuesday morning I was sitting at that window, rocking slowly and waiting.

A light-colored Ford had gone around the block three times. It crept down the street after a final pass and then parked a few houses away. The lights went out and for a while the Brooklyn neighborhood was calm again. It wasn't until 3:28 that Tony the Suit got out of the Ford, which was undoubtedly stolen, and made his way to A Mann's front door.

Tony had thought that I should kill Mann, for all the money I was insisting on. But I demurred.

"Killing is not my business," I told the mid-level gangster. "I traffic in information."

Now Tony was getting out of his car, a pistol resting in his pocket next to the key I had made for the ex-accountant's front door.

Tony crossed the street quickly, then silently walked onto the porch. And for a while everything was quiet again. Then lights came on all over the house. Five black cars with flashing red lights on their roofs converged in front of the place and a dozen men and women of law enforcement jumped out.

People surged out of A's small home, carrying with them Tony Towers, in handcuffs, followed by Mr. A Mann in a T-shirt and dark trousers, cradling the aged dachshund in his arms.

The accountant and the dog were the newest members in the witness protection program. He could only hope that they would keep him as safe as he kept himself.

Tony would probably be dead soon enough. Because of the information Mann could give them, along with the conspiracy to commit murder, GTA, and possession of an unlicensed firearm, the gangster would be their yellow bird before long. None of his business associates could live with that. I could only hope that this was the outcome Harris Vartan was looking for. But even if it wasn't, this was the only choice open to me.

"YOU LOOK TIRED, Pops," Twill said later that morning at the breakfast table.

Katrina had made the family buckwheat cakes along with broiled thick-cut applewood-smoked bacon.

"So that you might sleep peacefully, my son. How's Mardi?"

After they arrested her father, her uncle sent for her and her sister. They went to Dublin.

"She says she's happy," he said. And then, "I was thinkin' about what you said that day. And I promise that I will come to you with any more problems like that. At least till I'm twenty-one."

THE HOUSE WAS empty by noon.

I went down the hall to my den and sat down behind the desk, across from the little painting where a squiggle's face had abandoned him to become the sun. It was a lovely thing, beautiful.

I took out my cell phone and entered a code.

"Hello," she answered knowingly.

"Can we meet for a late lunch?" I asked Aura Ullman.

"A restaurant or my place?"

"I need to talk," I said. "But I think it should be in a public space for now."

"Okay," she said and I felt once more that I was falling, but I didn't mind at all.

ABOUT THE AUTHOR

Walter Mosley is one of America's most celebrated and best-known writers. His mystery novels, including the now classic Easy Rawlins series, are routinely on the *New York Times* Bestseller List, and his books have been translated into more than twenty languages. He has won numerous awards, including the Anisfield-Wolf Book Award (given to work that increases the appreciation and understanding of race in America), a Grammy, the Sundance Risk-Takers Award, and the PEN Center USA's Lifetime Achievement Award. Mosley served on the board of directors of the National Book Awards and is past president of the Mystery Writers of America. Born and raised in Los Angeles, he lives in New York City.